Also By *New York Times*
bestselling author Rachel Vincent

Shifters

STRAY
ROGUE
PRIDE
PREY
SHIFT
ALPHA

Unbound

BLOOD BOUND
SHADOW BOUND
OATH BOUND

Soul Screamers

MY SOUL TO TAKE
MY SOUL TO SAVE
MY SOUL TO KEEP
MY SOUL TO STEAL
IF I DIE
BEFORE I WAKE
WITH ALL MY SOUL

Coming In 2015

THE STARS NEVER RISE
MENAGERIE

For more information, please visit
www.rachelvincent.com

LION'S SHARE

Wildcats Book 1

RACHEL VINCENT

Cover design by Killswitch Media

ISBN-10: 0692390545
ISBN-13: 978-0692390542

To all the Shifters fans who wanted more.
This is for you.

ACKNOWLEDGMENTS

Thanks must go, first and foremost, to my husband, who has put countless hours into my career in the form of artwork, web design, brainstorming, and moral support. You are my anchor and I love you.

Thanks also to Rinda Elliott, my long-term critique partner, who critiqued *Lion's Share* as well as the entire Shifters series.

Thanks to Jennifer Lynn Barnes for untold hours of Panera-fueled writing and company, and for being the first to say the phrase, "You should write a new adult Shifters spin-off!"

Thanks to Rachel Clarke for invaluable beta reads and for endless cheerleading.

And thanks most of all to all the Shifters fans who asked for more.

ONE

Abby

What they don't tell you about college is how much time you'll have to spend dodging your Alpha's calls in order to get any studying done.

Or was that just me?

My phone rang again as I unlocked my dorm room, and a glance at the face that popped up on the screen made my chest ache. I wanted to answer the phone. I wanted to hold it to my ear and let the voice over the line rumble through me, touching me in places the man it belonged to never would. But that was a fantasy. He only ever called to talk business or deliver messages I didn't want to hear, and this end-of-semester phone call would be no different from the others.

I pressed the ignore button, even though I was all done studying, because I already knew what he was going to say, and my rebuttal wasn't yet ready.

But to be fair, I *did* feel a little guilty that time.

I exhaled with relief when the door closed at my back and warmth from my dorm room enveloped me. Three and a half years in Kentucky and I still couldn't get used to the cold or the snow. Where I came from, winter was little more than a cool breeze around the first of the year, and even though Kentucky liked to think of itself as a southern state, no one actually hailing from the Deep South could claim quite such a familiarity with the changing of the seasons.

In my part of South Carolina, we only had two: hot and slightly less hot.

I dropped my backpack on my unmade bed and took a resentful look at the bulging hamper in the corner of the room. Washing my clothes would be the mature thing to do. My laundry had been piling up all month while I studied for finals. But exams were finally over—I'd aced them, thank you very much—and the last thing I wanted to do was more work.

"Abby!" My roommate, Robyn Sheffield, pushed the door open with her elbow, carrying a steaming paper cup in each hand. Her eyes were bright and her cheeks were red. She looked happier than I'd seen her in two months.

She looked healthier too. Her appetite had come back almost a month before, and her steady hands told me she'd just about put the trauma at the campground behind her.

"Thanks," I said as she handed me one of the cups. "Hot chocolate?"

Her smile rose higher on one side as she took a sip from her own. "*Irish* hot chocolate."

"Because it was made by leprechauns in a pint-sized sweatshop on the outskirts of Belfast?"

"Because it's liberally spiked with Irish cream. Gary's Christmas present to the entire floor."

Our RA was a pain in the ass nine months out of the year, but he was generous around the holidays. God bless him.

"All done with exams?" I sank onto my bed, then leaned across my nightstand to press the ratty old scarf farther into the crack in the windowsill. No matter how high we set the thermostat, the draft froze the tip of my nose all night, every night.

"Finally!" Robyn sipped from her cup. "You?"

"As of twenty minutes ago. Seven semesters down, one to go." In six months, I'd have a bachelor's degree—only the second ever awarded to a female werecat. In the whole world. Ever. My brothers were proud. My parents were happy for me, but they were also ready for me to be finished with my education so my "real" life could begin.

The life wherein I would move back home, marry a future Alpha, and have his shifter babies while he trained to take over our Pride from my father. That's the way it had been for every tabby who'd come before me. All but one, anyway.

My cousin Faythe, the world's only female Alpha, had broken the mold. But that mostly just changed the way people saw *her*. Faythe was the exception. The tabby who could not be tamed. The rest of us were still expected to follow the rules, because the numbers hadn't changed. There were still only a handful of female werecats capable of bearing children, and if *any* of us refused to do that, the strength of our species would be compromised.

We could literally go extinct.

No pressure.

I took a long, deep drink of my spiked hot chocolate, suddenly wishing I had an entire bottle of Irish cream. Sans the cream.

I had taken Faythe's advice and I'd always been grateful to have it. Insisting on going to college had given me the opportunity to be myself—to *find* myself—before I had to become a wife and mother. But now my sojourn in the human world was almost over.

The clock was counting down toward graduation, and with every dreadful tick and inevitable tock, I could feel fate's vise tighten.

"What's wrong? Your hot chocolate doesn't have enough whiskey?"

"The *world* doesn't have enough whiskey," I muttered. "Nothing's wrong. Just family crap." After what she'd suffered during our fall break camping trip, I wouldn't feel right burdening her with my problems.

Robyn only knew a little about my home life—just the parts it was safe for me to tell her. She knew I had five highly protective older brothers and that my parents had very "traditional" expectations for me. She knew that I could handle myself in a fight, thanks to summers spent with my cousin Faythe. She knew I was still in touch with my high school boyfriend, Brian, but that I only answered about half of his calls, because neither of us knew what to say to each other over the phone.

She also knew that a good friend of my father lived less than an hour from campus, and that he acted as my emergency contact and *de facto* guardian while I was at school.

What she *didn't* know were words like Alpha and

enforcer. And Pride, at least in the shifter sense of the word.

"So, the semester's over!" I drained my spiked hot chocolate and stood to toss the cup into the trash, then turned to my closet, where my party clothes had been neglected for the better part of the term. "Last one dressed has to find us a designated driver!"

Three minutes later, I zipped up my shortest skirt and was just stepping into my highest-heeled boots when movement out the window drew my eye. A familiar black Pathfinder was pulling into a spot in the parking lot two floors below.

Nooooooo!

I leaned over the nightstand for a better look, and even with my breath fogging up the glass, I recognized the tall, broad figure who stepped out of the car. "Son of a *bitch*!"

I *knew* I should have answered my phone.

"Done!" Robyn stood up in the middle of the room, fully dressed. "Get ready to sweet-talk Julie Cass, because she's the only teetotaler on this floor who has her own car."

When I didn't reply, my roommate rounded the end of her bed and leaned over my nightstand to follow my gaze. "What are we looking a…" When her question faded into drooling nonsense, I knew she'd spotted him. "Who is *that*, and why the hell haven't you called dibs?"

"That's Jace Hammond." I stood, trying to slow the automatic jump in my pulse. She wasn't wrong. He was *gorgeous*, in a carved-from-stone perfection kind of way.

"Wait, *that's* your dad's friend? Shouldn't he be…old?"

"He's old enough." Though in truth, thirty was too young for the authority he wielded and too old for what I secretly, wake-up-aching-in-the-middle-of-the-night wanted from him. Which was why I avoided him as often as possible. "And he's not supposed to be here until tomorrow."

Jace never came to pick me up until the day after my last final. I'd thought I'd have the evening to talk him out of it this time.

In the parking lot, he leaned against the side of his SUV and pulled his phone from his pocket. Mine rang second later, and for the fourth time in the past two hours, his name and picture popped up on the screen. I answered the call and pressed the phone to my ear.

"You're early," I snapped, and Jace stood up straight to scan the side of the dorm building, surprised.

"How did you…"

"Fourth from the left, third floor."

When he found my window, Jace took off his sunglasses and grinned up at me. Even from two floors down, his eyes shone bright blue and his grin lit little fires deep inside me, as it had since I was fifteen years old.

I stomped those tiny flames until they were nothing but embers keeping me warm. Jace smiled the same way at every woman who looked at him. That grin meant nothing, I could not afford to forget that.

Robyn had identified the problem without even knowing it. Alphas weren't supposed to be young and hot. They were supposed to be old and wise, like my father.

"I'll be up in a second." Jace's voice surged

through me, stoking the flames I'd just trampled.

"No! I'll come down. Stay there." I hung up before he could argue, and Robyn looked at me as if I'd just threatened to cut off my own arm.

"What the hell are you doing?"

"Looking for my coat." I eyed a suspicious lump beneath my comforter, but it turned out to be my pillow.

"You know what I mean. If that guy promised my dad he'd look out for me, I'd sure as hell let him. He looks like he could take *really* good care of you."

A quick search of my closet floor revealed a cardigan, four bras, and the hair clip I'd been looking for all month. It was the only one strong enough to hold all of my curls out of my face at once. "Stop staring, Robyn. He's compulsively unavailable."

Her hopeful expression collapsed. "Wife?"

"Yeah, but not his own. His heart belongs to my cousin. My very *married* cousin." And his body belonged to whatever human girl was warming his bed on any given week. I'd met at least a dozen of them in what little time I'd spent at the lodge during holidays and long weekends.

He'd never failed to introduce me as "kiddo."

I found no sign of my coat, but Robyn's white down jacket was hanging over her desk chair. *Perfect.* "Hey, can I borrow that?"

"Sure." But she clearly had no idea what I was borrowing, because she was still staring at Jace. Not that I could blame her. I'd had years to practice not-drooling over him, yet I was still tempted to stare.

"Be back in a sec," I said on my way out the door, but Robyn never even glanced away from the window.

I flew down two flights of stairs and through the common room, and a burst of cold air hit me when I threw the door open. Shivering, I ran across the grass toward the parking lot in my boots, suddenly wishing I'd chosen lower heels. And pants.

Jace turned when he heard me coming, and a little thrill of satisfaction warmed me from the inside when his scruffy jaw actually dropped a little. But then he spoke, and that warmth died. "What happened to the rest of your skirt?"

"I left it in the nineteenth century."

His blue eyes flashed in amusement, and I caught my breath. "Okay then, where's your suitcase?"

I had to look up at him, even in my highest heels. "Um, I'm going to stay here with Robyn this time. It's only for a month, and ours is the dorm they have to leave open for international students." Though I hadn't met a soul, other than Robyn, who was planning to stay.

Jace's smile faded and the Alpha peeked from behind bright blue eyes and full lips I'd known my entire life. "You want to stay on campus alone? During the holidays?"

"No, I want to stay with *Robyn*. I was gonna call you, but..."

"But you forgot how your phone works. Right? That's why you never answer it?"

"I was busy with finals. I was going to check in tonight, I swear. Jace—"

"The council's called an emergency meeting at the ranch." The Lazy S, of course, which was still the council headquarters, even after the death of the previous council head. Mostly because the Texas ranch had more room than the other territorial capitals. "Our flight leaves in three hours."

"I'm not on the council," I pointed out in as rational a tone as I could summon. "Ergo, I'm not needed at the ranch."

"Your dad's already there and he wants to take you home for the holidays."

"Well, I'm an adult and I belong to *your* Pride, so he doesn't have the authority to order me home." Even if he *was* the head of the council, a position formerly held by his brother-in-law, my late uncle Greg Sanders.

Jace frowned, and I resisted the urge to give in just so I could see him smile again. "Your father's not ordering; he's requesting. Nicely."

"Well, I'm declining." I crossed my arms over my chest to hold Robyn's jacket closed. Also to illustrate my determination. "Nicely."

"Fine. Then *I'm* ordering you to go upstairs and throw whatever you need into a bag. Now."

"Why? Are you scared to stand up to my dad?" I knew I'd stepped over the line when a growl rumbled from his throat and my head tried to bow. Because my Alpha was angry and my inner cat knew that was my fault.

Jace had grown into his position quickly, and as the youngest male Alpha in the world, he was also among the strongest. His leadership had been challenged three times in the four and a half years since he'd taken over the Appalachian Territory, and none of the challengers had come close to beating him. There were only a handful of werecats in the world who could hold their own with him one-on-one, and I was not among those. Nor did I want to be.

He mirrored my stance with his arms crossed over his broad chest, and I could hear the warning before he even spoke. "Abigail Wade, if you're not in the car in ten minutes, I'll…"

"You'll what? Drag me out by my hair? Wouldn't be a first for me."

That was a low blow and I had no right to aim it at him, but the moment the words left my mouth, his anger crumpled beneath the weight of something much worse.

Sympathy.

I found pity and awkward compassion everywhere I turned in the werecat world, because all my fellow shifters could think about when they looked at me was what had happened to me the summer I turned seventeen, and how damaged I must be because of it. Which was why I preferred the human world, where I was presumed whole until proven broken.

"Sorry." I bowed my head and stared at my boots. "I shouldn't have—"

"No, you're right. We all let you down when you were just a kid, and *I* let you down in October. You could have been killed out there in the woods, and I can't let that happen again. So, I'm *ordering* you to go get your things and come with me to the ranch. For your own safety."

That was without a doubt the most overused phrase in any Alpha's repertoire, and it sounded strange coming from Jace. As if he didn't really believe what he was saying. But further argument would do me no good, so I sucked in a deep breath and made myself meet his gaze. "Fine. Give me ten minutes." Then I turned and headed back to the dorm without another glance at him. No matter *how* badly I wanted to know if he was watching me walk away.

What had happened on fall break wasn't Jace's fault. If I'd told him I was leaving campus, as I was technically obliged to do, he would have sent a pair of enforcers—probably my own brothers—to watch out for me, hidden in the trees in feline form. I'd kept Jace out of the loop because I didn't want to be watched, and he had probably caught hell from the other council members for letting one of the country's few and precious tabbies put herself in mortal danger.

But he must have taken full responsibility for what I'd done, because no one had yelled at me for my lapse in judgment. Not even my parents, during our bi-monthly video chat.

I owed Jace, even beyond the normal respect due an Alpha from one of his pride members, and paying him back with insolence was unacceptable.

In our dorm room, Robyn finally turned away from the window to watch me throw clothes into my duffel. "You're leaving? Now?"

"My dad wants me to come home for Christmas." I threw my toothbrush, its charger, and a nearly empty tube of toothpaste into my toiletries bag on top of the small, square box I hadn't unpacked after my previous trip home. Then I scooped my makeup into the bag with one swipe of the counter. "Will you be okay here on your own?" Since she was staying on campus over the holiday, we wouldn't have to pack up all our stuff and vacate the dorm room, a convenience I hadn't truly appreciated until that moment.

"Yeah. The nightmares are practically gone. I'm

fine, Abby. Really."

I studied her in the mirror, trying to decide whether or not that was true. She had few physical scars from what had gone down in the woods over fall break, and those bastards hadn't gotten the chance to molest her. Still, she'd seen three of our friends slaughtered right in front of her, and most people weren't used to witnessing violence or death, up close and personal.

More than anything in the world, I wished I wasn't either.

"Okay. Knowing my parents, I'll probably be gone for most of the break, but I can come back sooner if you need me." I pulled her into a hug. Robyn had been through so much in the woods, and no matter how fine she claimed to be, I knew better than most how long that kind of trauma could take to overcome. If she was staying over the holiday, I should be staying with her. Reluctantly, I let her go. "Call if you want to talk. Okay?"

"I promise." She smiled at me in the mirror. "Now go have Christmas with your family."

Christmas with my family.

My mother would hover over me and analyze everything I said for evidence that I hadn't recovered from that summer four years before. My father would watch me out of the corner of his eye and not so subtly mention what an accomplished enforcer Brian had become, looking for any sign that I was ready to settle down and turn my parents into grandparents.

My brothers would follow me into town so I couldn't get snatched off the street during any last-minute Christmas shopping, and they'd mentally dismember any guy who had the balls to even look my way, in spite of my large fraternal guard detail.

Going home for Christmas sounded about as pleasant as Thanksgiving spent in prison.

On the bright side, there'd probably be ham.

"So, what's the big emergency?" I threw my duffel onto the rear floorboard, then slid into the passenger's seat of Jace's SUV. His gaze landed on my thighs, where my skirt had ridden up, and the sudden jump in his pulse was…gratifying.

He'd seen me naked—and I him—a million times, but nudity means little to most shifters because it's required for the transformation to and from feline form. Shifters are aroused by what they *don't* see. What they *almost* see. By the intent implied by flesh displayed behind or beneath strategically placed panels of lace or silk. Flesh that is put on display in private, for a specific intended audience.

Jace had never looked at me like that before. As if he wondered what my underwear looked like. As if I might be something other than a child in need of protection.

I desperately didn't want Jace to think of me as a child. I was old enough to hold his attention. I was old enough to *warrant* his attention.

Wait.

I shook my head, jarring loose dangerous thoughts and foolish desires. An Alpha held an authority equivalent to a corporate manager, a parent, and a ruler all rolled into one, and even if dating an authority figure wasn't completely inappropriate, Jace was too old for me. Too experienced for me.

And then there was Brian.

Not that any of that mattered. One glance south of my neck didn't mean Jace was actually interested. It just meant he was a guy.

I shifted in my seat and Jace's gaze snapped up to my face. He looked flustered for a moment, then he stared straight out the windshield and made an obvious, concerted effort to slow his pulse.

I decided to call that a compliment, even if it didn't really mean anything.

"Jace?"

"Hmm?" He slammed the gearshift into reverse and made a production of looking into the rearview mirror as he backed out of the parking space.

"The emergency? Why are we going to the ranch?"

"Oh. Someone's killing humans, and the local news has picked up the story."

"Local?" I fought to control my own racing pulse. "How local?"

"For us? Very. The victims have all been killed in the Appalachian territory." Jace checked both directions on his way out of the parking lot. "Right now, the cops think there's a wild animal on the loose, but if we don't find the rogue and take him out, they're going to start suspecting foul play. Or they're going to shoot one of our guys while they're out hunting this mythical black cougar, then they'll have biological proof that humans aren't the most dangerous thing out there. The council's in self-defense mode. They'll do whatever it takes to keep us from being outed."

My mind raced as the details began to coalesce into something that almost made sense. "You're sure the killer's one of ours? Couldn't it be a thunderbird or a bruin?" Please *let it be a thunderbird or a bruin.* Bird- and bear-shifters could be every bit as vicious as werecats, and if it wasn't a cat, it wasn't our responsibility.

"Definitely a cat." Jace took a turn too hard, and I had to grab the door handle to keep from landing in his lap. He still didn't drive like an Alpha; most of the rest of them were old. "But probably not ours."

"You think it's a stray," I said, as more of the pieces fell into place.

"We didn't get to examine the bodies, because the cops got there first, and we don't have anyone on the inside. But we know for a fact that there are no natural wildcats in Appalachia." Or anywhere else heavily populated with shifters. Natural cats avoided us like the plague. "So, it *better* be a stray," he continued. "Because if one of our own's gone rogue, we're all in big trouble."

But what he didn't say—what I could see etched into the brand-new Alpha lines on his otherwise youthful forehead—was that we couldn't afford for it to be a stray either. Not when they were so close to voting on the resolution he and Faythe had sponsored in the territorial council.

For the first time in US history, the council was being asked to formally acknowledge a Pride made up entirely of strays who wished to carve out a territory of their own in one of the free zones. Faythe's husband Marc, a stray adopted as a teenager by her father, had been acting as ambassador to the potential new Pride, helping them get all their t's crossed and their i's dotted, in order to present themselves at the next meeting.

If the council discovered that the murderer was a

stray, that resolution would never pass. The project Jace, Faythe, and Marc had hoped would bring lasting peace between strays and Pride cats would fail before it ever even had a chance.

"That's why I have to go with you to the ranch," I guessed, and Jace gave me a small nod. With a murderous stray loose in the Appalachian territory, my dad wouldn't want me to stay at the lodge for the holidays, even though Jace had probably tripled his security measures to protect his mother and sister.

Tabbies were too rare and too precious to risk and having two of them of childbearing age in the same house would only strengthen the temptation for a stray who'd probably never even met a female of his own species.

"So, this is history repeating itself? The big, strong tomcat has come to drag the helpless council chairman's daughter home from school for her own good?"

"It was the right thing to do for Faythe, and it's the right thing to do for you. But you're *far* from helpless." Jace's voice rang with admiration that warmed me all over. "I know a few hunters rotting in shallow graves in the woods who could attest to that." His pride in me morphed into misplaced nostalgia, and alarms went off in my head. "Faythe taught you well."

The warm smile he gave me would have felt wonderful—if it were meant for me. "Jace, I'm not Faythe."

He laughed again, and those inner alarms began to fade. "Glad to hear it. Things never seem to work out in my favor when she's involved. You, however..." He aimed another blue-eyed glance at me, and I caught my breath. "*You're* my new lucky charm. Kiddo."

TWO

Jace

During my first four years as Alpha of the Appalachian Pride, I'd struggled with many things. Expelling my own half brother. Convincing my baby sister that she doesn't have to voice *every* thought that pops into her head. Assembling and training my own team of loyal enforcers from scratch. But sitting next to Abby for hours at a time had turned out to be its own special challenge.

She'd transferred into my territory as a withdrawn but determined college freshman interested in nothing but personal barriers and schoolwork. Which made sense, considering what she'd been through. But at some point since, little Abigail Wade had come out of her shell.

I'd first noticed her new grit during her fall break, when she took out three homicidal human hunters without waiting for backup. But it wasn't the reckless disobedience that stood out. It was her relentless insistence that she'd done the right thing. The thing *I* would have done in her situation. She wasn't afraid of the hunters, and she sure as hell wasn't afraid of me, and I found something captivating in her unflinching confidence. Something *exciting*.

Even if it led her to question every decision I made.

Her disposition wasn't the only part of her that had come out of its shell. After hours in a car and on a plane with her, I still couldn't decide whether she had no idea how amazing she looked in that skirt or she knew *exactly* how amazing she looked in that skirt.

It only took me five minutes to realize I had no business knowing which of those was true.

We were three miles from the ranch, stuffed into the cramped front seat of my rental car, when Abby turned to me with a familiar look in her big brown eyes. That look said she knew that curiosity would eventually kill the cat, but she really didn't give a damn. "When was the last time you saw her?"

I squinted at the windshield as a car passed us with its brights on. "Saw who?"

As if I didn't know.

"Faythe. You guys have been working together to present this new resolution, right? To officially recognize a Pride made up of strays?"

A long rope of red curls fell over her shoulder, and I had to stop myself from reaching out to touch it.

"They prefer to be called 'wildcats.'" Even though Pride cats had a slightly different definition for the same term. "But yes. Most of that's been done over the phone, though." Thank goodness. "If the resolution passes, we'll be making history."

For the first time ever, strays—werecats infected by a scratch or a bite rather than born into our world—would have a place to go for help, sanctuary, and company. They'd have an official presence and a *voice.* And their Pride would have a vote on the council, of equal worth to that of all the other Prides.

This potential new Pride wouldn't have an official name until it was formally recognized, but unofficially, we were calling it the Lion's Den.

"Working with her must be difficult for you," Abby said.

Understatement of the millennium.

As the first female Alpha in history, Faythe was practically a legend in every shifter society on the planet. She'd shattered the glass ceiling with her notoriously hard head and ripped the no girls allowed sign from the council's clubhouse. Faythe had paved the way, at least in theory, for every tabby who would come after her.

I, on the other hand, was the only tom in the world ever to have been dumped by a female Alpha, which had left certain members of the Territorial Council less than confident in my ability to lead. In a society where the respect an Alpha commands is crucial to the authority he wields, how were *they* supposed to have any confidence in me when *she'd* found me lacking?

Not that any of that would matter for long. My sister, Melody, was nineteen. When she married, I would be expected to train her husband so he could take over the territory with her at his side. Matrilineal inheritance had always been the norm so that our few tabbies could stay in their birth Prides, which would be run by the Alphas they chose as husbands.

Faythe had opened up new possibilities for female leadership, but the percentage of tabbies who would naturally develop into Alphas was no greater than the percentage of toms who would, and Melody… Well, my sister couldn't even pick a bottle of lotion without asking for a second opinion.

Regardless, I was little more than a temporary guardian of my future brother-in-law's territory.

But that was nothing Abby needed to be reminded of.

"The *truly* hard part is getting the other Alphas to understand the relevance of electronic communication in modern Pride leadership." I shrugged and forced a laugh. "You'd think email was synonymous with witchcraft, if you took Paul Blackwell's word for it." The old fart still hand-wrote letters to his fellow Alphas on honest-to-goodness carbon paper.

"That's not what I meant."

She'd meant that it must have been hard having to talk to Faythe so often after she'd picked Marc over me. Abby, like everyone else, was wondering if I'd gotten over losing the love of my life. Or whether I ever would.

According to the gossip from my own enforcers, the answer was no, and it always would be. But then, according to those clowns, Faythe had only picked Marc because she couldn't have any of them.

"So, you haven't seen Faythe in a while?" she asked.

I turned to see that an oncoming car's headlights had turned her curls into living flames. "Um, it's been about three years, I guess."

Three and a half, but who was counting?

"Seriously? But aren't most council meetings still held at the Lazy S?"

I nodded, and she frowned with the realization that I couldn't have gone so long without seeing Faythe unless I was consciously avoiding her. And that was true, but it wasn't just Faythe I was dodging. I was avoiding every memory I'd ever made at the Lazy S, because even the good ones were bittersweet in retrospect.

Especially with Ethan gone.

"About time," I mumbled as the gate appeared ahead, beneath a familiar capital S lying on its side. "I swear, the drive from the airport gets longer every time."

Abby groaned, as if she'd suddenly remembered something important. "Slow down!" She dove between our seats headfirst, placing her *very* well-shaped and barely covered hindquarters inches from my face.

"What the hell are you doing?" I pressed on the brake as I turned off of the highway, and it took every bit of willpower I could summon not to peek into the rearview mirror for an even more intimate viewing angle of what her skirt didn't cover. As the vehicle came to a stop, Abby settled back into her seat holding a small square box she'd dug from a bag in the back.

A ring box.

"I almost forgot," she mumbled, as she pulled her engagement ring out and slid it onto the fourth finger of her left hand. It was a single round diamond mounted high on a slim gold band, and the damn thing caught light from a pole on the side of the highway like rays from Heaven. I had to squint to see through the reflected glare.

"Why don't you wear it at school?" I was caught strangely off guard by the rare reminder that she had been spoken for a long time ago. Not that it mattered.

Abby frowned at her hand, which somehow looked completely different with that one simple addition. "Because Brian… It'd be hard to explain to humans."

Hell, her engagement would be hard to explain even to most shifters, who grow up knowing about the expectations placed upon a tabby at birth.

After narrowly surviving abduction, captivity, and gang rape the summer she was seventeen, Abby's senior year in high school was very difficult for her. A few weeks in, she'd dropped out in favor of homeschooling with her mother, and shortly after that, she'd gotten her GED. Around April of that year, her parents had sent her to the ranch to spend time with Faythe and Manx, who'd both survived similar trauma—a little less in Faythe's case, and significantly more in Manx's.

Faythe taught Abby to fight and talked her into starting college. Manx kept Abby from withdrawing from the world physically and helped her deal with nightmares.

That summer, she also got to know Brian Taylor, Faythe's newest enforcer at the time. Brian was young, and nice, and interested—I'd known him for years by then—and to everyone's surprise, Abby didn't shy away from his reportedly sweet and patient pursuit. By the end of the summer, she'd accepted his ring, to her parents' delight, on the condition that the wedding be put off until she finished college.

Brian was amenable and that was no surprise.

Engagement to Abby meant that he would be trained to take over her birth Pride. He would be an Alpha, a husband, and a father—opportunities rarely available to toms, because of the severe gender imbalance. Though their engagement was preposterously long by shifter standards, Brian was the envy of his peers.

But other than a few summer weeks spent on the ranch, he and Abby had hardly seen each other since she'd started school, and she only wore the ring when she went home. She was clearly no longer the shy freshman who'd joined my Pride, but neither did she act like a young woman eager for her wedding night.

Hell, my sister had subscriptions to three different bridal magazines, even though the face and name of her potential groom changed on a monthly basis, yet I'd never even heard Abby mention the ceremony her mother had been planning for years.

For his own sake, I hoped Brian was a very patient man, because no matter what she wore or how good she looked in it, Abby clearly wasn't ready for a physical relationship. And she had five huge brothers perfectly willing to break all two hundred and six of his human-form bones before they buried him in a shallow grave, if he so much as *thought* about breaching the clothing barrier without express invitation.

Five huge brothers and me.

My rental car's tires crunched on gravel as we drove through the gate, and my own troubles came into sharper focus. Unease sat like lead at the bottom of my stomach, yet somehow, returning to the ranch felt more like a homecoming than returning to my birth Pride had, four years before. Probably because I'd always been happy at the Lazy S, whereas taking over my birth Pride after I'd killed my stepfather had felt like launching a hostile conquest.

We passed the old barn, and even in the dark, I could see that it had been repainted. It was still red, of course, because Faythe would want to create continuity between her father's reign and her own to counterbalance the contrast in their leadership styles by keeping familiar landmarks familiar.

Smart. Greg had taught her well.

In front of the barn was the apple tree, naked for the winter season, and beneath it stood three headstones. They were equally weatherworn because both Ethan and Ryan had died within weeks of their father, the year of the revolution.

That's what people called it because we'd changed the world that year. *Our* world, at least.

Humanity was still mired in the same old shit because they did a lot more talking than acting. But as a political science major, Abby was more qualified to expound upon that truth than I would ever be.

I sat straighter when the main house came into sight, and for a second, déjà vu was strong enough to be disorienting. Had it really been eleven years since I'd driven that same path, both eager and terrified to pledge my service and loyalty—hell, my very *life*—to Greg Sanders and the South-Central Pride? In retrospect, my seven years as an enforcer felt like both an instant and an eternity, as if I'd somehow stuffed a lifetime's worth of experience and memories into a single bursting moment.

A moment I wouldn't give back for the world.

"Looks like everybody's home."

Abby's voice jolted me back to the present. The semicircle driveway was lined with cars, none of which belonged to the other Alphas. Marc would have picked them up at the airport.

I parked at the far end of the line and she was out of the car before the engine even died. "I'll come back for my bag," she called over her shoulder as she jogged toward the house.

For one embarrassingly long moment, I was captivated by the sway of her hips as she ran, highlighted by the beam from my headlights. Hell, even her shadow was alluring, with its exaggerated proportions and sleek outline. She really *had* grown up while I wasn't looking.

And you still shouldn't be looking.

Abby was my subordinate Pride member and the council chairman's only daughter. She was likely still suffering long-term trauma from everything she'd been through. And she was *another man's fiancée.* There was no of-age tabby in the country more off-limits to me than Abby Wade, and she deserved an Alpha who could respect that.

At least in action, if not in thought.

I got out of the car and made myself take the next few steps because if I hung too far back, everyone would think I was trying to avoid the inevitable, awkward reunion with Faythe. But the front door flew open before Abby even made it to the steps, and a tiny blur blew past her like that cartoon roadrunner, leaving a small dark smear across my vision.

"Uncle Jace!"

I knelt and braced for impact just as the child launched himself at me. "Logan!" I wrapped him in a bear hug, breathing deeply to take in his scent. Ethan's son smelled almost exactly like he had, but the lingering grief his scent triggered couldn't overcome my joy at seeing the boy. "What are they feeding you, kiddo? You got huge!"

"Meat *and* veg-ta-bles," Logan said as I stood with him seated on my forearm. "Mommy said nuh-uh, cotton candy is *not* healthy, even when it's green!"

I chuckled. "I tried, little man, but your mom's too smart for me."

His head bobbed solemnly. "Me too."

When I looked up, I found Abby watching me, her freckled forehead crinkled. "If you haven't been back in three years, why does Logan remember you? And call you Uncle?"

"I said I hadn't seen *Faythe* in three years. I come see *this* little monster at his mom's as often as possible." When I tickled Logan, his head fell into the light from the front porch.

Abby gasped. "He looks just like Ethan!"

I realized she probably hadn't seen him in months, and kids change so fast at that age. Which was why I visited as often as I could.

Logan nodded at her. "My daddy. Hero."

"Damn right he was." I squeezed the boy, and a smile took over Abby's face when his bright green eyes lit up. In spite of whatever genes he'd inherited from Angela, his human mother, Logan's resemblance to the father he'd never met was uncanny when he smiled.

"How old are you now?" Abby brushed a strand of dark hair from the boy's forehead. "Two?"

"Three." He held up four chubby fingers. "And a half!"

The conclusion surfaced in her eyes like an accusation when she turned to me. "You haven't seen Faythe since Logan was born."

I nodded. I'd moved on after Faythe chose Marc, but for a long time, seeing them together had stung. So, I'd stayed away to make things easier for all three of us.

Until now.

"No fair!" A new voice called as a larger but equally dark-haired boy stumbled to a stop on the top step, glaring at Logan. "You tripped me! And Grandma says close the front door 'cause she's not in the business of heating the great outdoors."

I took me a moment to recognize Desiderio, and if his eyes hadn't been identical to Manx's, I might not have. He was nearly five, by my count, and well-spoken for a kid his age. At least, judging by the standards my collection of younger half brothers had set.

Abby laughed and held her arms open, and Des ran into them.

"Abby! I didn't know you were coming!"

"I didn't know *you* were coming!" She scooped him up and held him on her right hip, unfazed by his size or weight. "Where's your mom?"

"Feeding the baby. Daddy said we could wait up for Jace. Tell him to let us stay up longer!"

"Ha! That's well beyond my authority," Abby told the child, and he glanced over her shoulder at me, still hopeful, even though he couldn't possibly have remembered me. He'd been less than a year old the last time I'd seen him.

"That's not up to me, bud," I said, and Logan pouted in my arms.

Desiderio looked puzzled. "But you're an Alpha, right?" He sniffed the air in my direction, scenting out hormones. "You smell like an Alpha."

"Dads trump Alphas every day of the week." I set Logan down and the boys ran into the house together to find Owen, who'd adopted Des when he and Manx had married a couple of years before.

"Ready?" Abby whispered, and I could tell from how intently she was watching me that she knew how nervous I was. If she could see that, so would everyone else, and Alphas couldn't afford to be nervous. Especially the junior-most Alpha—the one with the most to prove.

"As ready as I'll ever be."

She stepped into my path, facing me from just inches away, and her sudden nearness made my chest ache. *Damn*, she was beautiful. Light from the porch lit her curls on fire, and it took every scrap of willpower I had to keep from reaching for her. From leaning in...

"You're going to be great." She stared up at me as if I'd hung the very moon reflecting its light in her eyes. "All you have to do is let them see what I see."

My throat felt tight. What did she see?

"Strength. Confidence." Abby smiled up at me, answering a question I hadn't even voiced. "Passion. Dedication. Determination. You've given everything you have and everything you are to this job. They'll be able to see that." She stood on her toes to wrap her arms around my neck, and the easy contact caught me by surprise. My pulse spiked before I could check the reaction.

If Abby noticed, I couldn't tell. She snuggled closer, and as I wrapped my arms slowly around her, breathing her in, I told myself to keep it in perspective. Cats thrive on physical comfort from their Pridemates, and that was all she was offering. In fact, it had probably never occurred to her that anything else would occur to *me*.

Not that I was thinking of never letting her go.

I tried to relax into her touch, telling myself that this was more like hugging my sister than like touching…any other woman I'd ever touched. But my body didn't believe my brain.

"I hope you're right." So far, I'd run my Pride in a virtual vacuum, intentionally maintaining distance from the other Alphas and their territories while I worked to establish my authority and get things organized. This meeting would be my in-person debut as a leader, and Faythe would be there to see it.

Marc would be there to judge.

If I failed to impress the rest of the council, my authority as an Alpha would be weakened, and I could *not* afford for that to happen before Melody got married. Before I had a chance to train her husband.

"I'll be right beside you." Abby's breath brushed my earlobe, and again I lost control of my pulse. "For moral support."

When she finally let me go, I exhaled slowly, trying to deny disappointment I felt like a physical ache. What was wrong with me? She was *off limits*, and if I couldn't get my head in the game, the rest of the council wouldn't let me play for much longer.

I followed Abby into the house and pulled the door closed at our backs. For a moment, I just stood there, taking it all in. I felt like I'd gone back in time to an alternate past in which the floor plan of the house was unchanged but the rooms had all been assigned different purposes. And different occupants.

When Greg was in charge, the ranch had felt busy but structured. Orderly. Organized.

Faythe was an entirely different kind of Alpha, and under her leadership, chaos reigned. But it was a cheerful chaos, and that was actually a nice change.

A rocking horse sat in the entryway, still draped with a little boy's Batman cape in place of a saddle. Down the hall, one of the kids was crying, and behind the last closed door on the left, fast-paced, half-synthesized music blared from the room that had once belonged to Michael, Faythe's oldest brother. Kaci had moved into it more than four years before, after the South-Central Pride had taken her in as a lost and traumatized thirteen-year-old.

From the kitchen came the hum of both coffee pots running at once, along with the soft growl of the dishwasher and the clank of heavy pots. Faythe's mother was cooking chili, based on the scent. At ten P.M. Because a shifter's appetite knew no schedule.

Before I could absorb all the other nostalgic sights and sounds, the back door flew open and three large, broad enforcers came in, debating the benefits of one video game sniper rifle over another. Victor Di Carlo led the group and the moment he saw me, a smile took over his face.

He jogged down the hall, arms already open, and a second later, he was thumping me on the back. "Three years, you selfish son of a bitch! When we said don't be a stranger, we meant it!"

"Sorry, man." I gave his back an affectionate whack. "Things have been busy."

"I bet." He studied my face while his subordinate enforcers gave me a nod of respect, then filed into the kitchen for what could only be dinner, part two. "Responsibility looks good on you."

"Thanks." But my next thought trailed into

oblivion when I saw Brian Taylor coming down the hall, his gaze trained on Abby as if no one else existed.

"Abby." Brian's heartbeat spiked and he dared a brief glance down the length of her body, obviously caught between the desire to look and the enforcer's imperative to remain respectful, especially to his psychologically fragile fiancée. "You look *amazing.* Really beautiful."

Her cheeks turned pink and she smiled.

Irritation shot up my spine in a white-hot blaze. I'd never seen the two of them together and I hadn't spoken to Brian in at least a couple of years, yet I was suddenly certain that he wasn't right for her.

He wasn't good enough.

If Brian were truly Alpha material, shouldn't I feel threatened by him, on some level? Shouldn't my respect for his power and leadership potential be at constant war with my instinct to stomp them both right out of him?

I mean, sure, I wanted to shove him facedown on the floor and make him lick up the dirt I'd tracked in on my boots, but where was the *admiration* that was supposed to temper the demand for Alpha dominance coursing through my veins? If I pushed Brian down, he would stay there. I could *feel* that, just like my inner cat felt the call of the woods.

Abby needed a man who would get up. Who would push back.

She needed a man who couldn't be knocked down in the first place.

Don't start, I thought as I choked back an instinctive growl in Brian's direction. *She is not yours.*

But she *was* mine, at least on some level, and she

had been since the day she'd joined my Pride. And that wouldn't end until…

Until she swore she would have Brian as a husband, then later let him take her as his wife.

The thought of him touching Abby made every muscle in my body clench with rage.

Vic's brows rose in my direction and I realized he'd caught some small, revealing twitch. Or maybe he could sense fresh pheromones rolling from my body like smoke from a fire. He would have questions for me later.

Fortunately, both Brian and Abby seemed oblivious.

"Are you hungry?" he asked her. "Can I get you…"

"No, thanks, I'm…" Abby shrugged, absently twisting the ring on her left hand.

Could neither of them finish a sentence?

A door on the left side of the hall opened and Owen stepped out, mercifully drawing my attention from the poor junior enforcer who'd unwittingly inspired my disdain. Cradled in the crook of his right arm was a tiny bundle wrapped in a pale pink blanket.

"Abby!" The new father's eyes lit up when he saw her. "Come meet your new cousin!"

"Oh, let me see! Letmeseeletmesee!" She brushed past Brian on her way to view the new arrival, and his obvious disappointment soothed me. "I've seen a million pictures of her, but that's not as good as holding the real thing!"

Owen's baby was the first tabby born in the US in more than a decade—we'd *all* seen the pictures. But few outside of the immediate family had actually held her.

The proud papa put his daughter in Abby's arms, and she practically melted on her feet. "You named her Mercedes, right?" she whispered, obviously afraid to wake the infant.

He nodded. "Manx didn't want to, but I insisted she be named after her mother." He ran one rough finger gently down his sleeping daughter's cheek, love for his family stamped all over his face.

Owen was a lucky, lucky man. Manx was the first tabby in history, as far as I knew, who hadn't married an Alpha. She'd fallen in love with his gentle spirit and honest affection almost from the moment they'd met, and if not for him, she might never have overcome the trauma and grief that had brought her into the South-Central Territory from the war-ravaged Prides in South America.

Owen shrugged and smiled at Abby. "But Parker started calling her Sadie, and it stuck."

"Stuck!" the two-year-old in question echoed, and I glanced through the open doorway to find him curled up on the bed with his mother. He looked just like the pictures Owen sent out periodically. Tall for his age and gangly, like his father.

Manx waved at me over the top of the Spanish-language storybook she was trying to read to their middle child. They'd named him after Parker Pierce, the only South-Central Territory enforcer who'd died in the fight against my stepfather.

"Full house tonight," I said, watching Manx with her son. It was great to see her happy after all the tragedy that had preceded her acceptance into the Pride.

Owen laughed. "Yeah, we came up to watch the kids during the council meeting, but I'm starting to wonder if we don't create more chaos than we cure," he said as Des and Logan tore past us down the hall in matching superhero capes. Owen and Manx had built a house of their own on the other side of the property the year they were expecting Parker. That kept the kids close to their extended family, yet gave everyone some much-needed space and privacy.

"We should all be so lucky."

Owen's happiness was like a light shining just beneath his skin, casting its warm glow on everyone he came into contact with. He was perfectly content managing the ranch for his mother and raising his family, and I'd never in my life seen an existence fit a man so well.

"Hey, Ab—" Brian began, but the last half of her name was cut off by a shout from the office.

"Jace! Abby!" Rick Wade's voice boomed down the hall, startling baby Sadie awake. She began to fuss and Abby reluctantly handed her over to her father as we were summoned to the meeting. "We're about to get started in here!"

"She's beautiful, Owe," I said, as Owen took his daughter back. Then I gestured for Abby to lead the way toward the office, conveniently cutting Brian off before he could finish his sentence.

I could feel him glaring at my back all the way down the hall, and if he'd had the balls to call me out, I might have thrown my support behind his engagement to Abby.

Maybe.

But he didn't say one damn word.

THREE

Jace

I stepped back to let Abby head into the office first, and from the hallway, my eyes confirmed what my ears and nose had already told me—that several of my fellow Alphas hadn't shown up.

That was no surprise. The rogue was killing in my territory, which meant he was ultimately my responsibility. Those who'd supported my stepfather in the war would rather sit this meeting out so that if anything went wrong, they could legitimately blame me and my allies.

My least favorite part of leadership was the politics. Which was why Abby's choice of college major baffled me.

I stood back while she accepted hugs and greetings from Jerald Pierce, Ed Taylor, and Umberto Di Carlo, Alphas of the Plains, Midwest, and Southeast Prides, respectively. Faythe sat behind her desk at the back of the room, trying to tune everyone else out while she spoke on the phone, but she looked up when I stepped through the doorway. I could tell from the tension in her frame that she'd known the moment I walked into the house.

She'd probably heard my car before it had even turned into the driveway.

Faythe's green-eyed gaze met mine and I froze, bracing myself for the flood of conflicting emotions that had engulfed me every time I'd ever looked at her. Every time she'd ever looked at me.

Love. Lust. Jealousy. Frustration. I expected the entire toxic cocktail, and I was prepared to hide my pain behind the professional mask I'd been wearing for years. But instead of a flood of emotion, I got just a trickle. A mere echo of what I'd once felt and had long ago been forced to let go of.

My history with Faythe was now the rainy-day ache of an old wound.

I could live with an ache.

Still staring at me, Faythe tucked a strand of black hair behind one ear while Paul Blackwell spoke into her other one from the phone. For one long moment, she didn't breathe. When I was sure my heart wasn't going to implode—that it felt more bruised than injured—I grinned, and the tension drained from her frame. Her smile looked genuine. She was happy to see me, even under such grim, official circumstances.

Counting Faythe and me, we were still missing representatives from four of the ten US Territories, yet even from across the room, I could hear Paul Blackwell listing the litany of old-age complaints that were keeping him from attending. Faythe rolled her eyes, and I knew exactly what she was thinking—that if he was too old for the job, it was time he passed on his position to the next generation. It was *past* time, in fact. Blackwell's daughter and son-in-law already had a two-year-old grandson.

"Slim turnout," I said with a pointed glance around the room as Abby's dad, Council Chairman Rick Wade, came to greet me.

He shook my hand for the first time since I'd been confirmed as an Alpha, with his support. Wade was my unofficial—yet very real—ally on the council. "We only need six for a quorum."

And that was all we had since, as co-Alphas, Faythe and Marc had to share a single vote.

"How's school, Abigail?" Ed Taylor rose to engulf his future daughter-in-law in a hug. As unwise as *I* thought the union was, Abby's marriage to Brian Taylor would create a genetic, personal, and political alliance between her birth Pride and his. Their parents would share grandchildren. Brian would someday run Rick Wade's territory. When problems arose on the council, Ed Taylor would go to bat for Rick and vice versa.

"School's good," Abby said. "Just one semester to go."

I frowned at the reminder of how quickly time had passed. If she only had one semester to go, then she was, what? Six months from being married?

She wasn't ready. She still hardly wore the ring.

I made a mental note to talk to Rick about postponing the wedding on Abby's behalf in light of the fact that she clearly needed more time. And the equally important fact that her fiancé was a gutless asswipe.

Wait, that wasn't fair. Brian wasn't a coward. He

just wasn't an Alpha. But my point would stand.

"Well, I have one semester left for my *bachelor's*," Abby qualified, and her father looked up in surprise.

Ed laughed, but he didn't sound truly amused by the implication that his son's wedding might be postponed for another two years. "Sounds like she has plans for some more of your money, Rick."

"It's not *my* money." The council chairman smiled at his daughter, practically swollen with pride. "She's on a full academic scholarship."

"Three-point-eight GPA," I added.

Abby glanced at me with both brows raised, obviously surprised that I'd been listening to her chatter on the plane.

"That's our girl!" Marc called from the hall, and I turned as he strode through the doorway with a giggling, dark-haired toddler tucked under one arm like a sack of feed. "Clearly, spending summers on the ranch has paid off!"

"Are you seriously claiming credit for my academic accomplishments?" Abby demanded, but we could all hear the smile in her voice. She was happy to see everyone, even if the Lazy S was just a layover on an unexpected trip home to South Carolina.

"I claim only what belongs to me." He swung the toddler upright and the child squealed in delight as his father tossed him into the air, then caught him in both arms. "Go say goodnight to your mom!" Marc ordered with false sternness, setting his son on the ground. After a moment of wobbling on both feet, the child tottered toward Faythe.

He had her beautiful green eyes, but I could tell from the flecks of gold sprinkled through the striations that when he hit puberty and shifted for the first time, his eyes would look just like Marc's in cat form. It was kind of amazing how the boy could look so much like each of them, yet entirely like himself at the same time.

For one brief, unguarded moment, I wondered what a son of my own might look like. But that would never happen. I wouldn't be running the Appalachian Pride forever, and Owen and Manx's non-Alpha-marriage was an anomaly in our world.

Faythe hung up the phone and swiveled in her chair to face her son. She brushed a lock of dark hair from his forehead, then hoisted him up to sit on the desk in front of her, where tiny stuffed animals vied with pens, notepads, and a wireless mouse for the little available real estate.

"No bed!" the boy said, and from the corner of my eye, I saw Abby watching them. Her expression said she wanted to rescue the boy from both his parents and his bedtime. As if maybe she'd done that frequently when she was a guest at the ranch.

"*Yes*, bed!" Faythe laughed, then held up a pink striped tiger and a purple polka dotted bear for her son's consideration. "Who gets to sleep with Greg tonight? Felix or Fuzzy Wuzzy?"

"Fuzzy!" little Greg shouted, plucking the bear from his mother's grip so he could clutch it to his chest.

"He always picks the bear." Marc elbowed me with a grin. "Elias Keller gave it to him." Keller was a good friend of Marc's and the only bruin I'd ever personally met.

Marc pulled me into a hug as if he'd actually missed me, and before I could extricate myself, Logan flew past us with Des on his heels.

"Whoa!" Marc let me go and grabbed the back of Des's shirt as Rick Wade scooped Logan up on his rebound from a leather couch cushion. "Everyone under the age of…" Marc glanced at Abby. "Twenty-one?"

She nodded, and I frowned. Abby was legal for *everything*?

"Everyone under the age of twenty-one, out!" Marc called. "Manx is going to kick off this sleepover with a bedtime story in Greg's room."

"No bed!" the toddler shouted when Faythe set him on the floor.

She frowned at him firmly. "Gregory Sanders-Ramos, if you're not in your room in two minutes, you can go straight to sleep with no story." She handed him the bear he'd dropped, then spun him around by both shoulders and gave him a little push toward Marc. Greg toddled off with his arms crossed over his small chest and his tiny lips turned down in a pout.

Abby's dad put Logan down, and the older boys reluctantly followed little Greg into the hall in the direction of his room.

"We have Logan for the week," Marc explained. "Angela gets him for Christmas morning but promised to bring him over that night, then he's all ours again for the New Year."

"That's great." I watched as Ethan's son disappeared around the corner. "He needs to spend time with his own kind."

"We don't even know if he's a shifter yet," Abby pointed out.

"He is," Marc and I said in unison, and she laughed. Probably because he and I rarely agreed on anything.

"Abby, give me a hug!" Faythe stood, and my eyes widened at the sight of her small but distinctively rounded stomach as she pulled Abby closer.

She laughed at my expression. "Did I forget to tell you?"

I nodded, and I could tell from Abby's face that she hadn't known either.

"Dr. Carver says it's another boy. Due in April. We want to call him Ethan." She watched me from across the room, and everyone was silent, waiting for my response.

"No better name in the world," I said at last, and Faythe visibly relaxed as she pulled me into a hug.

"It's good to see you, Jace. I hope you know you're always welcome."

When I hugged her back, I found that leadership, marriage, and motherhood had changed her scent as much as they'd changed the rest of her life. She smelled like Marc now, even more than she used to. She smelled like the droplets of little Greg's apple juice on her blouse, and like whatever prenatal vitamin supplements she was taking, and like the earthy, healthy hormones her second pregnancy was producing.

And she felt strong. Steady. Resolute, as she always had, but now her determination was backed by four years of peaceful and successful leadership.

Faythe was gorgeous, as always. But she was no longer mine, and for the first time since she'd chosen Marc over me, I was okay with that, because I had truly let her go. Finally, it felt less like I had lost her than like the rest of the world had gained her.

"You look terrific. Healthy and happy," I said.

She let me go, grateful tears standing in her eyes. "Thanks. As it turns out, a woman really *can* do it all—if she's willing to give up sleep almost entirely."

I laughed, as I was supposed to, and we were making our way toward the center of the room when Kaci stepped into the office in snug jeans, a long sweater, and a cropped leather jacket.

"I'm leaving," she announced, jangling a set of car keys in one hand, and again the subversive passage of time smacked me over the head. How the *hell* could she be old enough to drive?

Of *course* she was driving. She had to be…seventeen?

"Hey, Kace." I braced myself to be attacked with another homecoming hug, but her gaze hardly even skipped over me.

"Hey." Then she turned back to Faythe. "Can I take your car? Marc's still smells like feet."

"Sure," Faythe said, while Marc grumbled something he probably wouldn't have said in front of the toddler.

"Kace." I ducked into her field of vision, trying to catch her eye. "When you get back, you wanna—"

"Don't wait up." Kaci shrugged. "I'll be late."

"No, you'll be back by midnight," Marc called over his shoulder from the couch.

She heaved a dramatic sigh, and I was all but forgotten. "My friends don't have curfews!"

"Your friends don't have claws, either," Marc pointed out, and Abby glanced back and forth between them, as if she wasn't sure whether she was supposed to identify with the oldish teenager or the youngish adult.

"That is neither relevant nor fair!" Kaci snapped,

but Faythe only smiled, as if maybe she agreed. Secretly.

"Midnight," Marc insisted. "That's an order."

Kaci growled and clutched her keys, then slammed the office door and stomped out of the house. Marc chuckled when the car started, then tore out of the driveway as if the gravel were on fire.

Faythe gave me a sympathetic look. "Don't take it personally. It was hard for her to lose both you and Ethan so close together."

Lose me? Kaci hadn't....

But hadn't she? It had been three years since I'd visited. That was an eternity in teen-time, and her crush on me hadn't exactly been a secret. She'd probably felt abandoned—an innocent casualty of my avoidance of Faythe and Marc.

I was almost relieved when Rick Wade cleared his throat, calling the meeting to attention. "Now that we're all—"

Light footsteps clacked from the hallway, then the door opened and Karen Sanders backed into the room, carrying a silver tray loaded with full mugs and a pot of coffee. A chin-length strand of gray hair fell across her face, and when she tried to blow it out of the way, Marc rose to take the tray from her.

"You don't have to do that, Mom," Faythe chided. "We can all get our own coffee."

"I've never *had* to do it," Karen—Rick's sister and Abby's aunt—said. "And I really don't mind." She distributed mugs and poured coffee but gave a Faythe a paper cup instead, with a glance at her daughter's pregnant belly. "But *you* only get hot chocolate."

"Because baby Ethan already has a sweet tooth?" I mock-whispered to Abby, who sat next to me on the leather couch.

She rolled her eyes and leaned closer. "Caffeine isn't good for a developing fetus."

"You know there's caffeine in chocolate, right?" I said as her father stood to address the room. Abby stuck her tongue out at me.

"Okay." Rick Wade cradled his full mug in both hands. "We've come together to discuss the recent rash of human murders in the Appalachian Territory, and with six council members present, we have the quorum required to put a plan into action." He turned to me. "How many murders have there been so far?"

"Three." I was acutely aware of each gaze trained on me. I'd arrived at the meeting with one strike already against me in the minds of my fellow council members. Even those who'd supported my takeover of the Appalachian Pride. After all, how good can an Alpha possibly be if he doesn't realize there's a serial killer loose in his territory until the bastard's already slaughtered three humans?

"And we're sure the killer is a stray?" Marc asked.

"Actually, we're *not* sure, because we haven't been able to inspect any of the crime scenes yet." I set my mug on the end table to my left, then leaned forward with my elbows resting on my knees. "The first two victims were killed last month, but the first didn't get much press until the second established a pattern. Until then, the first victim was assumed to have been mauled by one of his own dogs."

"How can we be sure that's not what happened?" Ed Taylor asked.

"The claw marks on first and second victims match, which means they were inflicted by the same animal. The state medical examiner ran some tests and realized the wounds are from feline claws, not canine." I shrugged. "We all know cougars won't settle into any region inhabited by shifters, and jaguars don't live as far north as Kentucky."

Abby's eyes narrowed as she thought aloud. "So, we know for sure that the killer is one of ours, but not whether he's stray or Pride?"

I nodded, and her father frowned. For a second, I thought he'd ask her to leave the room because she was neither an Alpha nor an official advisor to the council, like Karen. But before he could make up his mind, Faythe leaned forward, one hand resting on her stomach. "I assume the plan is to ID the killer and take him out?"

"ASAP. Assuming the vote tonight supports execution," I added. "The third murder took place three days ago, and that scene's the only one still fresh enough to be of much use. Now that the cops are done with it, I'll be checking it out personally as soon as I get home."

"In Manchester?" Abby sounded like something was stuck in her throat, and though she was staring at the rug, her eyes were unfocused.

Bert Di Carlo frowned. "What?"

"Manchester is where the third murder took place." I turned back to Abby. "How did you know that?"

"Um…TV." She met my gaze but seemed to struggle to pull my face into focus. "It must have been on the news. You're going there, what? Tomorrow?"

"That's the plan."

Rick took a sip from his mug, his focus still trained on me. "Just tell us what you need."

"If I recognize the killer's scent, I won't need anything. Mateo, Chase, and I will find him." I glanced at Bert Di Carlo, Mateo's father, in acknowledgment of his son's skill. Teo was the first enforcer who'd signed on with me, and he'd been my right-hand man since I took over the Appalachian Territory. "If I don't recognize the scent, I'll overnight each of you a sample for help with the identification and we'll proceed from there. Objections?"

I glanced around the room, waiting for an argument, but everyone seemed satisfied with the plan. Faythe looked almost as relieved by that as I felt.

Rick stood again, and every gaze followed him. "Sounds good, Jace. All in favor of capital punishment for the killer or killers, whenever he or they are found?"

I stood, and one by one, my fellow Alphas joined me. The sentence was unanimous.

"That went a lot better than I expected." I glanced at Abby, expecting to see her I-told-you-so face, but she looked away as soon as I made eye contact. She looked worried.

No, she looked scared.

I ducked to catch her eye, trying to decide whether I should ask her what was wrong in front of the crowd or wait for privacy. Then Jerald Pierce clapped me on the back, and the moment was over. "These meetings go pretty smoothly when we all have the same objective."

But I understood the part he'd left unspoken. The last time the council disagreed on something serious, my stepfather had started a war as an excuse to have Marc and me executed, and Faythe forced into marriage.

"Okay!" Karen stood and began gathering empty coffee mugs, and I noticed for the first time that I could see her veins through the skin of her hands. My mother's looked much the same. "Who wants chili?"

Anticipatory chatter accompanied the general movement toward the office door, and my stomach was already growling. I hadn't had Karen's chili in years.

"Wait." Abby spoke so softly that at first no one else seemed to hear her. She cleared her throat and tried again. "Wait. Dad, I can't go home with you tomorrow."

"What?" Rick Wade arched one brow at me, as if I had any idea what she was talking about, but I could only shrug. Suddenly, I had an all-new respect for the late Greg Sanders, who'd constantly been left out of the loop by the only young tabby in his Pride—Faythe, of course.

Wade turned back to his daughter. "Why not?"

"Because I belong with Jace."

My pulse jumped. Everyone turned to stare.

Abby's face flushed as red as her hair. "That came out wrong. I meant that Jace will need *all* his enforcers to catch the killer. Including me."

"*What?*" Rick turned on me, anger flashing bright in his eyes. "You hired my daughter? You had no right—"

"Hold on a minute," I growled as fire surged through my veins in response to the challenge from a fellow Alpha. I had no intention of fighting Rick Wade, but my body didn't know that. I had no idea what Abby was talking about, but there was a reason conflicts between Alphas escalated quickly—we were hardwired to exert our dominance whenever it was challenged. "In fact, I *do* have the right. Abby isn't yours anymore. She's mine."

Abby's eyebrows shot up and her flush deepened.

Damn it. "I mean, I'm her Alpha, and I don't need your permission to hire her." I would only need his blessing if I tried to hire a member of his Pride. Which Abby no longer was.

Shock rippled across his angry scowl, and I could see the brutal realization as it dawned on him. Abby was an adult and a member of someone else's territory; he no longer held any authority over his own daughter.

That had never happened before, because in the history of the US Prides, Abby was only the second tabby to leave home, and she was the first to actually transfer into another territory.

True, her membership in my Pride was intended to be as temporary as my leadership of it, but that didn't change the fact that she was now under my sole authority. Just like all the male members of my Pride.

"I..." Rick struggled to finish his sentence, while everyone else looked on in the tense silence. I almost felt sorry for him.

"There's really no need to get worked up," I said, when his mouth just kept opening and closing. I turned back to Abby with a scowl, silently demanding an explanation for why she would pit one Alpha against another. "I didn't hire her."

"The hell you didn't!" But the indignation in her voice didn't match the desperation in her eyes, which practically begged me to just go along with...whatever she was up to.

She should have known better.

Karen quietly closed the office door. Our council meeting had just gone into extra innings, and nobody wanted to miss a single pitch.

"*First* of all, don't *ever* curse at your Alpha," I growled, only slightly mollified when Abby lowered her gaze and took a small step back, accepting my rebuke with none of the resistance or hesitation she'd shown in the past, when we weren't in a room full of Alphas. Normally, I wouldn't have cared about her language; that particular courtesy was antiquated, in my opinion. But by shouting at me, she had challenged my leadership, and letting *anyone* get away with that would erode my authority. "Second, you do not work for me."

"I apologize." Abby still stared at the ground, yet her voice was neither soft nor weak. "But if you'll recall, after I freed my roommate from those ass—" She stopped abruptly for a rephrase, and one corner of Faythe's mouth twitched. "After I took out those hunters over fall break, you said there'd be a job waiting for me if I wanted it."

My eyes fell closed. *Son of a bitch!* I'd forgotten all about that because I hadn't intended it as a real job offer. When she'd gone back to school without even mentioning it, I'd assumed she'd taken the offer as the simple compliment I'd intended. As evidence that her Alpha had noticed and appreciated her abilities.

I scrubbed both hands over my face, stalling for time to think. "I meant for that offer to apply *after* you graduate." I hadn't thought she'd take it seriously, because she was supposed to marry Brian right after graduation.

"But you never said that."

Irritation narrowed my gaze at her. "You never

accepted the offer."

Her brows rose. "I'm accepting it now."

Damn it. I'd walked right into that one, and I couldn't get out of it without going back on my word.

A good Alpha *never* goes back on his word, and Abby knew that.

She'd just thrown me under the bus in front of half the territorial council.

FOUR

Abby

My heart thumped so hard, I felt the jolt of each beat in my bones. Jace looked like he wanted to *kill* me, and I couldn't blame him; I'd just made the council's junior-most Alpha look like a fool in front of his peers.

That hadn't been my intent, but if desperate times truly justified desperate measures, my conscience was in the clear.

At least, that's what I tried to tell myself.

For one long moment, nobody spoke or moved. Ed Taylor—who'd paid for the ring his son gave me—looked like I'd just ripped his heart out and handed it to him, still dripping blood. As guilty as I felt, I made myself look away from him so I could keep my eye on the goal.

Thoughts rolled across Jace's face like cards in a slot machine and I could hardly breathe, waiting to see where they'd settle. I knew the moment he realized I had him trapped, and his visible anger leached the warmth from my body.

Jace was *pissed*. He would make me pay for forcing his hand, just like he would if I were one of the toms. I was about to find out just how committed to feminism my Alpha really was.

"Fine. We'll swear you in tomorrow." His eyes narrowed and he crossed both bulging arms over a sculpted chest that strained against the material of his shirt. "But this is a full-time commitment, and you *will* give it everything you have." He marched toward the office door, and a path opened in front of him as everyone moved out of the way. "I'll expect your school withdrawal forms on my desk first thing Monday morning." Jace stepped into the hall and slammed the office door at his back.

I jumped, startled, and only once all the stares had settled on me did Jace's declaration sink in.

Withdrawal? I'd have to quit school, one semester shy of graduation?

Whether or not I *had* to quit, he had the authority to *make* me quit—especially if he thought that would change my mind. But it wouldn't. It *couldn't*, no matter how badly I wanted to graduate.

This was more important. Even if I couldn't explain that to anyone else.

"Jace, wait!" I threw open the office door and ran after him, heedless of the stares and whispers, but the back door was already closing behind him. I followed him onto the lawn stretching between the main house and the guesthouse out back, where he'd lived as an enforcer. "Please, just...wait."

Jace stopped but didn't turn around, so I had to

circle him to see his face. His eyes sparkled like ice in the moonlight, and they looked at me as if he no longer had any idea who I was.

"I'm *so* sorry." An hour before, his arms had held me as if I meant something to him, and now they were crossed over his chest, defining a tangible barrier between us. "I didn't mean for... That's not how the whole thing played out in my head," I said, already mentally cursing myself for the lame finish.

"What, you thought we'd celebrate you strong-arming your way onto my staff by throwing confetti and popping corks?"

"No, I..." I shrugged miserably. "I didn't think I'd have to strong-arm anything. I mean, you said you'd have a job waiting for me, if I wanted it." But we both knew that he hadn't actually meant that offer any more than I'd meant to take it.

I'd accepted out of the sudden terrifying realization that there was no other way for me to stay in the Appalachian Territory.

"I'm sorry for springing it on you, Jace." My real mistake wasn't accepting the job—it was *how* I'd accepted the job. "But I *really* need this." I'd had no other choice. Maybe someday he'd understand that.

"Be careful what you ask for, Abby," he growled.

Or maybe not.

The betrayal shining in his eyes bruised me all the way to my soul. I'd destroyed whatever trust he'd had in me, and that electrifying warmth his gaze had taken on recently? I'd *totally* killed that.

Not that that part mattered. I was going to marry Brian, even if his wasn't the face I saw when I closed my eyes or the voice that whispered my name in my dreams.

So then, why did the new chill in Jace's eyes sting like an ice dagger shoved straight through my heart?

Faythe sank onto the living room couch next to me, holding two bowls of chili. She moved gracefully in spite of the change to her center of gravity, and under any other circumstance, I would have asked if I could feel the baby move. I'd felt little Greg when she was pregnant with him, and that had been like laying my hand over a miracle.

Or over that incubating gut-monster from *Alien*.

Faythe handed me one of the bowls. She'd ringed the inside edge with a row of corn chips and had topped the whole thing with a layer of shredded cheddar.

"Thanks." I scooped up a bite of chili with one of the chips, then chewed slowly so I couldn't answer the question she obviously wanted to ask. For a while, we ate in silence except for the crunching, and I listened to the buzz of various conversations from the rest of the house, where the other Alphas and enforcers had gathered in small groups to talk about…well, me.

Jace's was the only voice I didn't hear. He'd gone for a walk in the woods.

"So," Faythe said when she'd eaten the last of her corn chips, "what was that all about?"

I pushed a bean around in my bowl with my spoon. "You're the last person I expected to criticize my career choice."

Her right brow rose, and I lowered my gaze in a gesture of apology. I'd managed to piss off three

Alphas in the span of an hour. I might have assumed that was some kind of record, if I hadn't known Faythe when she was a teenager.

"I'm not criticizing. In fact, I think you'll make a great enforcer." She scooped up a bite of chili with her spoon. "But you had no intention of becoming one until half an hour ago, and we both know it."

"Actually, I've been considering accepting Jace's offer after I graduate."

She studied me for a moment, looking past that partial-truth for the whole story. "When were you going to tell Brian? And your parents?"

I shrugged. "It didn't feel fair to upset everyone before I'd made up my mind."

"But it felt fair to spring it on everyone during a council meeting?"

"No, that just kind of happened." I stared into my bowl. The chili smelled amazing, but my appetite had fled. All I could think about was the look of betrayal on Jace's face.

"So, why the sudden rush to do it today instead of next June?"

I scraped cheese from the side of my bowl with my spoon while I considered my answer. The whole truth wasn't an option, and my best chance for getting away with the necessary lie was to keep it *close* to the truth. Though that didn't really assuage my guilt for being less than honest with her.

If there was anyone I wished I could confide in, other than Jace, it was Faythe.

"It's this case," I said while she chewed. "The murders. If I wait until this summer, that'll all be over, and I'll just wind up patrolling the territory on foot with Chase or Teo."

"And that sounds boring to you?"

Not really. I looked forward to any excuse to prowl in cat form. There weren't many chances for that at school. But it was too late to back out of the lie now, so I shrugged. "Yeah."

Faythe looked disappointed. "Abby, is the excitement of a murder investigation really worth quitting school? I mean, even if things *are* dull in June, that won't last long. It never does, unfortunately."

"I know, but—"

"And even if you start tomorrow, you'll only be in training. Jace isn't going to give you much involvement in something this dangerous as a rookie. Especially since..." She shrugged, leaving me to my own conclusion.

"Since I forced his hand?" I desperately wished I'd realized what I needed to do in time to give him a private heads up, but truthfully, that was only *one* of the do-overs the universe continued to deny me.

Faythe nodded. "I'm not sure whether to be relieved or disappointed that you know exactly what you just did to him."

"Yeah, me neither. As many lessons as I've learned the hard way, you'd think I'd be a little wiser."

Faythe exhaled slowly. "What's wrong, Abby?" She set her empty bowl on an end table and twisted on the couch to face me, folding one leg beneath the other. "What's this really about?"

"Nothing." But I was a bad liar, and everyone knew it. "I just want to help with the investigation."

My father chuckled, and I looked up to find him standing in the doorway, cradling a fresh cup of coffee. He didn't look irritated with me anymore, but that didn't mean much. His poker face was second nature. "Honey, Jace doesn't need your help."

"I know. I'm helping myself. I want to learn."

"About murder?" My dad glanced from me to Faythe, and I could practically hear his thoughts, even though they didn't show in his expression. He was thinking that whatever had gone wrong with his niece—whatever had turned her into an insurrectionist, no matter how well-intended—was contagious. He'd probably round up all the uninfected tabbies in the morning to keep them safe from themselves.

"Not murder specifically. I want to learn about Pride structure and management." Surely that was believable, considering my college major. "Dealing with the bad guys. Assisting my Alpha. Protecting the territory."

My father sank onto the chair across from us. "But that's enforcer business."

"*I'm* an enforcer."

"No," Faythe said, in the gentle tone she usually saved for small children. "You're a trainee."

"Speaking of which..." Brian stepped into the living room from the hall, and a sudden jolt of nerves made my pulse race. I should have told him about my new job in person, instead of relying on the Lazy S grapevine. I owed him that much. "It's time to get started." Brian's expression was blank and his voice sounded tense. "Jace asked me to take you on patrol."

Of course he had. First, he'd told me to quit school, and now, he was pairing me with my fiancé. He was trying to show me all the things I'd have to give up to work for him, convinced that I hadn't truly thought the whole thing through.

I understood the consequences of my decision,

and while they were harsh, they didn't matter. I'd done what had to be done, and really, wasn't that kind of the pillar of an enforcer's job?

I stood, and Faythe took my empty bowl.

Brian studied my face, but his was unreadable. "Change into something warmer and meet me out back." Then he stomped off down the hall. A moment later, the back door slammed shut, and I flinched.

My father chuckled. "Lots of doors being slammed tonight."

And each one felt like a potential life path being closed. I could only hope that somewhere, someone was opening a window.

"So, this is really what you want?" Brian held a bare branch out of the way for me, and even though I knew he was just being nice, probably out of habit, I almost wished he had let it smack me in the face. That was what I deserved, for blindsiding him with plans that would affect us both. But he was too nice a guy, which was what I'd liked about him from the beginning. Brian hadn't changed.

I had.

"You'd truly rather be out here chasing bad guys and tearing up your clothes on thorns and branches than married to me?"

I ducked beneath a low-hanging limb and stepped over an exposed root. "It's not an either-or situation. Faythe makes both work."

"You're not Faythe."

"Ouch." I'd reminded Jace of the same thing just

hours before, but hearing it from Brian stung.

He took my arm as I stepped over a cluster of brambles. "I didn't mean it like that."

"No, you're right." I pulled my arm free gently. "I'm not Faythe, and you're not Marc." But their arrangement only worked because they split the parenting workload just like they split the Alpha workload, and that was just as doable for Brian and me if he was willing to be an active parent.

But a big part of me was glad he hadn't suggested it.

"Brian." I put one hand on his jacket sleeve, and he turned to face me. Even if he hadn't been standing in a beam of moonlight, I would have recognized the hope shining in his eyes. "Listen. This is just like college—a learning experience. Self-improvement. You've always known I want to be very involved in the running of my Pride." I'd chosen a political science major with a minor in psychology for a reason: so I could learn from humanity's successes and mistakes. "I just didn't realize I want a physically active role until tonight. But I don't know that this is what I want for the rest of my life. I only know I want to try it." I shrugged, relieved to see that he relaxed further with every word I spoke, which meant that I was digging myself *out* of a hole for once. "And Jace wants me to quit, so when I've had enough, it's not like he'll try to keep me."

"So, this is for us?" Brian's eyes brightened. "For when we take over your dad's territory?"

I blinked, surprised by his conclusion, though in retrospect, I could see how he'd come to it. I'd meant that this was for *me*—at best, a partial truth—but Brian could only conceive of *us*. "Sure."

"Should I sign up for some classes? Maybe a leadership seminar?"

I almost laughed out loud. "I'm sure Faythe and Marc are teaching you everything you need to know."

Brian nodded. "And your father will take over from there, after the wedding."

The wedding. I'd been trying not to think about that for almost four years.

"We should really set a date."

I shook my head, and too late, I realized I should have at least pretended to give that some thought. "There's still plenty of time."

His frown deepened, and he suddenly looked younger than twenty-six. "I thought you'd get more excited as you got closer to graduation, but you still don't seem very interested in the wedding. Your mom and I are practically planning it ourselves."

My brows rose. "You're helping my mom plan the ceremony?"

"Someone has to." He crossed his arms over his jacket. "But, Abby, I don't know the difference between periwinkle and sky blue. You'd know that if you ever answered your phone."

"I'm sorry." I hadn't been fair to him, and I had to fix that. Brian was exactly what I'd needed when I was eighteen, and it wasn't his fault that I was no longer the girl I'd been when I'd agreed to marry him. That now I wanted more.

That when I closed my eyes, I saw a set of bright blue ones staring back at me.

I shook my head, trying to shake loose thoughts I had no business thinking. Brian would make a great father, and so what if he wasn't stellar Alpha material? Times had changed. *I* could be the stellar Alpha.

"Okay." I exhaled, mentally resigning myself to what I was about to say. "Send me whatever wedding stuff my mom gave you." I held my index finger up to stop his smile before it got out of hand. "But consider yourself warned—I don't know the difference between periwinkle and sky blue either."

"Well, I'm sure either of them will look beautiful on you." He frowned. "Oh, wait, the bride usually wears white, doesn't she?"

Usually. The word echoed in my brain until I couldn't hear anything else.

Brian looked horrified. "That didn't come out right. I didn't mean you can't wear white. *Of course* you'll wear white."

"Brian." But I didn't know what else to say.

"I'm so sorry." He hesitated. "You never talk about it, though. Don't you think we should—?"

"No." I said it too quickly, and he looked hurt. "I'm sorry, but no." The last thing I wanted was to discuss my very darkest memories in the middle of the woods with the man I'd be marrying in six months.

"If you change your mind…" He tried to pull me into an embrace but let go immediately when I didn't relax or hug him back. "Okay, you're not ready. That's okay. Sometimes, it takes a long time to get over—"

"That's not it," I snapped, irrationally irritated by his assumption that he knew what I was thinking and feeling.

He knew *nothing*. Because I'd never told him. Just the thought of how that conversation might go made me sick to my stomach.

"Is it me?" Brian frowned, studying my eyes. "Am

I the problem?"

"No."

"Then it's Jace." His gaze dropped to the ground, but not before I caught a fleeting glimpse of jealousy. "I should have known."

"What?" My pulse raced with a sudden burst of alarm. "No—"

He looked up sharply. "I see the way you look at him, Abby. He's so pissed at you right now that he can't even stand to be in the same house with you, but you still have that look on your face, like you want to take a bath in his pheromones."

My face flushed, and I hoped he couldn't see that in the dark. What I wanted didn't matter, because it wasn't reciprocated. Because it would be *extraordinarily* inappropriate. Because I'd already given my word and accepted a ring. "It's not like that, Brian. He's my Alpha."

"That's why you want him, isn't it? It's some kind of biological imperative. He's an Alpha, so deep down, you think he must be the best possible father for your kids, but—"

"Okay, that's enough!" I snapped, finished with trying to coddle his ego. "My biological imperatives are not the issue. I don't even *have* biological imperatives, because this isn't the *Stone Age* and I'm not some knuckle-dragging cavewoman, helpless to fight her reproductive urges."

Brian's eyes widened, and I could practically smell panic in the beads of sweat that popped up on his forehead. He'd never heard me yell. He only knew the Abby who'd been afraid of her own shadow. Afraid of *everyone's* shadow.

The Abby who would agree to almost anything

just so she wouldn't have to talk anymore.

But that Abby was gone, and *this* Abby was going to have to start talking her way out of trouble rather than into it.

"Jace is my Alpha and nothing more." I took another deep breath to cover the hitch in my pulse. "I'm wearing *your* ring." I held up my left hand, and the diamond glittered in the moonlight. "Does that make you feel better?"

Brian nodded. "I guess I just needed the reminder. Sometimes, it seems like everyone else knows you better than I do." He took my hand, running his thumb over my knuckles. "I love seeing that on your finger."

Yet somehow, I couldn't get used to the bulk of the ring, as if that one third of a carat weighed as heavily on my mind as it did on my hand.

Brian cleared his throat, then met my gaze with more boldness than I'd ever seen from him. "I'll be *so* good to you, Abby. I'll do everything I can to make you happy."

My chest ached as if he'd punched me square in the sternum, but my heart was the real target. Brian was sweet, and honest, and my parents loved him. Maybe someday I could too.

Maybe…

"I know you will," I said at last. His eyes lit up, and it worried me that a few words from me could change his entire demeanor. I didn't want to be responsible for his mental state. Hell, I didn't want to be responsible for my *own* mood.

"Okay. I need some space now, if you don't mind. I need to think."

Brian frowned and glanced around at the dense

woods. "I'm not supposed to leave you alone out here."

I made sure he could see me roll my eyes. "I'm an enforcer now. Besides, we're in the middle of the South-Central Territory, less than a mile from the ranch. I'll be fine."

He glanced in the direction of the main house. "You sure?"

"Yeah. I'll catch up with you before you even get back. I just need a few minutes. Please."

"Okay. But hurry." He took one last look at me, then walked off through the woods. When his footsteps finally faded from earshot, I exhaled and leaned against a tree, staring up at the moon between its bare branches.

Why did I find every conversation about my impending marriage *utterly* exhausting?

A twig snapped in the dark and I jerked upright, instantly on alert. I scanned the woods to my left and right, suddenly wishing I'd taken the time to shift my eyes. But then I inhaled to survey the ambient scents, and...

"How long have you been there?" I demanded in a whisper I knew damn well he could hear.

Jace stepped out of the shadows, his hands in the pockets of his jeans, his arms relaxed, as if he were on a casual midnight stroll. Through the deep woods, exactly where he'd sent me on "patrol" with Brian. "Long enough."

Shit. He'd heard everything Brian had said about him. "It isn't nice to eavesdrop."

Jace took a silent step toward me, and the gravity of his gaze belied his casual posture. "'Nice' isn't in an Alpha's job description."

"Brian just bared his soul, and he had no idea you could hear him."

"I gave him every opportunity to notice me." He took another step forward, his intense focus pinning me where I stood. Was that anger in the line of his jaw or…something else?

My heart hammered so hard, I was sure he could hear it. "Don't blame him. I didn't notice you either."

"You've been on the job for all of twenty minutes. Brian's been an enforcer for nearly five years. He should have noticed. And he should *never* have left you out here alone. Patrol *always* works in pairs."

"He was a little distracted." And now so was I. Jace was three feet away, and I could see every cerulean striation in his irises. Even in the dark.

"An enforcer can't afford to be distracted."

Was he still talking about Brian? Or was this about me now? "It wasn't his fault. I was…"

"Giving him false hope." He stepped closer, and I caught my breath. Something was different. His pulse was steady, but each beat of his heart sounded harsh and tight, as if the muscle was working harder than usual.

"No I… It might have been hope, but it wasn't false," I insisted.

"You're lying."

I'd heard his heart beat like that many times before, right before he pounced on prey. Yet he no longer looked angry enough to pounce on me. Maybe hungry enough, though.

That was it. Jace looked *hungry*. And not for food.

My heart jumped up into my throat. I'd seen glimpses of that craving in him before. When he'd seen the carnage I'd unleashed in the hunters' cabin.

When he'd seen the short cut of my skirt. But both of those times, professionalism and willpower had overruled any inappropriate appetite.

Now that hunger seemed to have been unleashed somehow, and I couldn't decide how to react. Surely, *anything* was better than the icy gaze he'd turned on me after the council meeting.

I was suddenly hyperaware that my idle hands wanted…something. "I'm going to marry him, Jace."

"Yes. You are." He stepped closer, and my pulse tripped, not in panic—I wasn't afraid of him—but with nerves. This wasn't the big-brother-Jace who called me kiddo and told me to wear a longer skirt. This was a pensive, intense Alpha I'd only seen glimpses of before. This was a predator closing in on his prey, and I couldn't tell whether he intended to devour me or simply play with his food.

"'Knuckle-dragging cavewoman.'" Jace chuckled, and each rich note resonated low in my stomach, then burned even lower. He took another step forward and we were a foot apart. "You're going to eat that poor kid alive. If he hasn't figured that out yet, he has my sympathy."

"Does he?" I wasn't sure how else to respond to the rapacious shine in his eyes or the way each movement he made suddenly felt tightly controlled, as if he were one overstressed thread of willpower away from reaching for me.

What would happen if that thread snapped?

What did I *want* to happen?

"No, you're right. I don't feel sorry for Brian." His voice was just a hint of sound, yet I heard every syllable. "Why did you railroad me, Abby?" Jace put one hand on either side of my shoulders, pressing me against the tree at my back with his very presence, and I couldn't tell if my sudden disorientation was because of his proximity or the rapid subject change.

"I didn't—"

"Don't even *think* about lying to me." His body was a torch blazing in the night, threatening to burn right through my clothes, though we had yet to touch. "You made a fool out of me in front of half the territorial council, and if Brian is the reason, so help me—"

"Brian? What?" I frowned up at him, confused.

"If working for me is just a way to delay your wedding, I'm disappointed in you. Faythe would never have used—"

"The hell she wouldn't!" I pressed myself so hard against the tree that the bark caught on my borrowed jacket and bit into my palms. "She would have done whatever it took to get what she needed out of life. She *still* would. But that's not what I was doing. I'm going to marry him. Eventually."

Jace stared down into my eyes, his breath warm against my cheek. Stirring my hair. "Your pulse didn't race while you were with him. Your pupils didn't dilate. There was *no* attraction."

Panic flooded my bloodstream like fuel dumped onto a fire. If he could hear what *hadn't* happened with Brian, surely could hear what *was* happening now. With my gaze caught on his beautiful mouth…

My face flamed, but I couldn't look away. "The job isn't about Brian."

"Then tell me the tru—"

I pushed up onto my toes and kissed him.

Jace went completely still, evidently as shocked by what I was doing as I was. Then he relaxed and slid one hand into my hair, not surrendering to my kiss but *guiding* it. He tilted my head and tasted my lower lip. I opened my mouth for a taste of him and Jace growled with pleasure, a sound so deep and strong, it triggered primal tremors all over me, lighting me up from the inside.

My entire body was on fire. I'd never felt anything like it.

Then Jace stepped back, ruthlessly severing all contact, and the space between us seemed suddenly colder than before. "What the *hell* are you doing?" he growled.

What was *I* doing? "It takes two." Yet the deflection of blame made me feel even guiltier.

Jace took another step back, and a brutal sense of loss settled over me with an almost tangible weight. "Abby, this can't happen. I'm your Alpha. Hell, now I'm your *boss*. And you're..." He glanced at the ring on my hand, which suddenly felt too heavy to lift. "Those are all lines I can't cross."

Can't cross. He hadn't said he didn't *want* to cross them.

I sucked in a deep, cold breath, trying to purge treacherous thoughts.

"I know." I had to fight to maintain eye contact. "I'm sorry." What the hell was I *thinking*?

"I mean it." He stepped back again, and his eyes closed. "I'm a mistake you don't want to make. I'm sending you home with your father. We'll start your training after the holiday, if that's still what you want."

Jace started to turn, but I grabbed his wrist and he froze. "I won't change my mind," I whispered, suddenly desperate to be taken seriously. Working for him had nothing to do with Brian or with my wedding. Hell, it had nothing to do with *him,* or with whatever had almost just happened between us. "You said I could start now. Alphas don't go back on their word. You *have* to keep me, Jace," I said, and his exhalation came on the tail of a frustrated growl.

His next words were a rumble so low and gravelly, I could hardly understand them. "Fine. But you're done for the night. Go to bed, Abby."

"Okay. I'm sorry, Jace." When he only growled at me again, I raced through the woods toward the ranch without looking back, silent tears trailing into my hair. I'd really messed up, and now Jace thought I was using him. Of course, I *was*, but he couldn't possibly understand why or how.

Or how much I hated myself for it.

Or the fact that I had no choice.

If I wasn't with him when he investigated the murder, I'd have *no way* to explain why my scent was at the scene of the crime.

FIVE

Jace

I followed Abby at a distance until she got to the ranch, then I shifted and headed back into the woods in feline form, trying to escape my thoughts. And give everyone else time to go to bed.

They could *not* get a whiff of Abby's scent on me.

What the hell was I thinking? Abby Wade was infuriating. She disobeyed any order she didn't agree with, then instead of apologizing, she would insist that she'd actually done me a favor. How could I ever have found that exciting? She was hazardous and unpredictable, like a bomb with a broken timer. Yet somehow, the more she pissed me off, the harder it was to get her out of my head.

I hadn't spent so much time thinking about a woman—especially one I'd hardly touched—since Faythe. But she'd never had the corrosive effect on my willpower that Abby had.

Back then, I'd crossed lines because I wanted Faythe and I was too young and stupid to give a damn about the consequences.

Now, consequences were all I ever thought about, but I'd kissed Abby back because I *couldn't fucking help it.*

I should have known better than to follow them. I'd sent her out with Brian to remind her of where she belonged, no matter how I felt about the pairing, but seeing them together had actually *hurt*, and an injured tomcat is a dangerous tomcat.

Even more dangerous was their complete lack of chemistry. Abby wasn't shy around him because of fear or inexperience. She was just completely unattracted to him.

I should *not* have been in on that secret. And I damn sure shouldn't have been happy about it.

I ran as hard and as fast as I could, concentrating on the feel of the earth beneath my paws rather than the images I couldn't seem to purge from my memory.

Abby leaning against that tree, crimson curls caught in the bark, breath puffing from her mouth in little white clouds.

Abby's eyes, deep brown, staring right through me as if she could see exactly what I wanted.

But what I wanted didn't matter. Whether or not she was attracted to Brian, Abby was taken. I'd been down that road before, and the emotional wreck at the end had nearly killed me. I couldn't go through that again, and I couldn't put her through it at *all.* Not to mention Brian. That spineless mouse didn't deserve Abby, but he didn't deserve to lose her either. None of this was his fault.

Keeping things professional would save their engagement and prevent my premature departure from the Appalachian Territory under a shroud of disgrace.

Cold air stabbed at my eyes and nose. Nocturnal mice, skunks, and rabbits fled from my path and I considered snagging one, since I'd missed out on Karen's chili. But to hunt, I'd have to stop running, and if I stopped, those thoughts would close in on me again.

Where the hell had she learned to kiss like that, anyway? Was that how she kissed Brian?

My blood boiled at the thought of him kissing her. Of his hands plunging into those fiery curls. Of him tasting her…touching her…

He had *no* right—

Except that he did.

She's not yours. My head was sure of that, but my body *vehemently* disagreed. My heart… Well, what the hell did my heart know? I hadn't even realized she'd grown up until a couple of months before.

A growl of frustration rumbled up from my throat, and rats skittered from a hidden den into the dark. The solution was simple, if unpleasant.

We would just pretend that kiss never happened.

"So, you and Abby, huh?"

I froze with the doorknob in my hand, the soft click of the latch still echoing in my head. I'd been sure everyone else was asleep.

"Kaci?" I blinked, and the guesthouse living room came into focus in the dark, another warp-speed race down memory lane.

Ancient springs groaned as her outline rolled over on the old sofa. "Yeah. Does Brian know?"

"There's nothing to know. What are you doing here?"

"Roughing it on the couch." She sat up on the farthest cushion, her shadowed silhouette clad in a baggy tee and yoga pants. "Abby's in my bed. In case you were wondering."

I ignored the inference and tried not to wonder how she knew whatever she thought she knew about me and Abby. "And you couldn't rough it on your bedroom floor, in your sleeping bag?"

"What am I, eight years old?"

I knew better than to answer that, with tabbies suddenly turning into women overnight.

The other Alphas had all been put up in the main house or at Owen's, but I'd practically grown up in the guesthouse back when Marc, Vic, and Parker all bunked there, so I'd voluntarily exiled myself. "Hate to break it to you, kiddo, but the couch is mine."

"I'll scoot. You wanna spoon or be spooned?"

I growled in warning. Shifters sleep in big piles all the time—even nude—but an authority figure sleeping alone with an underage tabby? That was yet another scandal I could not afford.

"Kidding." Kaci laughed. "You're not my type."

Thank goodness. "And your type would be?"

"Under twenty-five. Which is why Faythe and Marc put a moratorium on enforcers anywhere near my age two years ago."

"Good for them."

She scowled at me in the dark. "Whose side are you on, anyway?"

"Theirs." I didn't even have to think about it. "You're too young to—"

"I'm six months younger than you were when you came to the Lazy S. If you were a virgin at seventeen and a half, I'll bite off my own claws."

How was it possible that seventeen looked so much younger on her than it had felt on me? I'd thought I was ready to conquer the world, one human girl's bed at a time. But the thought of little Kaci…

"My point stands." I crossed my arms over my chest. "Don't tell me anything you don't want reported to your Alphas."

She clucked her tongue in mock disgust. "You've gone over to the dark side."

"Join me. I hear we have cookies."

Kaci pushed a flattened couch pillow onto the floor and patted the cushion next to her. "Don't worry. I won't bite." Her bitter undertone hinted that she didn't find her own joke funny.

Unlike most tabbies, my sister included, Kaci wasn't overwhelmed with attention from toms, because of her reputation as a man-eater, of the literal variety. A genetic anomaly, Kaci was born to two human parents who carried recessive shifter genes. During her completely unexpected first shift, traumatized and in shock, she'd killed her human mother and sister. In spite of four peaceful years, she still hadn't managed to shake the label.

"Ha! I'm more worried about your bark than your bite, kid."

"I hate it when you call me that. So does Abby."

"She told you that?" I sank onto the left-hand couch cushion, facing her.

Kaci snorted. "She hasn't told anyone a damn

thing since she got here. But you don't always need words to say something." Her brows rose, daring me to argue. "For instance, I can smell Abby on you. Which would explain why she came straight in and brushed her teeth."

I groaned. "It's not what it looks like."

Kaci's brows rose. "Oh, I'm sure you just slipped and fell, and your tongue landed in her mouth. Right? Happens to the best of us."

"It better *not* happen." I ran both hands over my face, then through my hair. "Isn't it past your bedtime?"

"That's your problem, Jace." She stood, her pillow tucked under one arm. "You still see children where none exist. I grew up when you weren't looking. So did Abby."

"She's marrying Brian."

Kaci snorted. "She will if you let her."

If I *let* her? When was the last time anyone *let* Abby do anything? And if I even *thought* about coming between her and Brian Taylor, the consequences wouldn't just be personal—they'd be political. Ed Taylor and Rick Wade would want my head. Alliances had been severed for less, and if I was voted out of the council, someone else would have to take over the Appalachian Territory until Melody got married and her husband was ready to protect and defend it.

Goodness knows, Melody couldn't protect and defend her own opinion.

"It's complicated, Kace." I leaned forward with my elbows on my knees, trying to figure out how I wound up taking advice from a seventeen-year-old.

"No, it isn't. Abby knows what she wants."

"No, Abby has wedding jitters, manifesting as a

crush on both me and my job. But if I let her act on those, she'll regret it later and hate me for the rest of her life. Because I derailed her future."

"That's the dumbest thing you've ever said." She hit me square in the face with a couch pillow.

I snatched the pillow and smacked her in the shoulder with it. "I'm an Alpha, you know!"

Kaci shrugged with an evil little smile. "If you treat me like a child, I'll act like one. So will Abby."

"When are you going to put this thing out to pasture?" Abby slid into the passenger seat of my Pathfinder, wearing another skirt evidently chosen entirely because of how inappropriate it was, both for the season and for a drive alone with her Alpha. And possibly because of how *incredibly* hard it was to look away from her bare, smooth thighs displayed against my dark leather upholstery.

Had she packed *nothing* else?

I twisted my key in the ignition and made myself focus on the gas gauge as the engine rumbled to life. "What are you talking about? This vehicle is in its prime."

"You're living in the sad, sad past," she said, and the previous night's conversation with Kaci came back to haunt me. "It's time to join the rest of us in the here and now, and you better hurry up, because in six months, I'll be good and mired in my inevitable future."

The flat note running through her typically upbeat chatter betrayed the cheerful facade she'd been putting forth all day. As if nothing had happened between us in the woods. But every time I met her gaze, I found it a little harder to look away. We might not be talking about what had happened, but neither of us had forgotten.

"So, how far are we from the murder house?" Abby flipped the visor down and used the mirror to apply pink-tinted lip balm while I backed out of the airport short term parking spot. With the scent of strawberries came a twelve-hour-old memory of what that lip balm tasted like smeared across my own mouth.

My hands clenched around the steering wheel. *Focus, Jace.*

"It doesn't matter how far we are from the scene of the crime." I was *not* going to call it "the murder house." "Because you're not going. I'm dropping you at the lodge when I pick up Teo and Chase."

Abby dropped the lip balm into her purse and flipped the visor back up. "I can help. You should take me."

"FYI, becoming an enforcer makes you even *more* obliged to follow orders, not less." Especially since she'd been sworn in that very morning, in the presence of five other Alphas. Everything was official.

I was stuck with her, and that was like staring at a bag of candy I would never, ever be allowed to taste.

"I'm just trying to help. Why hire me, if you're not going to use me?"

Take me. Use me.

She *had* to be doing that on purpose.

"You know damn well why I hired you." I'd had no choice. "And you can't go to the crime scene, because you haven't even started training yet. *You*, rookie enforcer, are going to spend most of your holiday break sweating through drills with Lucas and Isaac at the lodge."

Abby twisted in her bucket seat to face me, her full lips pressed together. "Okay, I get that I have work to do and dues to pay, and putting me under the supervision of my own brothers is a *great* way to remind me that you're still mad. So, bonus points for that. But isn't this crime scene actually *on the way* to the lodge? I mean, we're practically going to pass right by it."

I glanced at her as I changed lanes and found her typing furiously on her phone, shielding the screen from the glare of the sun with her own body. "How did you know that?"

"I have the internet and a functional understanding of my map app." She held her phone out to show me that she'd already plotted our route to the crime scene. And that it was, at a glance, almost directly on the way to the lodge.

"But where'd you get the address? They don't release stuff like that."

"The police and the news stations don't, but sicko crime scene junkies who run voyeuristic blogs do."

"Well, aren't you…" Exhausting. "…resourceful."

"Thanks. And since we're in a hurry to get this thing shut down before the killer exposes the existence of shifters to all of humanity, can you *really* justify delaying the investigation just to take me back to the lodge?"

"Nice try." Even if she had a valid point.

"Come on; you know I'm right. What's the harm in stopping on the way home to scope things out? The killer isn't there anymore, right? So, it's not like I'd be in danger or anything. And you just admitted

I'm resourceful. I might actually be useful if you give me a chance."

"No."

Abby scowled, and I caught the reckless gleam in her eyes too late to do anything about it. "This is because I kissed you, isn't it?"

My fists clenched so hard around the steering wheel that it creaked. "No." It was because she'd railroaded me into hiring her, which had started our working relationship off on the wrong foot. But I couldn't admit that without sounding petty and unprofessional. "Are you using humor as a self-defense mechanism, or do you have *no* verbal filter?"

"Why? You have a problem with me kicking the elephant in the car?"

"Kicking the… Are you speaking in riddles?"

She laughed, and the comfortable quality of that sound caught me off guard. "You know, the elephant in the room? Only we're in a car." She rolled her eyes at my blank look. "It means we're both avoiding a subject that makes us uncomfortable."

"I know what it means, but your rephrase was less than helpful."

Her laughter said she didn't believe me.

"And I'm *not* uncomfortable."

"You are *so* uncomfortable. But I can't decide if that's because you didn't like the kiss or because you *did*."

"It's not… I don't…" I was uncomfortable because we'd made a big mistake, and officially, I wanted to forget it ever happened.

Unofficially, I wanted to replay the moment over, and over, and over.

"Why don't we talk about something else," I

suggested. "*Anything* else."

"No problem. Let's revisit the issue of the murder house and how I'm going with you to investigate."

"You're not going."

"Seriously, Jace, who would be better at training me than you?"

"Flattery? You've struck a new low." But the daredevil look in her eyes told me that was only the beginning.

Abby laid one hand over her heart in mock horror. "This *is* because I kissed you!"

I swerved onto the shoulder of the road and stomped on the brake. When I turned to scowl at her, those big brown eyes were staring at me expectantly, but it was the anxious beating of her heart that convinced me. She wasn't just being a pain in the ass—this really meant something to her.

I exhaled slowly. "If I let you come, will you *please* stop kicking that poor elephant?"

Her triumphant smile could have lit up the Dark Ages. "What elephant?"

"Are you sure this is the place?" Abby held her phone up to compare the image on her screen with the one visible through the windshield: the last house on a street that dead-ended in front of a small wooded patch of land. "This house is the wrong color. Either you or the sicko crime scene junkies have made a mistake." She turned to me with a wicked smile. "My money's on you."

"O ye of no faith at all. That *is* the wrong house. The one we're here for is on the other side of those woods." I chuckled at her sheepish expression. "We can't park in front of the scene of a vicious, mysterious mauling and not expect neighbors—or sicko crime scene junkies—to be curious, can we?" I lifted one brow at her, ridiculously pleased to have struck her speechless, even momentarily. "Guess you're not quite ready to replace me as Alpha yet, huh?"

She pulled her hair into a poofy ponytail, avoiding my gaze. "I wasn't trying to… I'm just trying to help."

"I know. Grab that box behind your seat." I got out of the Pathfinder and circled it to open the back hatch, then dug through the junk for a few specific items. When I returned to the front of the car, Abby was staring at the small box in her lap.

"This is an ammo box." She held it up, and sunlight glared across the print.

"Yes."

"It's empty."

"It's just for show. Set it on the dashboard."

Abby frowned, but complied, and when she got out of the car, I draped a used paper shooting target over the arm of her chair. I dropped a receipt for the ammo and a trip to a gun range on the center console, then wedged a rolled-up hunting magazine into the space where my windshield met the dashboard.

"We're hunters?" Her brows rose.

"That's the idea. We're here to hunt for the beast who killed that poor man on the other side of the woods." Which was close to the truth.

"Clever."

"I have my moments." I eyed her white down jacket, the only one she'd brought from the dorms. "Are you warm enough?"

"Yup." Abby grinned. "I run hot."

Was that a double entendre? Or was she just pointing out the obvious—that a shifter's metabolism kept us both slim and warm?

She closed her door and I locked the car with my key fob, then caught up with her as she stepped into the woods. "So, what's the plan?"

"First, we scout to make sure no one's home. Unless there's an app for that too."

"Give it a couple of years, and there'll be one that scans for human heat signatures."

"Until then, we'll have to use what nature gave us." Our eyes and ears, of course. And our noses. Cats can't track by scent, but we have very well-developed senses of smell, and we can identify nearly every odor we come into contact with. "When we're sure the house is empty, I'll find us a way in."

"We're breaking and entering?"

I shrugged. "With any luck, just entering."

That's when I realized Abby was wearing hiking boots rather than the party heels she'd worn the day before. She'd known from the moment she got out of bed that she would talk me into taking her to the crime scene one way or another.

I'd never even stood a chance.

We made our way through the woods quietly, on alert for any sign that another shifter had been there recently. But I saw no claw marks on bark, which would have indicated that a cat had climbed the tree. Both the undergrowth and bed of fallen leaves and pine needles were too thick to show any paw prints. And the only other cat I smelled was Abby.

She smelled like warm flesh, airport coffee, and good health. And strawberry lip balm. And a little like whoever she'd borrowed her jacket from. The residual scent was familiar.

"Is that Robyn's?"

Abby glanced down at the jacket. "Yeah. I couldn't find mine."

I'd never formally met Robyn, and I'd only had the chance to smell her once. She'd been unconscious and bleeding by the time I'd arrived at the cabin where those sick hunter bastards had tried to lure Abby to her death, then hang her taxidermied head on their wall. But once was enough for any cat worth his claws, and I should have recognized Robyn's scent earlier.

"How's she doing?"

Abby rounded a clump of evergreens a few steps ahead of me. "Better. She was having nightmares for a while, but those have mostly stopped. Her parents call all the time now, and I know they just want to help, but she never wants to talk to them. I don't think she knows what to say. I offered to take her to a counselor on campus, but she wouldn't even discuss it."

"It's a good thing she has you to talk to." Post-traumatic stress could be a real bitch, especially for humans, most of whom rarely witnessed any death, much less the violent slaughter of several close friends at once. "But I guess it could have been worse." And no one knew that with more certainty than Abby.

She turned to give me a very grave look. "It was plenty bad."

The sudden change in her demeanor worried me.

In college, Abby had made friends and gained both independence and confidence. By the beginning of her sophomore year, she'd regained her sense of humor and had become almost compulsively cheerful, as if putting her trauma behind her was a conscious decision and one that required relentless reinforcement.

Seeing her somber now was jarring, and it did not escape my notice that the change was in response to her friend's recent trauma rather than her own. As far as I knew, Faythe was the only person she'd ever spoken to about her own ordeal, and that was because Faythe had been there for part of it.

"Hey, is that the house?" she whispered, and I followed her gaze to a low-pitched roof barely visible between the treetops.

"I think so." I stepped in front of her to assume the point position, and she didn't argue.

Listening carefully, I pushed my other senses to the back of my mind as we crept to the edge of the yard ahead, sticking to the cover of the woods for the moment. The house was small and one story, with a cellar. The exterior cellar entrance was secured with a padlock and chain, neither of which I could break through without bolt cutters.

We had several pairs back at the lodge, and I'd thought I'd have a chance to pick them up, along with a couple of experienced enforcers.

I glanced over the deserted, overgrown backyard and found a weatherworn shed in one corner, next to the obligatory old car on blocks. The only thing I could make out inside the doorless shed was an ancient and rusted riding lawnmower.

The back wall of the house boasted peeling paint, several grimy windows, and a metal door centered over a set of prefab concrete steps. I probably wouldn't be able to hear any heartbeats or pulses coming from inside, but by all appearances, there wouldn't be any to hear.

"Put these on." I took a pair of leather gloves from my right pocket and handed them to Abby, then I pulled an identical pair from my opposite pocket.

"They're too big," she whispered, tugging the first one over her fingers.

"Make it work."

A second later, she held up both hands hidden by a comically large pair of gloves, which hung limp over her fingertips by at least an inch. Her hands were tiny. But then, so was the rest of her. She shrugged. "If the police are gone, they've probably already tested for fingerprints."

"Maybe." I tugged her gloves down as far as they'd go. "But we don't even know if they know it's a crime scene yet. So, we take precaution."

I stepped into the yard and she followed silently while I tried the back door—it was locked—then peered through three grimy windows. They were all locked too, and I saw no evidence from the rooms beyond that anyone was home. Or had been in several days.

The locks on the back door were substantial. I probably could have broken them, but if the police ever came back to the scene, they would see that the locks had been forced rather than picked—a feat beyond human strength. "We'll have to break a window," I whispered, peeking carefully around the corner of the house to make sure no one was out front within human hearing range.

Abby grabbed my arm, and I followed her line of sight to see the kitchen window standing open just a fraction of an inch. "What about that one?"

"I can't fit through."

"*I* can."

"No."

"Jace—"

"*No.*"

She crossed her arms over her chest and lifted one russet eyebrow at me. "You'd really rather break the glass—vandalizing some poor dead guy's property—than let me climb through a window and open the door for you?"

Damn her and her faultless logic.

"Fine. But don't touch anything," I insisted, and she immediately started tugging on the fingers of her right glove. "And leave those on."

"They inhibit my fine motor skills."

"That's my condition. Take it or leave it."

Abby rolled her eyes. "Fine." She reached up and slid the glass panel open, then peered through the bottom of the window, gripping the sill in her clown gloves. At five foot nothing, that was the only part she could reach. "I need a boost."

A boost. There was probably no way to accomplish that without touching her.

My heart pounded as I wrapped my hands around her hips, achingly conscious of each point of contact, and I was suddenly glad I was wearing gloves. After my utter lack of willpower the night before, I wasn't sure I could trust myself with any more skin-to-skin contact.

Abby glanced at me over her shoulder and her hair brushed my face. "Sometime this month, Jace."

But that time, I recognized her words for what they were—a distraction from *her* rapid pulse.

Whatever she was thinking had triggered a physical response she wanted to hide from me, and it was probably a good thing I couldn't read her mind.

Yet I wanted nothing more in the world than to know what she was thinking and how I fit into that.

My hands clenched around her hips involuntarily, and Abby's soft gasp nearly *broke* me. That was the sound of unexpected pleasure, and it belonged in a much more intimate time and another place.

A time and place we would never be in together.

God grant me strength…

I lifted her and got a face full of red curls, and they smelled like sweetened strawberries.

With a nearly silent groan, I realized that from that moment on, I would mentally associate fruit-flavored desserts with the feel of her hips in my hands and her hair against my cheek.

Abby braced herself against the sill, then crawled onto the kitchen counter. "Okay, just give me a sec," she called as she lowered herself onto the floor.

I lost sight of her when she rounded the corner, and a second later, something scraped the interior of the back door.

"The door's padlocked from the inside," she called, and I probably wouldn't have heard her if not for the open kitchen window. "Whoever this guy was, he *really* didn't want anyone getting in."

"Or out, evidently."

"Yeah." Her voice sounded strained. "I'm gonna have to open a window for you instead."

Before I could reply, her footsteps echoed to the left, and I followed from outside the house.

Something clattered to the floor.

"What was that?" I called through the thick back

door.

"Sorry!" Abby whisper-shouted as she appeared behind a grimy bedroom window.

"I thought you went in first to *avoid* vandalism."

She unlocked the glass pane and slid it open. "This place is a wreck. There's crap everywhere."

"What happened to your gloves?" I asked as I climbed through the window.

She shrugged, and a long red ringlet fell over her left shoulder. "They won't stay on."

I swallowed another growl. "You're supposed to be helping this investigation, not hindering it."

"We're in, aren't we?"

"Yes, and now your scent is all over the windowsill." I leaned forward to sniff the metal latches. "And on the locks too."

"Sorry." And she truly looked remorseful. No, she looked *guilty*, as if she'd committed a much bigger breach than a little scent transference. Maybe she was serious about her training after all.

"This is why you need some experience before you start investigating crime scenes. Just be more careful next time."

"I swear." Abby shoved her hands in her pockets and glanced at the bedroom door. "But it may be a little late for that in the kitchen. And the living room. Also the bathroom."

"What?" I sidestepped her and walked through the house, sniffing furniture and walls. Her scent was everywhere except the second bedroom. Even worse, so was Robyn's, thanks to the jacket Abby wore.

"How the *hell* did you have time to touch the whole damn house in five minutes?" I demanded on my way out of the bathroom. "You contaminated the entire scene!"

I glanced around the living room, ready to give her hell, but Abby was gone.

"Ab—"

A sharp cry sliced through my anger.

"Abby!" Terror ignited my veins like a river of fire, and I raced through the small house, glancing through every doorway. The rooms were all empty. Abby didn't answer.

On my frantic rush for the back door, I noticed that the cellar stood open at the end of the hall. *Damn it!* "Abby!"

I ran through the doorway and down the rickety stairs. Her scent was on the doorjamb and the stair rail, along with those of at least half a dozen humans. Blood had been dripped on nearly every step, but the scent was dull. It had been dry for days, at least. Maybe weeks. "Abby!"

The *overwhelming* scent of blood hit me halfway down the stairs. It was mostly old and mostly shifter. Specifically, stray. And it had come from *many* sources.

I found her around the corner from the staircase, frozen in shock. Her pulse was racing, but she looked uninjured. There was no one else in the cellar, but it had clearly seen frequent, recent use.

Against one wall stood a scarred wooden table, ringed with an obviously hand-carved groove all the way around the edge. The table was stained with old blood and still sticky with fresh blood. To the right stood another, slightly cleaner table covered in barbaric-looking tools. Lined up against one wall were several fleshless, cougar-shaped mannequins.

But none of that was the source of Abby's fear.

I followed her terrified stare to the wall above the bloody table, where a framed corkboard had been hung.

The board was *covered* with photographs of Abby.

SIX

Abby

Nononononono...

There I was, in the top left photo, walking through the quad at school. The leaves were still green and I wore shorts. That picture was from early fall.

He'd been watching me for *months.*

"Abby." Jace tried to tug me toward the stairs, but I pulled free. My gaze was glued to the corkboard. I couldn't stand to see the pictures, but I couldn't make myself look away.

Bottom row, fourth from the left. I was in profile at a register in the dining hall, paying for three sandwiches and a cardboard tray of bacon. Robyn had always wondered how I ate so much and never got any bigger, but whoever'd taken that shot knew about shifters and our high metabolic rate. That's why he'd—they'd?—been following me.

"Abby. Look at me." Jace stepped in front of me,

his hands on my arms, but I stared over his shoulder, still searching the photos for an explanation. For some motivation that would explain why we'd found some kind of creepy Abby-stalker-board in the basement beneath the scene of a murder.

I'd come expecting to have to cover my scent upstairs, but I'd never been in the cellar. If I had been, the whole thing might have gone down differently. Maybe I wouldn't be in so much trouble.

Maybe Jace wouldn't want to get rid of me.

In a picture at the bottom left corner of the board, I stood in the parking lot next to Robyn's car, my pack hanging low and heavy on my back. Mitch and Olsen stood to either side of me, and Danielle was bent over the trunk, arranging luggage.

My eyes watered. I hadn't seen any of them since the day that picture was taken, no more than five hours before Mitch, Olsen, and Dani had been slaughtered. Before Robyn had been dragged through the woods to a disturbingly furnished hunter's cabin for no reason other than that she was my friend. She was bait, intended to draw me to the scene of my own murder.

Fear cooled my skin like a cold wind. My teeth started to chatter. How could I have missed so much? I was supposed to have everything under control!

I'd known since the day I'd killed the hunters that they'd been watching me. Their leader, Steve, had actually signed up for my psychology class just to get close to me. He was the one who'd suggested the campsite, luring us into his very backyard.

I'd fallen into his trap and my friends had paid for my mistake. Now their ghosts were haunting me from a full-color, glossy four-by-six photograph.

But some of those pictures were taken *after* I'd killed Steve and his friends. Two of them were taken during finals, just days before.

A strangling sound caught in my throat.

Jace took me by the shoulders. "Abby." That time, when I tried to move away, he pulled me into an embrace, his body pressed the length of mine—a physical shield against a visual horror. "Don't look," he whispered into my hair, gently guiding my head toward his chest.

My temple grazed his collarbone. My arms slid around him. I inhaled deeply, and in spite of all the blood—both old and new—the only scent I registered was Jace's. He smelled like the forest in winter. Like soap and coffee. And like something wonderfully, indefinably masculine.

He felt like strength, security, and power.

I relaxed against him, letting his scent and the feel of him eclipse the horrific implications of that repulsive stalker-board.

"I'll take it all down." The steady thumping of his heart intensified, and for a second, I thought I could feel it through his shirt and my jacket, but that was impossible. Right? "You won't have to see any of it again," he whispered. "Come upstairs with me."

But when he let me go, his gaze snagged on mine and I got caught on that fierce connection, like a bug drawn toward a light. I knew better than to touch him again, but I couldn't make myself back away.

"I never should have brought you here." His voice was so raw, it hurt to hear. "I'm sorry. You should never have seen this."

"It's my fault." But I knew before the words were even out that he wouldn't understand them. I wasn't giving him a chance to understand. I *couldn't* give him that chance.

Jace's brows rose. "Believe it or not, I know how to say no. Even to you." A small smile tugged at one corner of his beautiful mouth, and I was suddenly *crippled* by the memory of that midnight kiss in the woods.

I would never get to kiss Jace again.

All at once, the air seemed too thick to breathe. I was going to marry Brian, and he would want to kiss me, but that would never be like kissing Jace, and every time he tried it, I would remember what kissing was supposed to feel like.

I was going to spend the rest of my life married to Brian but thinking about Jace. Because that was the right thing to do, and I'd made far too many bad decisions recently. But before that happened, I *had* to know...

"Is it hard for you to say no to me?"

"You know damn well it is." He stepped closer, and I sucked in a short breath.

"I'll try to make it easier."

He chuckled, and the sound slid down my spine to pool in more sensitive places. "I don't think you even know how."

That was true. I had no idea what I was doing. All I knew was that Jace was the only thing in that cellar that didn't terrify me. As little sense as it made, he felt safe and right. Even though every word he said and every look he gave me shortened the fuse on a bomb that *would* eventually explode and take us both straight to hell.

"I'm not doing it on purpose. I just..."

"I know." Jace closed the space between us, and

his hand slid behind my head. "Some things just can't be helped." He leaned down, and I closed my eyes as his mouth met mine. Jace took a slow taste of my lower lip, and when he pulled away I rose onto my toes, chasing him without thought.

Wrong or not, I needed more.

I touched my lip, trying to pretend I could still feel his mouth on mine, and when I looked up, the heat in Jace's eyes burned right through me.

He bent toward me again, and that kiss wasn't sweet or slow. It was fiery, and hungry, and desperate. It was his hand in my hair and mine on his neck. It was lips, and tongues, and even a little teeth. That kiss was a problem—no use pretending otherwise—and no wrong in the *world* had ever felt more right.

Finally, Jace tore himself away from me and stepped back, panic alive in his eyes. As if that kiss might never have ended at all if it hadn't ended right that second.

My heart beat so hard, my chest ached. Everywhere he'd been touching me a second before felt suddenly cold and aching. I wanted nothing more out of life in that moment than to rise onto my toes and kiss him again.

"There. Now we're even." He was breathing too hard. His eyes were dilated and his fists were clenched, as if he wanted to reach for me but was fighting the urge. "You messed up, and I messed up. That couldn't be helped, but now it's over. This is over, Abby."

I nodded, because he was right. Whatever *this* was, it had to be over. "Okay. Now what?"

"Now I take care of that." He gestured over his shoulder at the bulletin board, and that time, when I stared at the creepy pictures of myself, it was to get him out of my head. To forget what we'd just done. Again.

"You don't need to see any of this. Go upstairs and let me—"

"No." I frowned, still staring at the board. Something was…off.

"Just let me clean this up, and you can..."

I didn't hear the rest, because he'd just identified the problem without even knowing it. "This shouldn't be here," I murmured, still scanning the pictures.

"That's why I want you to go upstairs."

"No, this shouldn't be here *now*," I insisted. "That bulletin board is proof of stalking, which would tell any cop worth his badge that what happened here was more than an animal mauling. If those pictures were hanging when the police came, they would have taken them as evidence."

"You think someone put these up *after* the cops left?"

I shrugged. "Or someone put them *back* up."

"Maybe they left a signature." Jace leaned over the table, careful not to touch it. He inhaled deeply, then moved down the length of the wood, taking in all the scents. "There are too many to distinguish. Strays. Several of them. And at least half a dozen humans. A couple match the scents from the bedroom—they probably belong to the occupant. I assume the rest belong to the police."

"Wouldn't cops have worn gloves?"

"Good cops would have. Assuming they recognized this as a crime scene. But if the pictures weren't here when the police were, they probably just saw this as some hunter's man cave." He shrugged, forehead furrowed. "I have no way of knowing which scents belong to the good guys and which belong to the bad guys."

"But the cops couldn't have touched pictures that weren't here." I leaned over one end of the table and sniffed the nearest photo, bracing myself against the wall to keep from brushing the gruesome surface of the wood. Something acrid and artificial burned all the way up my nose and into my throat. "Chemicals. These weren't printed. They were processed the old-fashioned way."

"There's no darkroom here," Jace said, still studying the pictures. "They were brought from somewhere else." He pointed at the image of me and my friends by Robyn's car. "Is that the day of the camping trip?"

I nodded.

"Well, that confirms it. This is the same group who went after you in the woods. We didn't get them all."

"We" hadn't gotten any of them. I'd killed all three of the hunters who'd slaughtered my friends, albeit against orders. By the time Jace and his men had arrived, there'd been nothing to do but clean up.

And be there for Robyn.

"I have to update the council."

Panic shot up my spine like electricity along a wire. "If you tell my dad, he'll call me home."

"And I'll comply. They're hunting you, Abby. You need to be as far away as possible."

"You wouldn't send any other enforcer away when there's a killer on the loose. You need every set of claws you can get."

Jace crossed his arms. "Don't try to paint this as a

gender issue. I'd send any untrained enforcer someplace safer if he was being specifically targeted. Even the guys aren't bulletproof."

"Okay, but if I'm being specifically targeted, won't they just follow me? I mean, if they know where I shop, eat, and get my hair cut"—I pointed to each picture as I described it—"don't you think they know where I'm from? And do you *really* think I'm safer with anyone else than I am with you?"

His left brow rose. "Flattery will get you nowhere."

But I wasn't just blowing smoke—my Alpha was *truly* a force to be reckoned with, and his hesitation said he damn well knew it. "Jace, you'd be sending me home to an Alpha twice your age who has a third of your strength."

"We're talking about your *father*."

"Who knows his weaknesses as well as his strengths." I crossed my arms over my shirt, mirroring his stance to drive my point home. "How many challenges have you lost since you took over the Appalachian Territory?"

He didn't have to answer; if he weren't undefeated, he wouldn't still be in charge.

My father hadn't been challenged in twenty years.

"Besides, two of my brothers are here, and they'd take a bullet for me." Not that I'd let them. "And I promise that what just happened..." *That kiss.* "...won't happen again. So, don't use that as an excuse to send me away. Please, Jace."

I needed to stay in the Appalachian Territory for reasons I couldn't explain to him. But I *wanted* to stay for reasons he already damn well knew.

He scowled, but my victory was reflected in the set

of his jaw. "You learned more from Faythe than just fighting."

"You're just now figuring that out?" I tried to smile, but my effort faltered with one more glance at the Abby-board.

"Fine, I'll talk to your dad." He dug his phone from his pocket. "Go upstairs and look around for anything we can use, but do *not* take your gloves off."

I gave him a halfhearted mock salute, then headed up to the main floor.

"There's mouthwash in the bathroom," he called after me, and I panicked until I realized that wasn't a comment about my breath. It was a way to cover his scent on my mouth. But it was a very *obvious* way, so after I rinsed my mouth, I took a soda from the fridge and drank half of it.

A minute later, Jace did the same thing.

While he called Teo and told him to put together a cleanup crew, I rifled through drawers and closets upstairs, wearing those absurdly large gloves. When he called my dad, I shifted the internal parts of my ears so I wouldn't miss anything.

"Yes, we found the scene of the mauling, but it's more complicated than we thought." Then Jace listened while my father asked the inevitable question. "The victim was part of the group of hunters who attacked Abby and her friends in October. Based on the tools and chemicals we found here in the cellar, I'm guessing he was actually their taxidermist. It looks like the last stray he tried to kill and stuff killed him instead, but without having seen the other crime scenes, I can't say how closely they're related. It could all be the work of one stray bent on revenge. Or it could be that the hunters got sloppy and several of their victims got smart. Which makes sense if the strays knew they were being targeted. I'll call my contact in the Lion's Den."

Still listening, I sank into the living room desk chair and began sorting through the crap piled on the dusty desktop.

"Yeah, it's pretty gruesome," Jace continued. "She's holding up really well, considering. But, Rick, there's one more thing."

I froze, staring at a drawer full of old bills.

"These bastards were watching Abby. For months, it looks like. There are a bunch of pictures of her pinned up on a corkboard above the taxidermy table."

"But the hunters are all dead now?" my father said over the phone, and I only understood the words because I knew what he was most likely to ask.

"We think there's still at least one out there. Someone must have put the pictures up after the cops left."

"Send her home," my dad said, and that time I understood him, loud and clear.

"I actually considered that." Jace's tone straddled the line between respectful and assertive—Alpha politics at work. Technically, he didn't need my father's permission to keep me. I belonged to the Appalachian Pride. But my father was the council chair, and Jace had butted heads with him less than twenty-four hours before. "But the fact is that she's safer here. My enforcers are younger than yours by a decade, on average, and they're strong and fast."

They'd had to be, to help Jace hold onto territory that had been hostile for nearly the first two years of his tenure as Alpha.

"Hell, two of them are your own boys, Rick.

Between me, Teo, Isaac, and Lucas, we're better able to protect her than anyone else on the planet."

There was another pause, and my father's silence over the line told me he was thinking. Hard. I couldn't understand what he said next, but Jace's reply filled in the blanks.

"I swear on my life, Rick. I won't let her out of my sight."

The guys arrived thirty-five minutes later, which told me they'd broken every speed limit between Jace's lodge, which functioned as the capital of the Appalachian Territory, and the dead taxidermist's house.

"Holy *fuuuuuck*," Chase Taylor breathed, glancing around the gruesome cellar. He ran one hand through his dark curls and for a second, he looked just like his brother Brian. Only older.

"Those sick *bastards*!" my brother Lucas said from the bottom tread.

A heartbeat later, Isaac pushed him out of the way and clomped down the last three steps. He followed Lucas's gaze to the Abby-board, and after a second spent processing, Isaac pulled me into a hug designed to block my view of the pictures. As if I hadn't already seen them. "You okay?" he said into the top of my head.

"No. You're smothering me."

Isaac finally let me go, and a second later, Lucas, my second-oldest brother, pulled me into an identical embrace. At six foot six, Luke was a full half foot taller than our father, and as I had, he'd inherited our mother's pale skin and red curls, though he kept his pretty closely cropped.

Isaac was the youngest of my brothers, yet still two years older than I. He had our dad's straight brown hair and no freckles at all, and at six foot two, he was practically dwarfed by Lucas.

"What is all this shit?" Chase ran one finger over the nose of one of the mannequins, which resembled a skinned cat about his size, in feline form.

"They're forms used for stuffing taxidermied animals," I explained. "As near as I can tell from an internet search, cat-shaped forms are kind of hard to come by. My guess is that they were custom-ordered from a company that specializes in safari hunting supplies."

"That is *so* fucked up," Mateo murmured.

Jace had left the cellar untouched so that his enforcers could grasp the full scope of what we were facing. He and I had spent the past half hour upstairs, combing through the information we'd gathered about the house's owner. His name was Gene Hargrove, and based on current pay stubs from a gun-and-archery range, taxidermy was just his hobby.

A very expensive, dangerous, time-consuming hobby.

Unfortunately, according to all the news stations, the name of victim who'd died in Gene Hargrove's house was Joe Mathews. Which meant that the gun-toting, shifter-stuffing Hargrove was still out there. Still hunting.

Teo whistled as he glanced over the taxidermy tools and a small supply of unfamiliar chemicals. "How did we not see this coming?"

Jace shrugged, but his grim expression and the

tight line of his jaw belied the casual gesture. "They've been targeting strays. Wildcats."

"Titus didn't say anything about wildcats going missing? I smell at least…what?" Teo glanced at the rest of us. "Six? More?"

"At least," Jace agreed. "I'm waiting for a call back from him, so we'll know something soon." Titus Alexander was Jace's contact in the Lion's Den—a stray who'd been infected several years before. I hadn't met him, but both Jace and Faythe spoke very highly of him.

"But I think if he knew about it, he'd have told me," Jace continued. "The most likely breakdown of information is between the other wildcats and the Lion's Den itself. As hard as Faythe and I have worked to open a solid line of communication with Titus, he's working even harder to get the other strays to trust him. Some of them see him as a traitor for working with us."

I couldn't blame the wildcats for their distrust of us, and I knew Jace didn't either. Though most of the other Alphas saw the need for and inevitability of a Pride comprised of strays in the free zone, few were as eager as Jace, Faythe, and Marc were to actually take that step, and the wildcats could no doubt feel that reluctance to accept them.

"Have Faythe and Marc heard anything?" Lucas asked, and Jace hesitated before answering.

"I don't know. Rick offered to call them and the rest of the council so we could concentrate on cleaning this mess up and finding the sick bastard who's been stalking his daughter."

Every gaze in the room found me again. "She shouldn't be down here," Isaac said.

Jace turned to me with the first hint of a smile I'd seen from him since we'd stomped all over that line we'd both known better than to cross. Again. "You wanna tell them?"

I sucked in a deep breath. "You're looking at your newest coworker. I was sworn in this morning with six Alphas in attendance." I shrugged. "The ceremony broke some kind of record."

For a moment, there was only stunned silence.

"Why would you—" Lucas asked, but Isaac interrupted him.

"Why would *Dad* let you do that?"

"It wasn't up to him." I gave them another shrug, and all four turned to Jace.

"She's right," Luke growled. "Why would *you* let her do that?"

Jace bristled as if even in human form, his fur was standing on end. "*I* make the decisions for this Pride, and I don't owe anyone an explanation." He cleared his throat, and my brothers shuffled their feet on the grimy concrete, obviously unaccustomed to being reprimanded by their Alpha. At least, in front of an audience. "You four bring in the cleaning supplies and get to work. Teo, I want every photo and scrap of paper filed and catalogued."

Mateo nodded, then gestured for the others to proceed him up the stairs.

"Abby," Jace said, loud enough for them all to hear, "you're on intel duty. Go through every file on Hargrove's computer. And all his emails. We need to know who the rest of the hunters are and how many of them are left. And where they live, because that may tell us where Hargrove is hiding."

And if he were smart, he *would* be hiding.

I nodded, already jogging up the steps after the guys. I would also go through Hargrove's search history and any online bank statements—we hadn't found any hard copies. But most of what I was actually looking for, I could never reveal to the others.

Not even to my Alpha, even though it *killed* me to be lying to Jace.

By the time the sun set three hours later, the guys had cleaned the entire house top to bottom—a skill most toms learned on the job yet rarely used at home. They'd made two trips to the county dump with trunks full of garbage, then had catalogued and packed up everything we would need to keep. Or have to bury. They'd found the desiccated remains of two headless shifters wrapped in tarps behind the shed.

When they came to pack up Hargrove's computer for further investigation at the lodge, I'd already uncovered the names of ten more members of the sick hunting club.

Six were already dead: Joe Mathews, who'd been killed in Hargrove's house, the three hunters I'd killed over fall break, and two more who'd been mauled to death in previous attacks, just like Mathews.

"Well?" Jace said as Teo and Isaac packed the cumbersome desktop and its accessories in one of the boxes they'd brought from the lodge.

I swiveled in the rolling chair to face him. "From what I can tell, the other maulings each took place in the victim's home, which suggests that the killer actually intended to hit Hargrove here, in his own house. Either Hargrove's guest—Mathews—was here alone when the stray broke in, or Hargrove survived the attack and escaped."

"One of the blood scents in the basement matches the owner's scent all over the rest of the house, but we can't tell how fresh it is, with so many other overlying scents." Teo shrugged. "He could have been injured in the attack, or he could have cut himself on one of his own tools months ago."

I blinked, sorting through both information and procedures that were new to me. "Whether he was hurt or not, you think he escaped, right?"

"Or the stray abducted him," Isaac said. "Maybe Hargrove missed the attack, and he's the one who hung the pictures afterward. Maybe he killed the stray. Or maybe he was taken and killed *by* the stray, and another member of their weird-ass safari club hung your pictures up as a threat. Or a warning."

"Okay." Jace nodded, obviously thinking it all through. "So, how many hunters are still out there?"

"As far as I can tell, four, counting Hargrove." I dropped the wireless mouse into the box Isaac held out for me, then spun in the rolling chair to face my Alpha again. "Two of them live down south, near the border of the free zone." The distance could explain why they hadn't been killed by the vigilante shifter yet, as well as how they were able to target so many strays, with their operation apparently centered firmly in the Appalachian Territory.

"And the third?"

"His name's Darren, but that's all I've found on him. They don't use his last name in any of the emails, and I haven't found any reference to where he lives or works, or even what he does for a living."

"That's not a lot to go on," Chase said on his way through the living room with another box.

"I know, but we could find more information at the other crime scenes."

He shrugged, brushing dark hair back from his forehead. "Or beat it out of those other two hunters when we find them."

"Well, we better hurry if we're going to get to them before Titus does. Or before they get to him." I turned to look up at Jace from my chair. "Your friend Titus is mentioned by name in a few of the emails. They seemed to think taking down a leader in the stray community would be a particular coup."

What I'd left unsaid was that they'd actually been arguing over who would get possession of his stuffed and mounted head.

Although, truth be told, that was only *part* of what I'd left unsaid...

Hot water ran over my head and down my face in scalding streams. I'd long since rinsed the shampoo from my hair, but the memory of my face on that creepy bulletin board refused to be washed down the drain.

Whoever the photographer was, he'd been watching me for months. He'd seen me eat, and study, and swim in the school's indoor pool. There'd even been a shot taken through my dorm room window—with some kind of zoom lens?—which had caught me walking behind Robyn and toward my closet wearing nothing from the waist up but my bra.

How could that have been going on for so long without my knowledge? Weren't cats supposed to have amazing instincts? What good were my super-sensitive sight and hearing without the instinct to know I was in danger?

Maybe I wasn't cut out to be an enforcer after all.

Frustrated, I turned off the shower and grabbed the towel I'd set on the counter before I got in. It was coarse, because both the bathroom and the cabin around it belonged to the enforcers, and no guy in the history of testosterone had ever taken the time to add fabric softener to a load of laundry.

Most of them would probably still be satisfied with beating dried sweat from their clothes with sticks if Jace's mother would let them get away with it. But the laundry room was located in the lodge—the main house—and what happened there happened according to her rules.

That was exactly why I'd kicked my brothers out of their own room in the west cabin rather than stay in the lodge. I had the strong suspicion that neither Jace's mother nor his sister really cared for me, no matter how polite they were to my face, but most of that probably had to do with the fact that my father had fought against Jace's stepfather, Calvin Malone, in the shifter civil war.

When Cal was Alpha, two rapidly disintegrating trailers had sat where the east and west cabins now stood. They'd been propped up on concrete blocks, which had been clearly visible between rusted panels of metal underpinning. One of Jace's first acts as Alpha was having the trailers hauled off, because he couldn't stand to see them.

He'd lived there with his stepfather's enforcers

from the time he was twelve, because Malone couldn't look at him without seeing Jace's biological father—his mother's first husband, and her true love, by all accounts.

Because Malone hadn't liked or respected Jace, his enforcers didn't either, and twelve is way too young for a boy to be kicked out of his own house. I could only imagine that Jace's life was truly hell before he'd turned eighteen and gone to work for my uncle Greg at the ranch.

I wrapped myself in the towel and wiped fog from the mirror with one hand, admiring the craftsmanship of the rustic frame holding it in place.

The cabins that now sat behind the lodge were built by hand, by Jace's men, under his supervision. When he'd moved back to Kentucky to run things, he'd taken a day job at a construction company and had risen through the ranks to become supervisor after just a year. Faythe told me that's the way it usually went for Alphas—their instinctive leadership shines through in their daily lives, and most of them find success both at work and at home.

While they were building the cabins, Jace and all his enforcers had slept on the living room floor in the main lodge. Jace thought it would help them bond, which was crucial for men expected to put their lives on the line for one another on a daily basis.

He must have been right, because I'd never seen a staff of enforcers as close-knit as Jace's were. Their unity and loyalty gave them formidable, noted strength.

Which, naturally, made me the outsider. And likely the only one who would chafe from using towels about as soft as dead grass.

I tightened the towel around my chest and had just grabbed my phone from the bathroom counter when it rang. Brian's name and number popped up on the screen. I groaned out loud.

I'd told him I would answer his calls. He'd probably heard about my psycho stalker and was worried, but the last thing in the world I wanted to do after seeing my pictures tacked up all over a murderer's bulletin board was talk to Brian. Though truthfully, the last thing I *ever* wanted to do was talk to Brian.

What did that say about the future of our relationship? How was I supposed to spend the rest of my life with him if I didn't even want to talk to him?

With a sigh, I sank onto the edge of the tub and pressed the button to accept his call. "Hey."

"Hey. Your dad just told me what you guys found today. Are you okay?"

"Yeah, I'm fine."

"Really? Because I think anyone else would be pretty freaked out." Brian sounded openly frustrated for maybe the third time in our entire engagement. Usually, he was careful to keep his tone so light and gentle that it just kind of floated over us both, never really dipping into the realm of true substance.

Evidently, after our "breakthrough" in the woods, he'd expected me to be more forthcoming. But I'd had a breakthrough of my own.

I couldn't spend every day for the rest of my life like that. Avoiding conversations. Ducking kisses. How was I supposed to give either of our parents grandchildren if I couldn't stand the thought of Brian touching me?

"Okay, it wasn't a great first day on the job." I shrugged at my reflection in the mirror. "But I didn't sign up to cuddle puppies and fluff pillows."

"Abby, it's okay to be upset. Do you want to tell me about it?"

I can't.

I was keeping too many secrets and telling too many lies, and letting the truth out—any of the truths—would mean losing someone. The only person in my life that I could stand to lose was Brian. That *meant* something. Right?

I took a deep breath. "Well, I do need to talk to you, but not about the crime scene."

"What's wrong?" Over the line, I heard the squeak of springs, which told me he'd just sat on the edge of his bed. Or maybe a large chair. I wasn't sure what the furniture in his room sounded like, because I'd never been there in all my time on the ranch.

Another deep breath. Then I decided to rip the bandage off and hope that was the break-it-to-me approach he favored, because I had no clue how he took his coffee, much less bad news. "Brian, I can't marry you." Even if a broken engagement had the potential to drive a wedge between our fathers. My dad wasn't unreasonable. I had to believe he would understand.

Though I wasn't sure about Ed Taylor...

Silence settled over the line for the span of a heartbeat. Then: "What?"

"I'm sorry. I thought I could. I thought that's what I wanted, because that's what I was *supposed* to want. But it's not."

"Is this about Jace?" Brian's voice sounded…heavy, but not truly angry. Nor surprised.

"No." Not technically, anyway. Jace and I obviously had chemistry—just the thought made me blush—but that didn't change the reality of the situation. I was too young for him. I was his employee, so any relationship between us would be a blatant conflict of interest for him. And if it even *looked* like I'd broken up with Brian for Jace, I would have dragged a third Alpha into the rift between my dad and Brian's.

Even if Jace was willing to risk that for me, I wasn't sure I could let him.

"Then why?" Brian asked. "We could be good together."

"Yes, I think we could. If either of us really wanted that."

"I want it," he insisted.

"Why?"

"What do you mean?"

I could practically hear his confusion. "Why do you want to marry me, Brian?" It wasn't because we'd connected physically or emotionally. Or even conversationally. "What is it you were looking forward to the most?" I gave him a moment, and when he didn't answer, I took a guess. "Sex?"

"No! I could have been… I mean, if we weren't together for the past few years… I gave up lots of opportunities."

"I'm sorry about that." I hadn't meant to dangle any X-rated carrots in front of him. "So, if not sex, what then? The Pride? Did you want to be an Alpha?"

"What did *you* want?" Brian snapped, and I realized I'd struck a nerve. "What did you get out of this?"

"I…" But telling the truth was a lot harder than

asking for it.

"If you deserve the truth, I deserve it. Why did you wear my ring?"

I exhaled slowly, preparing to put into words something I'd never consciously admitted, even to myself. "Because you were safe, and the ring was like a shield. As long as I wore it, other toms stayed away. That's what I thought I wanted. That *is* what I wanted, four years ago."

I'd needed to be left alone, when my species needed me to be propagating. Being engaged to Brian with the graduation clause meant I wouldn't have to think about getting married for four long years. Only those years had felt a lot shorter than I'd expected.

"And the truth is that I thought I *would* marry you. I thought that by now we would have fallen in love, because that was what made sense. But love doesn't make sense, Brian. It isn't easy, and you can't just decide to feel it. If we were in love, we'd want to talk to each other all the time, even if all we do is argue. We'd be pulled toward each other any time we're in the same room. We'd have to fight the urge to touch each other, because we're not supposed to, but ultimately, we'd lose that fight because when it's love, *it can't be helped*."

My hand flew to my mouth, as if I could take the words back, but it was far too late for that. I hadn't known what I was going to say until I was already saying it, and I hadn't known it was true until I heard it.

"Who are you talking about, Abby? Because it's not me."

"No one." I closed my eyes, horrified by what I'd just done. Conflicted by what I'd just then come to understand.

"It's Jace, isn't it? *Damn* it, Abby, please don't do this. You know what he's like. The man's never met a skirt he didn't want to lift. Calling himself an Alpha hasn't changed that."

A growl began low in my throat. "*Calling* himself—"

"You know what I mean. He's an Alpha with an expiration date. A placeholder. You deserve something better. Someone who will treat you like a treasure. He's using you—"

"He's not even doing anything!" Jace had pushed me away. Twice. That was the *opposite* of using me. "Listen, I'm so sorry that I said yes for all the wrong reasons. I'm sorry that I let it go this long when I knew we weren't in love. The best I can do to fix this is to tell you the truth now." I took a nervous breath. "I won't blame you if you hate me."

"I could never hate you," he said after less than a heartbeat, yet the words sounded hollow. "But I think you're making a big mistake. You're going to regret this when you see what he's really after."

"He's not after anything!" I stood to pace on the tile, my face burning with indignation. "This isn't about Jace. This is about you and me. I have no doubt you could have made our marriage work. But you deserve better than a marriage that has to be *made* to work. And *so do I*."

SEVEN

Jace

The rest of the west cabin was empty, but Abby was on the phone in Luke and Isaac's bathroom. I couldn't make out any of her conversation, though.

Not without trying, anyway.

It would have been completely inappropriate for me to eavesdrop on her, but almost everything I wanted to do with, or for, or to Abby was completely inappropriate. And anyway, I didn't actually want to know what she was saying; I just wanted to hear her voice. I wanted to know how she was holding up after seeing her picture plastered all over that sick bastard's wall, and if she didn't know I was listening, she wouldn't hide anything.

But I resisted the urge, because we'd agreed that she was an enforcer, and I was an Alpha, and there was nothing more to our relationship. Just like any other enforcer, if she needed to talk, she'd tell me.

Her overnight bag sat open on Luke's unmade bed with several articles of clothing hanging from it. Most of her stuff was jeans and cotton tees, but something green and silky peeked from one end of the bag, and I *really* wanted to know what it was.

Abby didn't strike me as the kind of girl who would wear sexy underwear, but then I was learning all kinds of new things about her.

Focus, Jace.

I glanced around the room in search of something to divert my attention from that green scrap. On one corner of Luke's desk, I found a gruesome and bizarre computer printout. I picked it up, scowling at the picture, and hinges creaked in front of me. When I looked up, Abby stood in the bathroom doorway, wearing nothing but a towel, and I forgot all about the grisly image.

Hell, I forgot my own damn name.

I'd seen her naked, of course. Most recently in September, before the Pride's annual fall group run. But in that setting, the last thing on my mind had been…

"Jace?"

My gaze snagged on her damp, plump lower lip, the gateway to indulgences forbidden to me on the basis of decorum, and professionalism, and many reasons I could no longer *quite* remember.

"Jace?" she said again, and I blinked.

"Sorry. I was just thinking about—" *Tasting. Touching. Breaking every rule I'd ever been bound by in my entire miserable life…* "—running. Together. Um…" I blinked again and cleared my throat, grasping for focus and control.

Get it together. You've seen many *nude human women.*

But Abby was neither nude nor human, and those two facts made all the difference. Wearing nothing but a towel, she seemed to straddle some erotic line between naked and clothed, and my mind couldn't quite fathom the temporary state.

Though the rest of me knew exactly how to proceed.

"I was thinking about a Pride run," I finally managed to say. "We should do one this month. Make it a winter tradition."

"Sure." Her towel slipped a fraction of an inch, and I realized I was holding my breath. I knew what she looked like beneath that white cotton, yet being limited to my own memory made me *ache* to refresh the mental image by removing her towel.

Slowly.

With my teeth.

Abby shrugged, and the cotton slipped a little more. "We could probably all use the physical release."

My cock stiffened and I *prayed* she couldn't see. "Release?" She was doing that on purpose. Again. She was a child playing a woman's game, and I wanted to *let her win.*

Abby nodded and dropped her dirty clothes into Lucas's already-stuffed hamper. "We're all under a lot of pressure, hunting the murderer. And the killers he's trying to kill. Ironic, isn't it?" She turned back to me, and my focus snagged on her mouth again, then followed the line of her throat. So pale. So delicate. I could see her pulse through her skin, and I wanted to lick it. I wanted to feel the thrum beneath my tongue.

I wanted to know that her heart beat, and her pulse raced, and her body ached for no one else. No one but me.

What the *hell* was I thinking?

"What's ironic?" I asked, and only my automatic recall of the past few spoken words gave me any clue what we'd been talking about.

"It's ironic that the killer's actually doing us a favor." Abby dropped the hamper lid, and I hardly heard the clatter.

Her chest was freckled. Hundreds of tiny reddish spots sprinkled her shoulders and collarbones, then disappeared beneath the cotton. How far did the freckles go? Were they still red that far down, where the sun rarely touched them? Were her nipples pink? Large and round, or small and cute?

I'd seen her wearing nothing but a thin sheen of sweat literally dozens of times, so why couldn't I remember? Why hadn't I memorized every single freckled inch of her skin—every curve and dip? Every peak and valley?

When the *hell* had she developed peaks and valleys?

"I mean, when we find the rest of Hargrove's group, we're going to kill them, right?"

I inhaled deeply, trying to focus on her words as she dug into her overnight bag at the foot of Lucas's bed.

That's right. Think about her brothers. All five of them. They were all big, and protective, and…

And I couldn't remember a single one of their faces or names. All I could think about was Abby, and how badly I wanted her.

My body told me I could have her. My brain told me I *should* have her. I was an Alpha. She was a tabby. It was only natural. And I *knew* she was interested.

She'd kissed me in the dark, in the woods, her body pressed against mine for balance and maybe for warmth. Then I'd kissed her, in that morbid taxidermy chamber, and she'd tasted like…life. Like everything vital, and warm, and vibrant. Like everything I'd always known I wanted, but could never have.

Because Abby. Wasn't. Mine.

"Jace?"

Damn it. She was still talking, and I hadn't heard a word, though I'd seen every shape her lips made as she spoke. "I'm sorry. What?"

"I said we'll kill them when we find them, right? The hunters?"

"Well, if we *can* capture them alive, we have to take them to the council for questioning before they're executed," I said, and Abby frowned. "But yes, ultimately, they'll all be put out of their misery for the good of the entire shifter community."

"So then, do we really have to find the stray?" She pulled a nightshirt from her bag and shook it out. It was blue and it already smelled like her, which meant she'd worn it the night before. "I mean, he's only doing what we're going to do anyway, and he clearly knows more than we do about the situation. So, maybe we should just wait and let him do his job."

Wait, what? I shook my head to regain focus. Her *laissez-faire* approach to crime prevention had woken me up.

"But it's *not* his job," I reiterated. "It's my job. It's *your* job, now. Vigilante justice isn't really justice, Abby. It's violence and chaos."

"You don't believe that." She raised one reddish brow at me as she shook out a pair of pajama bottoms. "I can see it in your eyes."

What else could she see in my eyes? They probably read like a thermometer at the moment. Could she see my temperature rise with every movement she made? Every glance she threw my way?

Beads of water still clung to her. The clean scent of her skin triggered urges I had no right to feel. No right to want. And the only thing that could possibly smell better than Abby fresh from the shower was the scent of her sweat mixed with mine.

I shifted subtly, trying to disguise the evidence of what I wanted. I needed to taste her. I *ached* to touch her.

I should have turned around and run, right then.

"If you didn't have an Alpha's responsibilities, you might be doing exactly what this stray's doing," she insisted. "He's taking out the men who were *hunting* me, Jace. Wouldn't you do that for someone you cared about?"

"In an instant," I growled, surprised when the truth rumbled out without warning. "And when I find Hargrove and the rest of the hunters, I will personally rip them limb from limb, one bone at a time." *For you.* Because they'd watched her. Stalked her. They'd photographed and threatened her. They'd terrorized and murdered her friends, then lured her to their sick-ass slaughtering cabin and come after her with a knife.

They'd tried to kill *my* Abby…

Another growl rumbled from my throat, unbidden, and her eyes widened.

While part of me was embarrassed by the possessive notes of aggression I couldn't hold in, a deeper part of me was pleased that she'd heard and understood them, because I could never articulate those thoughts. No matter what my instinct was telling me—no matter what kind of potent hormones some ancient biological imperative was dumping into my bloodstream with every beat of my heart—she was *not* mine. She would *never* be mine.

But she *was* my responsibility.

"I would do anything for someone I cared about, Abby. But there's a process. As an Alpha, I have to dispense justice rather than vengeance." Though there were days when I'd *much* rather be a vigilante. "And even if we weren't going to take action against the stray, we'd have to find him and question him, because you're right—he probably knows more about the hunters than we do, and we need to know everything he knows."

Abby bent over her suitcase again, her shoulders stiff. She didn't like my answer. "I just think it's messed up that we're after this poor stray for doing exactly what we're going to do to the monsters he's hunting."

"We're not—"

She untucked her towel and let it fall, and I choked on the rest of my sentence. I had to focus on each breath after that to make sure I hadn't forgotten the entire respiratory process, but that didn't help, because every breath smelled like Abby. The rest of the room slid out of focus until I saw nothing but the curls tumbling down her back, ending just above the narrowest part of her waist. Even her lower back was freckled, but below that, her skin was smooth and pale, leading toward taut, rounded muscle.

Look at something else. Anything *else.*

I glanced around the room, desperate for something to latch onto. Something to talk about other than how her *very* well-toned backside tapered to slim, powerful thighs that could probably squeeze…

No, no, no. There was no hiding how badly I wanted her, and if she looked, she'd see.

My gaze landed on the computer printout I'd found on the desk, forgotten with my first glance at Abby in her towel, still wet from the shower. The gruesome image was jarring, but it did the trick.

"Where did you get this?" I held up the page.

She turned as she pulled her nightshirt over her head, then froze when her gaze landed on the paper. Her eyes widened and the hem of her shirt fell past her navel. "I should have shredded it," she whispered.

Staring up at me from the page was a picture of Abby's head mounted on a wooden plaque sloppily nailed to a paneled wall. Cartoonish blood dripped from her severed neck in the image, and her human eyes had been digitally overlain with cheesy cat pupils. She'd been smiling in the original photo, and the grinning severed head was well beyond disturbing.

"I printed it at Hargrove's house before they packed up his computer." Abby stepped into that green underwear and crossed the room toward me slowly, each step deliberate, as if she wasn't sure she wanted to be any closer to the gruesome image but was too stubborn to give in to fear. And she *was* afraid. Terror danced in the coppers and browns of her eyes, but the line of her jaw had been chiseled by determination.

She was *so* strong. I'd never met anyone who'd been through as much as Abby had and had come through it with half as much resilience and determination.

"Why?" I frowned down at the page, then studied her face again, convinced I'd see more there than she would say aloud. "Why would you even want to *print* this, much less keep it?"

She glanced at the floor, obviously struggling to put into words an idea that probably hadn't even been clear when she'd first thought it. "I need to remember why I'm doing this. I can't afford to forget what will happen if I get sloppy or careless. If they catch me."

She'd needed to keep the threat fresh in her mind, because the passage of time breeds complacency. Given enough distance from them, we start to forget how badly pain hurts and how scary fear feels, and when that happens, we lose our edge. I could understand that.

But… "You're not in this alone."

"I know. That's the problem. They've already killed several toms, including one of your enforcers."

Leo. We'd found his head stuffed and mounted on the wall of the cabin the hunters had lured Abby to with her human roommate as bait.

"After they get me, they'll go after someone else. If they *can't* get me, they'll go after someone else. We can't let that happen. *I* can't let that happen."

Did she think killing the first three hunters made their entire sick club her responsibility? "Abby, you can't hold yourself at fault for what the hunters do. This is *my* territory. I'm responsible for killing them and catching the stray, and I will never let any of them near you."

"I know you won't." She stared up at me, and her eyes were swimming with an overwhelming mix of fear, trust, and determination.

I pulled her into a hug. The printout floated to the

floor, face down. "They'd have to go through *all* of us to get to you. Luke and Isaac included."

"I know." She laid her head on my chest. Moisture soaked through my shirt from her damp curls, and suddenly I was humiliatingly aware that she was still pressed against me. Half naked. "But I need to remember that I'm capable of defending *myself*. You need to remember that too." The warmth from her breath made my heart beat harder.

"I've never forgotten." I inhaled the clean scent of her hair and my arms tightened around her, pressed flat to her warm lower back. "I saw what you did to those hunters. That's why I offered you this job in the first place."

"Bullshit." She pulled away to frown up at me, and I felt the sudden distance as if the earth had split between us. "You offered me a job because you didn't think I'd take it."

"That's not—" But I bit off the lie, determined not to insult her with it. "Okay, that's true, but I meant the offer as a compliment. I wanted you to know that I saw what you were capable of, and that I respect the skill. You're this fierce little ball of fur and claws, and I pity any idiot who goes up against you."

Her frown deepened. "That makes me sound about as vicious as a hissing kitten. I'm not a child, Jace. That was the point of keeping the stupid printout." She knelt to pick it up, and her forehead furrowed when her gaze focused on the image. "Sick *bastards…*"

"Hey." I pulled the paper from her grasp. "I'm not going to leave your side until we've buried the last of them in at least a dozen shredded pieces."

"You're going to stay with me every minute?"

"Every single"—agonizingly platonic—"second." My tongue suddenly felt thick and clumsy. "I swear I will be with you every second of every day, until everyone in the *world* who wishes you harm is dead and buried. And I *know* you're not a child." She'd made that very clear. But it didn't matter, because Abby was Brian's fiancée, and I could *not* take another man's fiancée.

Even if she clearly wanted to be taken.

I had alliances in place, people dependent upon me, and responsibilities to uphold, and just because Abby obviously didn't understand the consequences of what she was asking for didn't mean *I* could ignore them.

"*Do* you know?" She bit her bottom lip, and I couldn't have looked away if a tornado had ripped through the cabin at that very moment. "Prove it."

There she went, playing a woman's game again, and suddenly, I was *certain* I was going to lose, even with the wisdom of hindsight on my side. She was an adult, and I was an adult, and she wanted me, and I wanted her, and was there really anything else that mattered?

I was *starving* for a taste of her, and a starving man can't think straight. A starving man is a mindless force driven by impulse and need, and at that point, a starving man would have made me look rational and patient.

You won't be able to take this back, a voice whispered from deep in my mind as I bent toward her. That voice was right. Abby wasn't a temporary scratch for a casual itch. Alphas and tabbies do *not* hook up. They get married, and start families, and run territories.

But Abby was already taken. If I touched her

again, I'd be crossing a line I'd sworn never to even approach again.

Yet the moment my mouth met hers, all the warnings and consequences faded into blissful silence. There was no longer room in my head for anything but Abby.

EIGHT

Abby

Jace kissed me, and my entire life seemed to grind to a halt, as if the planet had suddenly stopped rotating. His hands grazed my jaw to cup my head, his fingers sliding gently into my hair. Chills followed in the wake of his warm touch.

He tilted my head to one side and his mouth opened against mine. A satisfied sound slid up my throat, and I stood on my toes, wordlessly asking for more. Then brazenly taking it.

My head spun. All of the rules, and warnings, and consequences blew away like dead leaves in the wind, and what remained was fresh, and new, and green. I could breathe without that claustrophobic feeling in my chest—*the wedding is coming, you're all out of time, the wedding is coming*—for the first time in years.

I wanted to touch and be touched, and that had never happened with anyone other than Jace. That was a fucking *miracle*, all on its own, and I jerked back with surprise at the realization.

Jace's hands stayed at the back of my jaw, his fingers still curled into my hair. "You okay? Is *this* okay?"

"Yes. Don't stop." I turned to kiss his palm. "Please."

His heartbeat spiked. "You sure?"

"*So* sure. I just…" I could feel my face flush. "You're the only person I've ever kissed, and..." I shrugged. "I like it."

His eyes widened. "Brian never…"

"Just on the cheek."

"That boy is a *fool*," Jace growled. Then he bent toward me and tilted my face up, and *that* was the kiss that changed my life. The kiss that opened my eyes and woke up my body, and showed me exactly what I'd been missing. That kiss was gentle, but it built with steady intensity toward a frantic climax that left me breathless, and astonished, and eager for more.

I'd never felt so desired in my entire life.

I kissed Jace back, taking my cues from him, and a primal sound of satisfaction rumbled from deep in his throat. His hands trailed over my cotton-clad shoulders, then guided my arms around his neck, where my fingers intertwined out of some instinct I hadn't known I'd possessed. I only knew I didn't want to let him go.

His tongue greeted mine, teasing lightly, and when I realized I could tease too, he made that sound again. It was more feline than human—a carnal growl of pleasure and fulfillment. He nibbled my lower lip, and I slid my hands into his hair as he kissed a slow, hot trail over my chin toward my neck, waking me up inch by blissful inch.

"Jace," I whispered when his tongue reached my collarbone, and when he froze, I realized I'd broken whatever spell had possessed him. He took an abrupt step back, and the sudden loss of him shocked me like a bucket of cold water thrown over my head. "What's wrong?" I asked, and his expression was carefully, horribly blank. "Am I messing this up?"

"You're doing this *exactly* right." His voice was the barely restrained rumble of a man about to lose control, but he didn't look mad. He looked *ravenous.*

A tantalizing heat unfurled within me. He was telling the truth; I wasn't the problem.

Yet there *was* a problem.

"You're perfect. But I can't do this again, Abby." He turned away from me, and my heart fell into my stomach with an ice-cold plop. "Things are different now."

Again? Now?

He was talking about Faythe, and that had ended badly for him. "But I'm not…" *Faythe. Taken. In love with someone else.*

"I can't put my needs above the needs of the Pride."

"You need me?" I whispered, stunned.

Jace turned to me again, and his eyes had shifted. The feline pupils were impossibly dilated—a testament to how desperately he was clinging to what little control he had left. "But it doesn't matter," he insisted. "I can't have you." Yet he reached for me without seeming to realize what his hands were doing. His fevered gaze trailed down from my face, and his pulse raced so fast, *I* got dizzy from the head rush. "I can't even…"

He blinked, and I saw his willpower snap like a cord under too much pressure.

Jace took two steps forward, then his arms were around me. I gasped when he lifted me until my bare legs wrapped around his waist, and suddenly we were eye to eye. He kissed me again, and the angle was different.

Better.

Perfect.

I forgot about whatever pointless objection he'd been making. It couldn't possibly matter, because nothing that felt this good could ever be wrong. I knew what wrong felt like. I'd had nightmares about wrong for years, and there wasn't a single thing about Jace that didn't feel *exactly right.*

His kisses grew deeper, bolder, and every stroke of his tongue made me want more. I slid my fingers into his hair and his hands cradled my thighs, a supportive touch that promised everything I could ever want, yet demanded nothing.

Jace worked his way down my neck, tasting, teasing. Electrifying me in ways and places I'd never even been aware of before. When his tongue flitted into the hollow between my collarbones, I groaned, and Jace tensed against me as if I'd flipped that regret switch again. He set me down, and the floor was a cold shock beneath my feet.

Conflict raged behind his eyes—a storm of rivaling needs. "I'm sorry. I'm *so* sorry, but I can't let this happen." Every muscle in his body was taut, and I found that intoxicating. Jace gave orders and kicked asses on a daily basis, and the thought that *I'd* put that tension in him made me feel powerful. Wanted. *Needed.*

"I have to…" Obligation battled desire in every word he said. In every movement he made. "You need to go home. To your parents."

"You still want to get rid of me?" The heat that had built up again inside me dissipated in a sudden wash of cold shock.

"I don't *want* to. I'm trying to do the right thing." He swept one hand over his hair, then clutched the doorframe as if the solid reality of it were a lifeline. "If you stay here, we'll… I'll…"

"No!" I reached for him, and he backed away, fleeing from my touch, even as his gaze seemed caught on my fingertips. "You said you wouldn't leave my side!"

"Abby, this is dangerous." His gaze found mine and I couldn't have looked away if I'd tried. "I see you, and I want to touch you. I touch you, and I want to taste you, and then…." He shrugged miserably. "Propriety aside, this isn't fair to Brian, and it *damn* sure isn't fair to either of us."

Oh. Brian.

I held up my left hand with a small smile.

Jace frowned at my bare finger. "Taking off the ring doesn't make the problem disappear. And the fact that I'm thinking of Brian as a problem should tell you what a dangerous frame of mind I'm in. This will end badly. I've been here before, and I can't *do* this again."

I stood on my toes to kiss him, and he groaned and pulled me closer. "I'm not going to marry Brian," I whispered.

Jace stood up straight. "What?"

"I just told him. Like, fifteen minutes ago."

He glanced at the open bathroom door, and I

realized he'd heard me on the phone but clearly hadn't caught much of the conversation. "You're serious?"

"*So* serious."

Relief spread across his features, and for a second, he looked so happy that my chest ached. Then some new concern lined his forehead. "Does he know about *this*?" He ran his hands up my arms, and delicious chills followed his touch.

"He has suspicions, but you're not the reason I called off the wedding, and that's exactly what I told him. With or without you, I don't want to marry Brian."

"That won't stop Ed Taylor from blaming me," Jace said, and though that fact should have made him hate me, he only held me tighter. "My stepfather's allies have just been waiting for an excuse to take my territory, and if the council thinks I've abused my authority to seduce *another* tabby—someone else's *fiancée* this time—"

"Hey." I put both hands on his face to make him look at me, and the short stubble on his chin was a foreign yet fascinating sensation. "You're *not* the reason we broke up, and if I have to shout that from the roof of the lodge, I will. I ended it with Brian because I finally realized that all the time I spend dodging his phone calls and avoiding his touch would make for a *really* miserable marriage for both of us. So, you're in the clear." If anyone was in trouble, it was me. *I'd* kissed Jace first.

"And for the record..." My face burned with the admission perched on the end of my tongue. "You're the only person in the *world* that I've wanted to be touched by in five years." The heat flashing in his eyes gave me enough courage to say the rest of it. "I don't know what that means beyond the fact that you make me feel beautiful, and powerful, and wanted. But four years spent avoiding the man I was engaged to has taught me that this"—I put one hand on his chest, and his heartbeat spiked beneath my fingers—"doesn't happen every day. So, if you want to try this in spite of the political complications, I'm in."

"You're in?" The upward tilt of his lips said he was teasing me, but his intense gaze said he knew how much of a risk I was taking.

"*All* in. All of me."

Jace studied my gaze for a second, and my own heartbeat thundered in my ears. Then he nodded firmly. Decisively. "I'm in too."

"You are?"

"I am." He leaned down for another kiss, as if to prove that he meant it, and my head swam. The moment felt surreal. Jace wanted me, and not just as the girl of the week. He wouldn't risk his alliances and the fate of his Pride over a fling he planned to be over in a few days.

He was serious. He was risking *everything* for me.

But I was still lying to him.

Guilt swelled inside me and my smile faded. But if I told him what I'd done, he would hate me. I would lose him and everything else I'd ever cared about.

It was *far* too late to come clean and hope for the best. I had to stick to the plan. I had to keep covering up what couldn't be fixed, then find a way to explain what couldn't be ignored.

Finding out that Jace cared about me hadn't given me more options. It had given me more to lose.

"What's wrong?" He tilted my chin up and stared

down into my eyes.

"Nothing. I'm just... I didn't mean to make things difficult for you or for Brian."

"We'll make it work. How'd he take it?"

"He wasn't thrilled, but once I pointed out that we were both really just using each other, there wasn't much left to say."

Jace's arms tightened around me. "How were you using each other?"

"Well, it wasn't intentional, but…" I shrugged. "He wanted to be an Alpha and a father." Not that I could blame him. Toms had very few opportunities in that regard. "And I wanted a magic ring with the power to keep unwanted suitors at bay."

His eyes widened. "*That's* why you said yes to him?"

I nodded. "I know that makes me sound horrible, but I knew I'd have to get married at some point, and the sooner I said yes to someone, the sooner the others would leave me alone."

"It was self-defense," Jace said, and his simple recognition of the position I'd been in eased a fierce tension I hadn't even realized I was feeling.

"Yeah, I guess it was." I'd only been able to heal from my abduction on my own timeframe because being engaged officially took me off the market. "And Brian was sweet, and cute, and I figured—worst-case scenario—I had the next four years to fall in love with him. But that never happened."

That heat was back in his eyes when he pulled me closer. "In my experience, chemistry is either instant or nonexistent." He leaned down for another kiss, and I wanted to melt into him. "I'd call this pretty damn instant."

"You've known me all my life," I pointed out.

Jace rolled his eyes. "When we met, I was a nine-year-old and you were a squalling infant." He held me at arm's length and gave me a lingering once-over. "Things have changed."

"And when, exactly, did you realize that?"

"In October, when I showed up at that cabin to rescue you and you'd already killed all the bad guys. And looked great doing it. I've spent the two months since then trying to convince myself that I don't want you, or that I can't have you, or that you're still just a kid. By the way, short skirts and late-night kisses very nearly blew all those arguments out of the water."

"Very *nearly*?"

"I was trying to be a responsible Alpha."

"And now?"

"Now I'm off the clock." He lifted me again, and that time, my legs encircled him on their own.

"Alphas are never off the clock," I said as his mouth trailed down my neck, and each breath I took seemed to stoke the flames kindling deep inside me.

That was what had been missing with Brian. That spark. The visceral certainty that nothing in the world was more important than touching and being touched.

"Then I'm on call," Jace murmured against my skin. "They know how to reach me." He kicked the bedroom door shut, then kissed me again as he carried me across the room, my legs still wrapped around his waist. In the middle of the floor, he looked up to scan the room, and I realized, at the same time he seemed to, that other than the desk chairs, there was nowhere to sit except for the beds.

I tensed in his arms before he could sink onto the

edge of the nearest mattress, with me on his lap. "That's my brother's bed. They both are."

He made a face. "Yeah, that'd be weird. Living room?"

"Yes."

He set me down and tugged me by one hand to the front of the cabin, where he bolted the front door while I closed the blinds, praying no one was peeking through the rear windows of the lodge at that moment. Once everyone else found out about us, the opportunity for privacy would expire.

Butterflies danced in my stomach, and I had a tight, tingly feeling deep in my chest. Making out with Jace was one thing. One mind-numbing, body-quivering, forbidden-fantasy-come-true kind of thing. But keeping that a secret pushed our tryst into the realm of scandal.

No one would ever have thought damaged little Abby Wade capable of such shocking behavior with the country's only single—and notoriously philandering—Alpha, and that fact heightened my excitement until I could hardly breathe. I felt like someone else. Someone powerful, and beautiful, and in control of her own life.

Someone that a man like Jace Hammond would want.

"So, were you just going to let me marry Brian without saying anything?" I asked, as we settled onto a couch I'd sat on dozens of times in my three and a half years in his Pride.

"I wasn't going to be what came between the two of you." He bent for another taste of my neck. "Not on purpose, anyway..."

His kisses burned across my skin, and my

heartbeat set the tempo. Every touch sent tendrils of warmth to pool in sensitive places, but the best part was the satisfaction of long-held curiosity. After years of wondering what it would feel like to be touched, to be kissed, to be savored with a patient but eager passion, I was at last living in that moment.

And finally, I dared a bold touch of my own.

Jace made another guttural sound when my hand trailed from his hair down his neck, then over his chest, slowly. Feeling every flat plane and hard ridge. He was *made* of muscles, each one tense with anticipation, as if he craved contact, but was determined to let me forge my own path. I closed my eyes and let my hands wander while his mouth explored every inch of my neck and shoulders, pushing just past the neckline of my shirt to lick or nibble a neglected surface.

His tongue felt amazing, but the landscape my hands had discovered was equally compelling—Jace's arms were bulge upon bulge of restrained power. I slid the cotton of his sleeves over each ridge as they bunched and stretched beneath my touch. Then, suddenly, I was *sick* of his shirt.

"Jace."

"Mmmm?" he murmured against my collarbone, his breath cooling the warmth his tongue had just left there.

"Can I…" I tugged on the hem of his shirt, and he sat up to look at me.

"You can do anything you want."

Anticipation buzzed beneath my skin as I slid my hands under his long-sleeved tee. My fingers bumped over each defined ridge of his stomach, and his eyes fell closed as he leaned back to let me explore. A low, pleasant sound rumbled from his throat. "I don't know whether to tell you to stop or to go faster," he growled, and the need in his voice echoed low and hot inside me.

"What if I keep going?" I said as my fingers found the lower ridge of his pectorals. "What happens after this?"

His eyes flew open, and his gaze burned into me like deep blue flames. "Lots of other things we don't have to do tonight."

I took a deep breath. "You said I could do whatever I wanted."

His hands settled around my wrists and his focus on my eyes intensified. "Abby, there's no hurry. Are you sure this is what you want?"

"No. But how can I know unless I try?" I kissed him, and my hands slid down his chest again, reaching impatiently for the hem of a garment I wanted to rip from his shoulders.

"Wait," he said against my lips, and I growled when he removed my hands firmly but gently. Jace laughed, amused by my impatience. "We have plenty of time."

"What about Luke and Isaac?"

"They're patrolling for the next two hours."

"Is that long enough?" I murmured against his neck.

Jace laughed again. "It's a hell of a start." He cradled the back of my head, his hand buried deep in my hair, and kissed me again. Then he leaned back against the arm of the couch and looked right into my eyes. "We can do whatever you want. We can stop any time you want, and if you *do* want to stop, I won't be mad or disappointed. I don't want to do anything you don't like—if you're not having fun, I won't be either. And if you just want to sit here and hold my hand, I'll still consider myself the luckiest son of a bitch on the face of the planet. Okay?"

I nodded, and the warmth spreading through me had nothing to do with desire or chemistry. Jace was giving me safety. Security. Power. Choice.

"So…now what?" My heart thumped so hard, I was sure it was all he could hear.

"What do you want to do?"

I thought about that for a second, and my gaze snagged on his shirt. I was fascinated by the way the material clung to him, highlighting every plane and angle in light and shadow from the end table lamp. "I want to touch you." He was the first man I'd ever voluntarily touched and the only one I could imagine ever wanting to touch.

Jace's gaze burned through me. "Say it again."

My pulse swooshed in my ears, and I felt a little dizzy. "I want to touch you."

"I'm all yours." He leaned back against the arm of the couch and spread his arms, giving me free rein.

I hesitated, nerves constricting my throat. But then hedonistic curiosity got the better of me. I climbed onto Jace's lap, holding his gaze, and sat with my knees on either side of his hips. The warmth of his legs beneath me felt both intimate and contained, filtered through a layer of denim. I lifted his shirt, and his heart thumped harder. His arms rose when I tugged the material up, and I realized he was truly going to let me do whatever I wanted.

I slid the shirt over his arms, letting my fingers trail over his flesh, feeling him breathe beneath me. Each inhalation was slow and controlled. Jace was raw power contained by impervious restraint, like the depths of the ocean raging beneath a calm surface. I could dive deeper whenever I liked, or I could float on the top, skimming untold potential until I was ready.

I grew more ready with every second.

Jace's shirt hit the floor, but his gaze stayed glued to mine, watching each thought flit across my face as I explored. Tested. His body was a miracle, tight, and hard, and smooth. And—like all shifters—*so* very warm. I ran my hands over his shoulders and chest, memorizing the feel of features I'd seen a million times.

Then, I needed a taste.

I leaned forward, and he shifted beneath me, giving me greater access. My hair skimmed his arm. My lips touched the warm skin above his left nipple, and he stopped breathing. His hand twitched against my arm, as if he wanted to reach for me, but his restraint was ironclad. He would not touch me until I asked him to.

Emboldened by that knowledge, I dared a taste of his skin. Jace groaned. Something twitched beneath me and I sucked in a breath. He was *unmistakably* aroused.

I froze, unsure what to do, but he didn't mention it, and he didn't seem uncomfortable, so…

I bent to kiss his chest again, which made me rock against him. When he clutched the back of the couch, I felt an intense rush of power. This was because of me. Because he wanted me. If I wanted to see the proof that he wanted me, he would let me, and if I wanted to touch it, he would let me do that too. And if I didn't want any of that, none of it would happen.

He would just hold my hand while I fell asleep next to him, fully clothed.

There were no rules. He would not hurt me. I could leave whenever I wanted.

Or I could stay.

I licked a light path down his chest, and the lower my tongue traveled, the shallower and faster his breaths became. To give myself better reach, I slid down onto his thighs, and the brush of my most sensitive places against his denim-clad leg triggered a new and intimate ache. When that ache echoed in my breasts, I realized my nipples were hard—and that Jace could see them through my thin pajama top.

My heart thudding almost painfully, I pulled my shirt over my head and dropped it on top of his. Jace's pulse rushed faster and his pupils dilated, but he only watched me, waiting to see what I wanted.

I licked my lips, suddenly nervous. "I…umm…." My cheeks burned, and trepidation tripped through my veins with every beat of my heart. I was scared, but not scared enough to stop. "I want something."

Jace's gaze was glazed with desire, as hot and heavy as my own private ache. "Name it."

"I want you to touch me."

For a second, I was afraid he'd ask questions I couldn't answer, like how or where, but Jace only gave me a smoldering smile and slid one hand around the back of my neck, then gently pulled me down for a kiss. He sucked lightly on my lower lip, tracing it with his tongue, and his free hand grazed my side. His palm slowly brushed the side of my breast, his fingers curling around the back of my rib cage, and I held my breath, alive with exhilaration. But his hands stayed steady as we kissed, and that ache inside me swelled.

"More," I whispered, as his mouth trailed down my throat again. That time, when his erection twitched beneath me, a jolt of anticipation shot up my spine from the heat gathering low within me.

Jace's hand slid forward to cup my breast, lifting it, and my nipples tightened into aching points. His thumb brushed over one and my head fell back. I pressed myself into his grip, wordlessly requesting more contact. Jace's hands slid up my back, supporting my weight, and his lips grazed the underside of my breast.

I clutched his arm as he licked a hot, slow path toward the peak. Anticipation throbbed within me, and when he finally took my nipple into his mouth, I groaned, instinctively shifting against his leg in search of friction I hadn't even realized I wanted. I'd never felt like that before. Hot and swollen, and in need of something I'd never expected to want.

"Lower," I whispered. "Please."

Jace groaned around my nipple. His hand slid down my stomach, slowly, giving me plenty of time to change my mind, while my anticipation built, and *finally* his fingers landed where I wanted them.

With that first delicious, brazenly intimate touch, I understood what I'd been denied before.

Desire.

I was overflowing with it. Swollen with it. I wanted Jace like I'd never wanted anyone or anything in my entire life.

His fingers stroked slowly, gently through the satin, and the pressure building inside me rose toward some mysterious carnal conclusion. "Under," I gasped, my voice a breathless whisper.

Jace's tongue trailed toward my neglected nipple as

his thighs spread beneath me, making more room for his hand. His fingers pushed aside the strip of cloth I still wore and he groaned against the swell of my breast. "You are *so* wet."

I hardly heard him. I heard only the frantic rush of his pulse. I felt only the steady pace of his fingers, stroking, teasing, building. "Oh!" I breathed, and he sucked my nipple into his mouth. "Jace! More!"

He gave my breast one more quick lick. "Do you want my fingers inside you, Abby?"

"Yes," I moaned. "Please. *Now.*"

His hand shifted between my thighs, then his thumb stroked gently as one finger slowly slid deep inside me. "Ohhh…" I moaned, as he pressed forward and up, and this new pressure found a hidden sensitive spot. "Jace!" I rocked against his hand and that delicious friction exploded in wave after wave of a throbbing pleasure I'd never imagined. Every muscle I had tightened, clinging to that sensation. Riding it. The world unraveled all around me as he stroked, and sucked, and drew from me a release I hadn't known my body was capable of.

And as the pleasure finally faded, ebbing with little aftershocks, Jace's hand withdrew and I fell forward against his chest, resting my cheek on his shoulder. "That was incredible," I whispered, and his chuckle rumbled through me.

"It was a good start."

"You're saying it gets better?"

"Well, generally, as a couple gets to know each other physically, they get more comfortable, and as they learn things about each other, their sex life can reach all new…heights."

Couple. Jace was saying he and I were a couple.

With a sex life. That concept seemed unbelievably normal and healthy, and almost too good to be true.

He shrugged. "Although you seemed like you had a pretty good time, and they say a good first time can be pretty hard to beat."

"First?" I sat up and frowned, trying to understand. "But we didn't even have sex. And I'm not technically a…."

"A virgin?" Jace said, and I could only nod stiffly. His hand slid into my hair again and his gaze locked onto mine. "Abby, sex is intimate and consensual, and neither of those descriptors apply to what happened to you in that cage. But I hope you see how they apply here, with us. And how they always will, as long as you want me."

I nodded. I did understand that.

"And as for virginity…" He shrugged. "That's an archaic concept anyway, and a hazy one at best. There's no biological or physical definition. If you don't believe me, just *try* telling a woman who's only ever enjoyed the company of another woman that she's still a virgin."

"So, there's no such thing as virginity? Seriously?" Why had no one ever *told* me that?

"Well, *I* like to think of virginity as a state of sexual inexperience, and I believe that it can't be taken. It can only be *given*, in exchange for a consensual, illuminating, and hopefully *really* fulfilling introduction into the carnal arts," Jace said, and the heat in his eyes burned right through me.

"So, then…" My heart thundered in my chest, and my cheeks burned. "I just gave you my virginity."

Jace pulled me close enough to whisper into my ear. "And I will treasure it for the rest of my life."

NINE

Jace

Something buzzed in the dark, and it took several seconds for me to recognize the sound of my phone bouncing on a hard surface. At some point, I must have put it on vibrate.

I rolled to my right, reaching for the nightstand, and the soft creak of the mattress beneath me was unfamiliar. I blinked, suddenly wide awake. Unfamiliar beds were nothing new, but I never stayed out overnight unless I had pressing Pride business elsewhere, because an absent Alpha makes for a vulnerable territorial capital. And I would *never* leave the Pride during a crisis like…

Abby!

I inhaled as my phone vibrated again, and her scent was suddenly everywhere, and it was *deliciously* multifaceted. I smelled her skin, and her hair, and her sweat, and another, more intimate moisture that had already soaked into her panties by the time I…

My phone clattered again, and when I reached for it, my hand landed on Abby's warm arm instead. I'd slept on the wrong side of the bed, because the bed was actually the foldout couch in the living room of the west cabin.

I hadn't left Abby; I'd stayed with her. All night.

Irritated by the buzzing, I reached over her to grab my phone from the end table, my eyes perfectly adjusted in the dark, even in human form. With a glance at the number on the glaringly lit screen, I accepted the call as I slid out of bed, trying not to wake her.

"Just a second, Warner," I whispered into the phone. I stepped into my underwear on my way into Abby's brothers' bedroom, then pulled the door closed at my back. "Okay, what could possibly be wrong at…" I pulled the phone away from my ear to glance at the on-screen clock. "…five in the morning."

"You mean *other* than the fact that I'm locked out of my own cabin?" Warner Green and Chase Taylor shared the bedroom across from Luke and Isaac, but I'd asked them both to take a shift in the main lodge overnight as part of the security step-up for my mother and sister. And to give me and Abby some privacy. "Let me in, boss."

"Abby's asleep on the couch."

He huffed. "What a shame cats aren't famous for their silence and stealth."

"Smartass."

"It's important," he insisted. "I won't wake her up."

I hesitated until I realized that even if I went out

instead of letting him in, he'd smell Abby on my skin. I'd known our secret wouldn't last long, but I'd hoped we'd at least get a chance to shower off each other's scents before morning.

Reluctantly, I crept back into the living room and quietly unbolted the door, then closed and rebolted it after Warner stole in on bare feet in spite of the near-freezing temperature. He had Hargrove's laptop and a manila envelope tucked under one arm.

Abby groaned in her sleep and rolled over, but neither the noise nor the cold gust woke her up.

I gestured for Warner to follow me into Luke and Isaac's room, then closed the door behind us. "What's so important?" I said, as he opened Hargrove's laptop on Lucas's desk.

"Sorry about the timing." Warner's face was lit only by the glow from the screen. "Especially…considering." His pointed glance strayed south of my navel, but my near-nudity wasn't the issue. I never slept in clothes, and even though Warner preferred guys, he knew I did not.

His point was that he could smell Abby on me.

"She's none of your business," I growled, already resentful of the cold air against my skin, where Abby's warm body had been seconds earlier. "None of anyone else's either. If she gets even a *hint* of judgment or criticism from you, I'll—"

Warner held up both hands, palms out, protesting his innocence in advance. "I'm happy for both of you. Brian was never her type."

I lifted one brow at him in surprise, and Warner rolled his eyes.

"No, he's not my type either. I'm just saying they were never really right for each other. But Brian may not know that yet."

"He knows," I mumbled, and Warner snorted, scrolling through a menu with Hargrove's mouse pad. "But he doesn't know about me yet."

"And maybe if you hadn't locked Brian's brother and two of Abby's out of their own cabin for the night, that secret might have kept for a while."

"They're already talking?"

He shrugged. "There's no such thing as privacy for an Alpha. Or for a tabby, for that matter."

Our situation was delicate, politically speaking. We'd have to make an official announcement at some point, and it would be the first of its kind. The US Prides had never seen an unmarried Alpha, which meant that even if Abby hadn't just dumped her fiancé—the son of one of my allies and brother of one of my enforcers—our fledgling relationship would be under considerable scrutiny.

"What the hell am I doing?" I sank onto the end of Lucas's bed. "This is crazy, isn't it?"

Warner turned from the laptop to grin at me. "The Spanish poet Pedro Calderón de la Barca reportedly said, 'When love is not madness, it is not love.'"

"So, that's a yes?"

Warner laughed and clicked another key on the laptop, then turned it to face me more directly. "Okay, I've been up all night, going through Hargrove's computer. Abby did a good job, but she doesn't have the tools or the training to access password-protected files and emails. Including this." He tapped a few more keys, then clicked the trackpad, and an email appeared on the monitor.

I frowned at the screen. "What am I looking at?"

"This is an email from someone named Darren.

I'm not sure who that is yet..."

"Yeah, Abby said the same thing."

"...but let all learned men be warned—the grammar is painful. According to this message, Darren was writing to Hargrove from some place they call the 'lakeside cottage,' where there's evidently spotty Wi-Fi. I haven't found any other property in Hargrove's name or any other mentioned in his correspondence, so this cottage could very well be where he's hiding out."

"And that would be helpful, if we knew where this cottage is." I stood and came closer to scan the email.

"I think we do." Warner clicked on the trackpad again, opening an email attachment before I'd finished the first paragraph of text. "Darren sent this picture with the message. Look past all the carnage," he said, when I scowled at the image of a stray I'd never met, stuffed and posed in cat form, like a grizzly bear at some redneck's hunting lodge. "Through the window behind that poor bastard, you can see the 'lake,' but it's really not much more than a big pond in the woods. Jace, *I know that pond.*" He glanced up at me, then turned back to the image. "It's in Knox County. I used to run there. There are only three cabins within sight of the water, and only two of them face the western shore." He looked up at me again, excitement gleaming in his brown eyes. "We can be there in two hours."

"Be where in two hours?" Abby asked, and I looked up to see her standing in the threshold of her brothers' bedroom, draped in a throw blanket my mother had crocheted. Her bare knees peeked from beneath the blanket, and I could tell from the flesh showing through small holes in the afghan that she wasn't wearing much beneath it. If anything.

I hadn't even heard her get off the couch.

"Warner thinks he's found Darren's lake house, and that Hargrove might be hiding out there."

Abby's eyes widened. "I'll be ready in ten minutes." She ran for the living room, the blanket flying out behind her. I groaned, then snatched her duffle from the end of Lucas's bed and followed.

"Abby."

"What?" she called from the floor beneath the sofa bed, where her legs stuck out.

I dropped her bag on the mattress, then squatted and ran one hand lightly down her thigh, wishing I had the time to linger. Then I pulled her out from under the couch by her ankles; her afghan cape slid easily against the wood floor.

Abby laughed and turned over to look up at me, clutching the shirts we'd discarded several hours before. "Here." She shoved mine at me, then leapt to her feet. "I just have to brush my teeth."

"Abby, wait. I need you to stay here."

"No way! I'm an enforcer now, and this case affects me. It's *about* me, at least in part."

"Both of which are good reasons for you to stay here. Enforcers follow orders."

Her copper brows dipped low over angry brown eyes. "Then give me a good one, and I'll follow it."

I growled, realizing for the first time that our relationship would be more complicated than I'd anticipated. Brian was no longer in the way, but I *was* still her boss, and that was one hell of a conflict of interest.

"What?" Abby cocked her head and gave me a smile. "You didn't think this was going to be *all* kissing and cuddling, did you?"

I groaned, and Warner burst into laughter from the bedroom.

"Okay, we're going to have to draw a couple of boundary lines," I said. "When I'm the Alpha and you're the enforcer, there will be no kissing, and you will follow orders." Which would not in *any* way be affected by the fact that I could still taste her on my lips. Really. "When we're off duty, there will be plenty of kissing, and whatever else you want to do, and you won't have to follow any orders."

"But an Alpha is never off duty," she pointed out. "We've been over this."

"Fine, then, when *you're* off duty, there will be all the kissing and none of the orders. Okay?"

Abby propped both hands on her hips, and when her afghan fell to the floor, it took every bit of self-control I had to keep my focus on her face. "Let me draw a boundary line for *you.* If I don't go, *you* don't go, because you swore to spend every single second at my side. So, which is it going to be? We stay here and do off-duty things, or we go catch this son of a bitch—together?"

Warner laughed again, then pretended not to hear my growl of warning.

"Damn it, Abby," I grumbled, but she only shrugged.

"I don't make the rules. Yet. So what's it gonna be, *Alpha*?"

I exhaled slowly, clinging to patience. "Get dressed. We're going to the lake."

"If I could make a suggestion…" Warner's nearly silent footsteps came toward us from the hall. "Take a shower. No, take *separate* showers. Unless you're both ready to confirm the rumors buzzing in the main house."

Abby raced across the back yard in faux-fur-trimmed white winter boots, with little leather tassels hanging from the shoestrings. We were going to have to talk about her work wardrobe. Enforcers do *not* wear tassels. But then, none of my other enforcers had ever sat on my lap, nearly naked, and asked me to slide my fingers…

Focus, Jace. There's still a job to do. And a good deal of the upcoming work would involve defining the line between Abby-the-enforcer and Abby-the…girlfriend? I wasn't really sure what to call her other than the woman whose very scent provoked an X-rated Pavlovian response in me.

She clomped up the back steps, red curls bouncing against her roommate's white down jacket, highlighted by what little moonlight remained. A cat's eyes don't need much light, even in human form, and Abby practically *glowed.* My right hand and I would have liked to claim at least partial credit for that, but the truth was that she wore her most recent victory well, and something told me I wouldn't be winning many arguments in the near future.

That wasn't a problem many Alphas faced, but I could *not* give less of a shit.

None of the other Alphas had Abby.

I caught up with her as she turned the doorknob, but the door didn't open. "We're locked out." She turned and stared over my shoulder to where Warner was crossing the lawn from the west cabin, with

Hargrove's laptop under his arm. "Do you have your keys?"

He shook his head. "Left them in the cabin."

Before I could tell him to go get them, the doorknob rattled, and I looked up to see Chase Taylor opening the door. "You locked us out." Abby stepped past him into the kitchen, rubbing her hands together for warmth.

"Turnabout's fair play," Chase returned, as Warner and I followed her in. "Did you really need the *whole* cabin? *All* night?"

Abby flushed, humiliated by the insinuation, and my temper sparked into an instant blaze in defense of her. My vicious growl surprised even me, and Chase and Warner instinctively backed away, eyes wide.

Abby slid her arm around my waist as mine curled protectively around her shoulder. I'd never in my life felt such a powerful protective instinct, and the strength of my unexpected reaction triggered memories of Marc's fury anytime anyone had threatened Faythe. Ever. What had seemed irrational and excessive when the shoe had been on his foot suddenly felt perfectly appropriate. The last thing Abby needed was to feel guilty or insecure about her sex life, and I wouldn't tolerate a *single* insult hurled at her.

I turned back to Chase. "You ever take that tone with her again, and I'll consider it a personal challenge to my authority."

"Whoa." He took another step back and bowed his head in respect for a second—the strongest submissive gesture a werecat could give in human form. He was surprised but clearly not confused by my reaction. "I meant no offense," Chase insisted, and I nodded, acknowledging the apology.

"Chase, listen," Abby began as Warner closed the door behind us.

When she didn't seem to know how to finish the thought, Chase laid a hand on her shoulder, with a quick glance in my direction to make sure I had no plans to rip it off. "No worries, kid. Brian told me the wedding's off. But he didn't mention this." He glanced cautiously from her to me.

"He doesn't know," I growled.

"Chase, Jace didn't... He's not the reason..." She let go of me, as if downplaying our connection would help. "I broke up with Brian before we..."

"It's okay, Ab," I said. She was nervous and upset, and that made me want to kill someone. "What's between us is none of anyone else's business." But we all knew that was wishful thinking on my part. Warner was right—there was no such thing as privacy for an Alpha. Or for a tabby.

Abby nodded but looked unconvinced as she turned back to Chase. "How is Brian?"

Chase shrugged. "More embarrassed than anything, I think."

Having been dumped by the world's most powerful tabby, I knew how he felt, but the truth was that in a way, Brian had lost much more than I had. Along with Abby, he'd lost his chance to be Alpha of her territory, and he'd almost certainly lost his chance to be a father. Toms were forbidden from procreating with humans, in order to keep our existence secret from humanity at large. Logan was a happy accident and one hell of a cute kid. But if Ethan were still alive, he would have been sanctioned for breaking a very serious rule.

Michael, Faythe's oldest brother, had married a human, but he'd had the good sense to fall in love a woman who didn't want children.

As both my past and my present illustrated, I had much less control over my heart and what—or who—it wanted.

"Will you give him this and tell him I'm sorry?" Abby pulled something from the front right pocket of her jeans. Her engagement ring glittered in light from the back hallway as she placed it in Chase's palm.

He nodded. "So, what's with the predawn invasion?" He slid the ring into his pocket and turned to pull open the refrigerator, signaling his willingness to dismiss the subject.

"Warner thinks he's found Hargrove," Abby said. "We're going to take him out."

"We're going to bring him in," I corrected, and she frowned at me. "The council wants to question him, and our job is to make sure they get that chance." But she still seemed to be having trouble with the idea that we wouldn't be killing him on the spot.

"We?" Chase pulled a soda from the fridge and popped the tab with a pointed glance at Abby. "Are we sure that's a good idea?" He looked more hesitant than usual to question my judgment, so I made a conscious effort to relax, because my mood influenced all of theirs. No Pride was a democracy, but any good Alpha would listen to advice from a respectful and knowledgeable source, and my enforcers needed to feel free to advise.

Though so far, my newest hire had had no problem voicing *her* opinion.

"No, taking Abby along is a horrible idea," I admitted. "But we're going to make the best of it, because I'm not letting her out of my sight until every one of those bastards is in the ground."

"She won their first fight," Warner translated as Chase tossed him a soda.

Abby caught the next one. "It wasn't our first."

"And no doubt it won't be our last. Let's round everyone up. I'm taking Teo, Warner, Lucas, and Abby. Chase, you, Isaac, and the others will stay here, and I want at least two of you in the lodge with my mother and sister at all times." My half brothers would be there as well, but they were untrained because neither of them wanted to serve as my employee. "Respect their privacy, but keep them safe. Got it?"

"Loud and clear."

"And double the patrol. If there's a foreign scent in the woods, I want to know about it. Abby?" I turned to give her instructions, but she was gone. Based on the echo of her boots in the hall, she was headed for the great room, where the displaced west cabin residents had probably camped after their patrol. "Damn it, Abby, you can't just walk out when I'm…"

Chase and Warren laughed as I stomped after her.

I got to the great room just in time to see her launch herself across the room like a cat in human form. She landed on the couch on all fours, and Lucas made a pained *oof* sound beneath her. "Damn it, Abby!" He pushed her over and sat up. "That was only funny when you were four."

"Get up!" She grinned in response to his scowl. "We're going to ki—I mean, *catch* Hargrove. Warner found… Hey," she said, with a glance at the three empty sleeping bags on the floor. Two of them belonged to Warner and Chase. "Where's Isaac?"

Luke tossed back the blanket, which wasn't long enough to cover his feet anyway. He always got the couch, because there wasn't a sleeping bag invented that was long enough or broad enough to fit him. "Isaac?" he called, standing to stretch.

"He's probably in the bathroom." My sister Melody appeared in the doorway in a halter top and short sleeping shorts.

"Go put on some pants," I snapped when she flopped into a chair and propped her bare feet on the coffee table. "It's twenty degrees outside."

"Well, it's plenty warm in here," she purred, stretching just to provoke me. Or to catch Lucas's attention. She was successful on both counts.

I growled, and Lucas blinked, then looked away. They'd all seen her naked, of course, but this wasn't nudity for the purpose of a shift or a run. This was flesh intentionally put on display because she lived for attention. "Go!" I shouted, and she jumped, startled.

Her eyes narrowed as she stood, moving as slowly as possible to obey my order, and as she passed Abby, Melody's focus took on a riling gleam. "So," she whispered, loud enough for the whole planet to hear, and I realized what she was going to say an instant before the words came out. "Are you sleeping with my brother?"

I was about to start shouting when Abby pulled herself up straight and propped both hands on her hips. "Would that make us even?" she asked softly. "Since you're sleeping with *my* brother?"

"Whoa, *what*?" Lucas snapped.

A murderous growl rolled up from my chest.

Abby slapped both hands over her mouth, as if

she wished she could take the words back.

"You!" I glanced from Luke to my vindictive little sister. "She's only nineteen years old!"

"Okay, wait, that's not the point." Abby stepped in front of me and turned my head by my chin until I looked down at her. "Only nineteen is nineteen enough," she insisted gently, and I knew she was right, but I found it really hard to give a damn in that moment. Melody was nineteen in chronological years, but psychologically, she was as stunted as my remaining half brothers, who'd been raised by their psychotic father.

Calvin Malone had ordered Alex, his second-youngest son, to murder Brett, his oldest and the closest thing I'd had to a real brother. Four years under my leadership were nowhere near enough to mop up the mess Cal had made of their lives.

"Hold on." Lucas held both his hands out, palms facing me, as if to show me he was unarmed. "Nobody's sleeping with anybody. Right? I've been on the couch all night. Alone. And Abby would never..." He glanced at his sister, waiting for her to fill in the blank with the expected denial. "Because she's engaged to..."

And that was when I realized he'd slept right through the rumors about me and his sister.

Abby frowned at Luke, and I read the impending subject change a second before she spoke. "Not you. Isaac. He's in the bathroom, probably brushing his teeth in the shower. To wash off her scent," she added, with another glance at Melody.

"Isaac? But that doesn't—" *Luke* was the Wade brother Melody always flirted with, and he'd clearly spent the night on the couch. Abby was mistaken.

Simple enough.

My temper began to cool as I turned to Lucas, trying to figure out the best way to tell him that I was, in fact, sleeping with his sister, even if he wasn't sleeping with mine.

Abby rolled her eyes. "Your sister's window lit up as soon as I knocked on the back door," she said. "And the shower came on while we were in the kitchen. Melody's still wearing yesterday's makeup, and she just brushed her teeth. She hasn't been to bed yet tonight." Abby shrugged. "Well, she's been to *bed*, but not to sleep."

An angry pressure began to build up in my jaw until I realized I was clenching it. I turned from Abby to Melody, who suddenly looked terrified. "Mel?"

"Okay, Jace, don't freak out." She backed toward the staircase, and I realized that Abby was right—the shower was running. Specifically, *Melody's* shower was running. Her bedroom and mine were the only ones on the second floor.

I turned and ran for the stairs.

TEN

Abby

"Jace, *no*!" Melody shouted, but he was already halfway to the second floor, and the tight clench of his fists was *not* a good sign. Though that did seem to indicate that he hadn't sprouted claws yet.

"Wait!" I raced after him, and from the sound of the stampede, everyone else in house was behind me.

"Abby!" Lucas called from half a flight below. "What the hell's going on?"

"Not now!" I yelled as Jace hit the second floor landing. There'd be plenty of time to avoid talking about my private life once I was sure Isaac wasn't going to be killed, or fired, or...systematically neutered. I should never have said anything about Melody and Isaac, but she could be *such* a little *bitch* sometimes, and I'd struck out with the only weapon I had.

As I raced up the last half of the first flight of

stairs, a door creaked open on the third floor, and Garrett, Jace's youngest half brother, leaned over the railing overhead. Garrett was my age, and he was the only one of the Malone brothers I'd never wanted to punch. "What the hell? It's barely six in the morning."

When Foley Malone peeked over his shoulder, I realized the entire house was awake except for Patricia, and with the level of noise our stampede was causing, Jace's mom couldn't possibly be asleep for long.

"Jace is going to kill Isaac!" Melody squealed, as I followed Jace across the landing toward her closed bedroom door. "You guys do something!" She gave Chase a shove and he stumbled past me, but our Alpha's growl of warning stopped him cold.

"I'm not going to kill him," Jace snapped, and when he tried to open her door, he pulled the doorknob right off. *Not* good. "I'm just going to rip his balls off and—"

"Jace!" I grabbed his arm, then wrenched the amputated doorknob from his grip. I briefly considered recruiting Lucas for help, but if any of the guys touched Jace while he was seeing red, this would escalate too quickly for me to control. "That's my brother!"

"In a minute, he's going to be your sister," Jace growled, and my stomach clenched miserably.

"Okay, wait. Let's talk about this calmly. Melody's an adult. Just like *I* am," I said, hoping he wouldn't need me to spell out my point. And maybe he wouldn't have if the knobless door hadn't swung open at that very moment to reveal Isaac standing in the middle of Melody's bedroom floor, his hair wet and dripping, a towel tucked around his hips.

Jace's gaze narrowed and his face flushed. "What the *hell* did you do to my sister?" he growled, and I could tell from the sound that his throat had already started to shift.

Uh-oh.

"Do *to* her?" Isaac stood his ground, his hands raised, palms out. "I didn't do anything *to* her."

Melody raced past us and threw herself between her brother and mine, her back pressed to Isaac's chest. She held her arms out to protect him like a human shield, her brown eyes flashing in anger like I'd never seen from her. "Don't hurt him, Jace. I *love* him," she said as Garrett and Foley stomped down the stairs from the third floor.

I gaped at Melody, still clutching her broken doorknob. She loved him? She could *not* be serious. Melody was as self-centered as a tabby could get—which was saying a lot, considering that most of us were treated like precious cargo from birth—and she'd thrived on attention from tomcats since she was fourteen years old. From *all* the toms.

She'd claimed she was only trying to find the right match, which her father had told her was her one and only duty to the world, but her kiss-a-hundred-frogs approach had left more than one of the guys with a broken heart and a chip on his shoulder. Jace had traded two miffed enforcers for two of my brothers a couple of years before, just to patch the rift Melody had carved in his carefully bonded brotherhood. Now she was doing it again.

Or was she?

Tears stood in her eyes. Every muscle in her body was tense. And she wasn't trying to defend herself; she was trying to protect Isaac.

"You love—" Jace shook his head, and I realized he couldn't see the change in her. Or he wouldn't, anyway. "You were in *love* with Chase this past summer, and Nate Blackwell back in the spring. You don't know what you want yet, because no matter what year is stamped on your birth certificate, you're still just a kid. I'm trying to give you time to figure out what you want."

He'd been encouraging her to get to know herself before she threw herself at the next tom. Or to at least get to know the next *tom* before she threw herself at him. But she couldn't be the only one who'd noticed he was preaching one thing but practicing something else entirely, with his endless string of human women.

At least, until me.

"Things are different now," he insisted. "You don't have to get married at nineteen and have six kids by thirty. You could go to school. You could get a job. You could even travel—"

"I don't *want* any of that!" Melody shouted. "Not all girls are like Faythe and Abby, you know, and just because you want a woman who'd rather throw a roundhouse than a dinner party doesn't mean every tom wants that. *I* just want a pretty wedding and a bunch of redheaded babies, and you obviously want the same thing," she said with another pointed glance at me. "So, stop being a hypocrite."

"Wait, *what*?" Isaac looked past Jace to me. "You and *Jace*? Since when?"

"It's new," I said, trying to avoid his gaze.

"What about Brian?" Luke demanded from my right.

"We broke up."

"Oh. Well…good for you!" Isaac said, though I got the distinct impression he was only saying that because he knew he was currently in no position to criticize his Alpha's private life. "I hope you're happy together." Isaac turned back to Jace. "The least you can do is wish us the same."

"She's nineteen years old and she doesn't *know* what she wants!" Jace shouted. "You're taking advantage of her!"

"No, he isn't!" Tears rolled down Melody's face, but she stood her ground, still pressed against my brother's bare chest. "Being an Alpha doesn't mean you know everything. We're going to get married, and I'm going to have this baby, and you can't—" Melody slapped one hand over her mouth, shocked by what she obviously hadn't meant to say, and astonished silence descended over the now-crowded bedroom.

"*Baby?* You—!" Jace lunged for Isaac, but I grabbed his arm again as Melody burst into sobs.

"Wait! Let's talk about this calmly," I insisted, though I was as stunned as everyone else.

"Well, so much for letting *me* break the news to him gently," Patricia Malone said, and I turned to find her standing in Melody's bedroom doorway, both arms crossed over her long, gray robe, dark brown hair perfectly straight and in place, as if she slept sitting up on a shelf. She glanced around at the gathering of shocked shifters and sighed.

"You knew about this?" Jace pulled free from my grip.

"Of course I knew. She's my daughter."

"How could you let this happen?"

"*Let* it happen?" Patricia bristled—that was new. When I'd joined the Pride, she'd been a quiet, almost cowed woman accustomed to doing what was asked of her and mollifying her husband to keep the peace. "I didn't *let* anything happen, and I'm no happier about it than you are, but I *do* know that killing your nephew's father"—because the baby would almost certainly be male—"won't help."

"He's not going to kill Isaac," I insisted, and when Jace didn't immediately agree, I elbowed him. "Right?"

"No, I'm not going to *kill* him."

"You're not even going to *touch* him!" Melody shouted. "Get the hell out of my room. This is none of your business."

"I'm your Alpha, and he's my employee. And this is my house. This is *most certainly* my business."

Melody's eyes narrowed, and I saw the verbal bullet coming before she fired it. "You're only my Alpha because you killed my father!"

Jace recoiled, and I could see how much that hurt him, even if she couldn't. The truth was that Calvin Malone had only been the Alpha because he'd killed Jace's real father—according to the rumor mill, anyway—but Jace would never say that to her, even in his own defense.

"Melody!" Patricia scolded.

"I don't want you here! Get out!" she shouted at Jace, in spite of her mother's censure. "Not just out of my room; I want you to get the hell out of my Pride!"

Shocked gasps echoed behind me.

Jace was the only Alpha I'd ever heard of who'd taken over his father's territory rather than his wife's, and we all knew that someday he would lose both his territory and his home. Again.

But for her to throw that in his face, after everything he'd done for her…after he'd rebuilt the Pride, practically from scratch…

"What did you just say to me?" Jace demanded, and my hair stood on end. He loved Melody in spite of the constant pain in the ass she'd been most of her life, but no Alpha could take a challenge like that lying down. Even if it came from his little sister.

"Okay, wait!" Isaac tugged Melody back and stepped in front of her, shielding her from Jace through a protective instinct surely everyone in the room recognized. "She doesn't mean that."

"The hell I don't!" Melody shouted, standing on her toes to glare at Jace over his shoulder. "He wants to keep me a child forever so he never has to give up my territory!"

"No, he's only trying to protect you," Isaac told her, without ever taking his wary focus from our Alpha. "Jace, your complaint is with me, not with her. She's just upset."

"Of *course* I'm upset!" Melody screeched, and when Isaac reached back to put a gentle hand on her arm, she actually seemed to calm. Their contact looked familiar and easy, as if they were very accustomed to touching each other, and not just for sex. Melody and Isaac weren't just fooling around, and their relationship wasn't new. Not *brand*-new, anyway.

With one glance at Jace, I realized he saw it too. And that he was kicking himself for not seeing it earlier.

"How long has this been going on?" He sounded at least a little calmer with the understanding that this wasn't just a hookup gone wrong.

Isaac stood straight and tall, and unless I was

imagining it, his chest was puffed out a little. "We've been together almost three months. But she's only about six weeks along, if our math's right. You'll be able to smell the hormones soon. I can already, but I think that's because I know what to look for. Or because the baby's mine, or…" Isaac shrugged, and with that one simple gesture, the reality hit me.

"I'm going to be an aunt!" I grabbed Jace's hand and squeezed it. "You're going to be an uncle. Jace, this is *good* news!"

He didn't argue, but neither did he agree. He was still caught up on how young and self-involved Melody was, and he was probably upset because she'd just deprived herself of a *world* of newly available choices.

"We were going to tell you soon. We really were." Isaac held Jace's gaze boldly, and I could hardly contain my surprise. Refusing to drop his eyes meant he was rejecting the subservient role. That was Alpha potential showing itself. Faythe had told me Jace went through the same thing—instinctively refusing to follow Marc's leadership—the year of the revolution.

Alpha potential is innate; some shifters are born with it, some aren't. But often, those who do have that potential don't show it, or even realize it, until some major life event triggers a psychological shift. Jace's was triggered by a combination of his feelings for Faythe and his grief over her brother Ethan, his best friend.

Melody's pregnancy had obviously kicked Isaac's Alpha development into overdrive.

I wondered if our parents had any idea.

The silence from the crowd gathered in Melody's bedroom told me none of the others had realized it either. And that no one other than Patricia had known about Isaac and Mel's relationship.

"Okay." Jace nodded slowly. "What's done is done, and we all have work to do, so we'll have to address this later." He glanced around the room. "Chase, go to the east cabin and wake everyone up. Luke, Warner, Abby, be ready to go in an hour." With that, Jace leaned down to kiss me—drawing a surprised look from his mother, who'd missed that part of the discussion. Then he marched across the second-floor landing into his own room and slammed the door without another word.

I was brewing coffee in the kitchen of the lodge when Patricia came in and started pulling cartons of eggs and packages of bacon from the fridge. "If we're all up, we might as well eat," she said, twisting her long brown hair into a loose knot at the back of her head.

I'd never mastered that particular skill. I had way too much hair.

"How do you take your eggs?" she asked, as I began pulling travel mugs from an overhead cabinet. Which I could barely reach. Being short sucks.

"I take them as an unavoidable ingredient in cakes and brownies. Or fully grown and in the form of nuggets or tenders," I added with a glance into the backyard, where the rising sun was painting the east cabin with bright streaks of light. So much for getting an early start.

Patricia turned to me with one brow upraised, a strip of bacon dangling over a heated skillet from between her thumb and forefinger. "You don't like eggs?"

"Not as a main course. Sorry." The coffee pot gurgled, and I leaned closer to let the scent help wake me up. I'd been fired up and ready to kick serious ass, until the emotionally exhausting drama-fest had drained my energy like pulling the plug from the bottom of a full tub.

Bacon sizzled and grease popped, and I realized I *was* hungry.

"So, what *do* you eat for breakfast?"

"Oh, don't go to any trouble for me. I'll just grab a few strips of bacon on the way out the door."

"It's for future reference." Patricia was facing the stove, but something in her voice—some softer-than-normal quality—told me that was as close to a "welcome to the family" as I'd ever get.

"I like breakfast meats and breads, mostly. Bagels. Pancakes. Scones."

Jace's mother huffed as she cracked another egg over the skillet. "Scones are just fancy biscuits. Do you like biscuits?"

"Yes!" I said, disproportionately pleased to have what felt like good news to give her.

She nodded firmly. "I can do biscuits. Thirty minutes." With that, she left eggs and bacon sizzling on the stove and headed into the giant, well-stocked pantry.

Melody came downstairs a minute later, her eyes still red from crying. She looked exhausted. "No coffee," her mother said, carrying a ten-pound bag of flour under one arm and a can of baking powder in the opposite hand. Evidently, she was going to make biscuits from scratch. In thirty minutes. "Caffeine isn't good for the baby."

"Turns out there's caffeine in chocolate too," I whispered to Melody while her mother dug in a drawer full of metal measuring spoons. "But I won't tell if you won't."

Jace's sister looked at me as if I were a piece of gum stuck in her hair, and I turned back to the coffee pot as it spat the last of the coffee into its carafe. I decided to have a cup *right* in front of her.

But guilt got the better of me as I stirred sugar and creamer into my steaming travel mug. "Listen, Melody, I'm so sorry." I sank onto the bar stool next her. "I should never have said anything about you and Isaac. I had no idea it would set off such a shitstorm."

"That *was* kind of bitchy." She shrugged. "I was almost impressed. But they were all going to find out eventually anyway." And that was clearly as close to an acceptance of my apology as I was going to get. Like mother, like daughter.

It was a miracle Jace had survived childhood.

"So, you and Isaac are getting married?" I said, and when Melody turned to me with stars in her eyes, I realized I'd just said the magic words.

"Yes, and you *have* to be my maid of honor. No one else will do it."

"Oh, I'm sure someone will."

"No." Patricia dumped a cup of white flour into a big metal mixing bowl. "They won't."

"The other tabbies all think I'm a total bitch," Melody whispered, as if that information might come as a shock to anyone. "You *have* to be my maid of honor. I'll *totally* return the favor for you, if I'm not hugely pregnant when you and Jace get married."

When Jace and I got married?

We'd only been together for nine hours, but everyone seemed to take for granted that there was a wedding to plan. "Oh, we're not… We haven't really talked about the future yet," I said.

Melody frowned. "What is there to talk about other than picking a date? But I've got dibs on Valentine's Day, so don't even think about it."

I held my hands up in a defensive move. "All yours. Like I said, we're not really…" Another shrug.

"You're almost through with school, right?" she said, and I nodded. "And it's not like you're getting any younger. You may have to go through five or six pregnancies before you get a girl, and I hear childbirth is really hard for older—"

"Okay, I really just came down for coffee, but thanks for the chat!" I stood so quickly that my barstool tipped over and slammed into the floor. Melody rolled her eyes and made no attempt to help me right it, so I picked up the barstool, then hurried out of the kitchen and up the stairs.

I'd been standing outside Jace's door for nearly a minute, trying to work up the nerve to knock, when he opened the door on his own. "How'd you know?" I asked, as he stepped back to let me in.

"I could see your shadow under the door. And hear your heartbeat." He pulled me into a hug as he kicked the door shut, and he smelled *so* good. "What's wrong?"

"Other than the fact that my brother knocked up your sister?" I laid my head against his chest, trying to come to grips with how much had happened in the past twenty-four hours.

New job. Psycho stalker. Overdue breakup. Sex. Melody's pregnancy. And now hunting the hunters—

the only thing I'd truly hoped to accomplish during my winter break.

"You sounded fine with the whole thing earlier." Jace seemed to be inhaling the scent of my shampoo with every breath.

"Well, I don't think a baby's ever *bad* news, but it's certainly something we'll have to get used to. Quickly." I let him go and sank onto the edge of the bed, briefly wondering how many women had been there before me. But then the answer came unbidden. *None.* He'd only brought a few of his women home, and they'd never spent the night, because our lifestyle would be incredibly difficult to explain to anyone who couldn't know about shifters or the werecat social structure. Which was the vast majority of humans.

"Abby?"

"Your sister just asked me to be her maid of honor. Then she offered to return the favor. I didn't have the heart to tell her that technically, she'd be a matron of honor."

Jace snorted. Then he sat next to me and took my hands. "Hey, I need you to understand something."

I nodded, unexpectedly nervous.

"What happened between us last night—what I'd like to *continue* to happen between us—has nothing to do with your father, or your birth Pride, or me losing my position here. This is about nothing and no one but the two of us." He slid one hand into my hair, cradling the back of my jaw in a gesture that made me want to crawl all over him. "I want you to know, especially after what happened with Brian, that I'm not using you. I'm not going to pressure you into any kind of commitment, and I have no intention of taking over your father's territory."

"You don't?" My chest ached, and I wasn't sure why. He was trying to reassure me, yet for some reason, I felt almost rejected. "Do you not *want* the East Coast Pride?"

He shook his head, but not in answer to my question. "That's not what I'm saying—I've never even really thought about it. What I'm saying is that I've known all along that I'd be losing my position here, and I'm not counting on you or your father to give me somewhere to go. I've worked very hard to make sure I'm not dependent upon *anyone* for that."

"You have?" I felt like I was missing something. "What's your plan, Jace?"

Instead of answering, he held my gaze for a moment, waiting for me to puzzle it out on my own.

"Oh, shit…" I covered my mouth with both hands, then spoke through them. "You're going to the Lion's Den!"

And just like that, I understood his involvement in the wildcat resolution. Jace wasn't just backing the motion in the Council; he and Faythe were the ones who'd *proposed* it, and the idea had probably been his originally. His intent hadn't just been to establish a good relationship between Pride cats and strays—he'd actually been creating a future home for himself.

As an Alpha who'd already been leading a Pride for years, Jace couldn't *possibly* serve beneath another tom in another territory. Even if one of the other Alphas wanted him—and none would; they would all subconsciously recognize him as a threat—his own instincts would keep him from peacefully submitting to another tom's will.

Faythe and Marc's connection to the project was obvious. Genetically, Marc was a stray. What I hadn't realized was that Jace thought of himself as a stray too, because that's practically what he would become when Melody claimed her territory. With Isaac.

But Jace knew that if strays were allowed to form their own officially recognized Prides, he would still have a legitimate role to play when he had to leave the Appalachian Territory. His plan was altruistic, and radical, and *brilliant.*

His plan was breaking my heart.

"You're going to leave." We'd *just* connected. He *couldn't* leave.

He exhaled deeply. "I don't really have a choice."

"You could—" I said, but Jace cut me off with a gentle squeeze of my hand.

"Abby, your dad's not ready to retire. He was expecting you to wind up with an inexperienced *potential* Alpha. Someone he could spend the next few years training to take over. That's not me. I can't serve under him, and he's not ready to step down."

"You don't know that."

He took my hand. "I do. Think about the big picture. If your father steps down, the council will have to elect a new chair. Your dad wouldn't just be prematurely losing control of his own Pride; he'd be handing leadership of the council over to someone else, and that could very well put the—"

"Okay, but Isaac's not ready to step up yet. I think he *does* have Alpha potential—"

"That much is crystal clear," Jace agreed.

"—but he won't be ready for years."

"At least a couple, probably. But Melody doesn't want me here. And if I could learn on the job, so can Isaac."

"He could, but why should he, when you could

train him? He's about to get married. And he's going to have a baby soon. That's a lot for any man to take on at once, and you know damn well that the Pride will be better off if you stay on, at least until he's truly ready to take over."

Jace shrugged. "Well, I guess that's up to Melody."

"And Isaac," I insisted. "If he's going to be the new Alpha, he should get a vote, and I *know* he'll want to do what's best for the Pride."

Jace nodded. "Like I said, I suspect I have at least two years left here."

"And I'll be here with you." We could figure out the rest then. Assuming we were still together, and I couldn't imagine that not being the case. I knew enough about what didn't feel right to recognize what *did* feel right with Jace.

Though there were still things I couldn't tell him.

"Abby…"

"No. I've made up my mind." I crossed my arms over my chest, shutting down whatever argument he'd been about to make. "As long as you're here, I will be too. We'll have plenty of time to sort out the rest. This is just the beginning, Jace." I took his hand, and his fingers wove between mine. "We don't have to figure it all out right this second."

"Speaking of beginnings, since Melody knows about us, there's a good chance every other shifter in the country will know in a couple of hours. Especially since making it sound like I broke up you and Brian will take some of the focus off of her premarital pregnancy. Don't you think your parents should hear about us from you first?"

"I guess." I was assuming the fact that I hadn't already heard from them meant that Brian hadn't yet told his parents, who would *definitely* have called mine. "Any particular way you want me to spin this?"

Jace shook his head. "It's your news. Tell them whatever you're comfortable with. As long as it's true." He stood when I pulled my cell phone from my pocket. "I'll give you some privacy."

While he went downstairs to round everyone up for the mission, I autodialed my parents' home number. But what Jace and I had both failed to realize was that if you call your parents before breakfast, they *will* assume someone has died.

"Abby?" my mother screeched into the phone, and for a moment, I regretted showing them how to set up caller ID. "What's wrong?"

"Nothing." Although I seriously considered selling Isaac out, just to take some of the pressure off my own news. "I broke up with Brian last night, and I just thought you guys should know."

"Oh, honey, what happened?"

"She broke up with Brian," my father snapped in his groggy voice. "If *I* can hear her, why can't you?" He wasn't gracious about having his sleep interrupted for anything less than death or dismemberment.

Springs groaned over the line as my mother got out of bed, making irritated clucking noises at my father. "I meant to ask *why* you broke up with Brian," she said as her footsteps transitioned from carpet in the bedroom to the creaky floorboards in the second floor hall. "He's a really nice young man."

"Yes, he is, but I don't love him. I don't ache to see him, and I don't want him to touch me, and—"

"Well, honey, that could take some time after…" Her voice trailed into nothing. She meant well, but she was never really able to talk about what happened to me in that cage.

"Mom it's *been* some time, and that hasn't changed."

"Okay, but that doesn't mean you can't marry him. There's more to a marriage than sex, and lots of women don't really *like* it, so—"

"Mom, please listen to me." I exhaled slowly, fighting for patience. "This isn't about sex. I like sex. I just don't like *Brian*."

"Well, hon, who on earth did you have sex with?" She said it just like that. As if we were discussing my preference for one tomato sauce over the other, and I might be able to suggest a new recipe.

It was kind of weird.

"Um, I'm actually with Jace now."

"You're with…"

When a familiar door squealed open, I realized that she hadn't moved far enough from their bedroom. And that my father had only been feigning disinterest. "Did she just say she's with *Jace*?"

"She *did* say Jace, and she says she likes sex."

"Oh, good Lord, Mom, tell Dad to go back to bed." I could already feel my face flaming. "This conversation is awkward enough already."

"I can't go back to bed after that!" my father blustered, and I wanted to crawl into a hole and die.

"Okay, listen. All you two really need to know is that I gave Brian's ring back, and I…I think I love Jace."

"You *what*?" my father demanded.

My mother sighed. "Well, we'll have to order a larger groom's tux, but unless Jace has an aversion to chocolate cake or lilies, all the other wedding preparations should be fine. I'll call the tux shop after breakfast."

I had to fight the urge to pull out my own hair. "Before you do that, Mom, call Isaac. He has something to tell you." I hung up my phone and threw it straight at Jace's pillows.

ELEVEN

Jace

"I swear, Melody's going to put me in an early grave." With every word I spoke, my foot fell heavier on the gas pedal. Which was bad, because my Pathfinder was already chewing up the narrow backroad faster than the Tasmanian Devil on speed, in spite of the sun glaring in my eyes and the sharp, winding curves.

In the car behind us, Lucas was having trouble keeping up. I'd decided he should drive separately with Teo and Warner to give him time to adjust to my new relationship with his sister without having to see it up close and personal. After the uproar with Melody, I knew exactly what it felt like to discover that one of your friends has had his hands all over your sister.

Not that Isaac and Melody had *anything* in common with Abby and me. Ours was a much more mature and acceptable connection. In ways I couldn't put into words when Abby had asked me to. Many, many indescribable ways.

"She's just growing up, Jace." Abby's pulse raced as trees flew by on either side of the car, an irregular blur of dark green, casting shadows over the narrow road. She clutched the armrest. "Could you *please* slow down?"

I lifted my foot from the gas pedal, and the truck behind us swelled in the mirror until Lucas slowed to match our speed.

"Seriously, though," she continued, "you can't tell me that I'm old enough to make my own decisions, then deny her the same opportunity. She's an adult. Just like I am."

"You've *never* been as young as she is at this very moment." Melody was not ready to make major life decisions, and Isaac was damn well old enough to know better. And they'd gone behind my *back*! In my own *house*!

Yet Abby seemed perfectly calm about the whole thing. "It's not fair to compare me with your sister," she insisted. "She and I have led entirely different lives. And even if she's a little immature now, becoming a mother will change that."

"I wanted *life* to change that." I punched the steering wheel, and Abby winced as if her own fist hurt. "I wanted Melody to have a chance to grow up on her own *before* there was a baby." I'd spent years trying to undo what Calvin had done to his only daughter—trying to show her that she had options. And she'd just thrown the whole thing away.

"Well, that's not your choice to make, and she's made hers," Abby said, as a road sign sped by. "The best thing you can do is support her. She knows what she wants, which is more than a lot of girls her age can claim. Besides, having a baby doesn't mean she can't still do other things. Look at Faythe. She's on baby number two, and she's running a whole Pride."

"Melody isn't Faythe."

Abby rolled her eyes. "Oh, please. She's hardheaded and she knows exactly what she wants. Sounds like Faythe to me."

A growl rumbled up from my throat. "You're manipulating the facts."

"And you're manipulating *her*. You're giving your sister all the choices in the world except the one she wants. That's you trying to run her life for her, which is no better than what Cal was doing." I growled again, but she spoke over me. "If you could set aside your own ego for a second, you'd see that I'm right."

"My..." I glared at her through narrow eyes.

"Yes, your ego. By the way, I'm officially off the clock until we get there, so you can't play the boss card to shut me up."

But that had never really worked, anyway. The best way to stop Abby from talking was to kiss her, and since I was willing to rip the face off any other bastard who tried that, the rest of the world was just going to have to listen when she decided to talk.

Abby studied the map Warner had given her. She squinted at a gravel road up ahead, only barely illuminated by the morning sun. "I think that's it."

Her pulse was racing over what she assumed would be her first live takedown. Not that I had any intention of letting her get her hands bloody—that was the only thing Lucas and I could agree on without addressing the larger issue. Untrained enforcers don't see action.

I slowed as we approached the gravel path, then pulled as far onto the side of the road as I could. I got out and closed my door as Lucas rolled to a stop behind me, blinding me until he turned off his lights.

"It's about a mile through the trees to the north," Warner said on his way to the Pathfinder.

Abby slid out of the passenger's seat to the ground, shivering. She zipped up her borrowed jacket and shoved her hands into the pockets, and for the hundredth time, I wished I had gloves that would fit her. I could see clouds of my own breath with every exhalation, and according to the forecast, midday wouldn't bring much warmth.

She was going to freeze, and I wanted nothing more than to warm her with my own body heat.

"Okay." I clicked the button to lock my car. "If we were after shifters, we'd have to move quietly, but since we're after humans, I think we can emphasize speed over stealth for the moment. We need to be there before the sun's high enough to make us easy to spot. Fortunately, we don't have far to go." Even so, we'd have to hurry. The sky to the east was rapidly brightening over the treetops.

We took off into the woods, and after a few minutes of quietly crunching through the underbrush, I spotted a break in the trees. Just beyond the clearing stood the lake cottage.

At my silent signal, everyone stopped while I scanned the empty yard. On my right, Abby breathed into her cupped hands to warm them. She smelled like her roommate and like cedar, thanks to the borrowed jacket and every branch she'd brushed against during our short hike.

Lucas slid one huge arm around his sister and she snuggled close to him for warmth. As badly as I wanted to be the one she was snuggling with, I understood the gesture for what it was—a signal that he was no longer mad at her for failing to give him a heads up about her relationship with his Alpha.

I had yet to receive a similar signal from him, and that was fine, as long as his irritation at me didn't affect his job performance.

Teo and Warner stood to my left, silently studying the back of the small cottage. The top of the roof was brightly lit by the rising sun, but everything else was still deeply shadowed by the woods. Beyond the building, I spotted the edge of the pond and the thin, dark sheet of ice that had formed on top.

Warner nodded at an old blue Chevy freckled with rust spots. "That's Hargrove's truck." The whispered words puffed from his mouth in white clouds. "The license plate matches the one on file at the DMV. He *has* to be here." If not for Warner and his computer skills, we'd probably still be looking for Hargrove and Darren under rocks and piles of underbrush.

Lucas shrugged. "Or he left his truck here and went somewhere with Darren. There's only one vehicle."

"We'll know for sure in a minute. Luke, you and Teo make your way around front. When you hear us make our move, make yours." I turned and met Abby's gaze, her eyes shining a brilliant green, now that they'd shifted. "Abby, you're with me and Warner."

Abby nodded, but she looked distracted. And scared. Her pulse was whooshing too fast, her heart beating too hard. I wanted to reassure her that she would be in no danger, with Warner and me at her side, but if I did, she'd only insist that she could take care of herself.

Teo and Lucas headed around the side of the cottage, sticking to the woods as much as possible, while Warner, Abby and I watched for any movement or light from the house. When the others rounded the front corner, I took Abby's hand and squeezed it. "Stay behind me and keep your eyes open. Don't touch anything you don't have to touch." I met her gaze and held it. "I'm serious, Abby."

She nodded, and that time, I thought maybe she meant it.

Warner and I headed straight across the cottage's backyard, with Abby on our heels. I climbed the back steps silently and laid one ear against the door. The flimsy hollow-core door told me Hargrove and Darren weren't expecting a break-in—they didn't think the rogue stray would find their lake cabin, and they had no clue we were even looking for them.

When I heard only silence from inside the cabin, I gestured for Warner and Abby to give me some room. I shifted my balance onto my left foot and kicked the door, right next to the knob. Wood splintered as the frame broke. The door swung open to smack the kitchen counter, revealing a small table and a grimy linoleum floor.

A second crash of splintering wood came a second later, and the front door swung open. Lucas and Teo stepped into the living room, which was separated from the kitchen and small dining area only by an arch of stained wood.

A suitcase sat open on the floor next to the taxidermied tom Warner had found a picture of in

Hargrove's email. Mateo knelt next to the suitcase and inhaled deeply. "It's Hargrove's," he said. "Matches the most pervasive scent in his house."

I nodded and sniffed the air for myself. The only strong scents in the cabin belonged to Hargrove and another human man, whom we were assuming to be Darren.

At my right, Abby exhaled deeply. "I smell a few unfamiliar strays, but those scents are older and pretty weak. Other than a faint trace of the same chemicals we found in Hargrove's basement, I don't smell anything unexpected." Tension melted from her frame with the discovery—until her gaze found what hadn't been visible from outside. The top of the living room wall was *lined* with the stuffed, mounted heads of dead shifters. And not just cats. There were also a bruin and the bizarrely posed heads and long slender necks of two thunderbirds.

"Please tell me that's not Elias Keller," she whispered, nodding toward the mounted bear's head.

"It's not. But he'll need to know about it." Bruins were largely solitary creatures, but if anyone knew how to warn the other bear shifters about the hunters, it would be Keller.

I studied the kitchen, looking for anything out of the ordinary, but other than a vertical gun rack on the floor next to the refrigerator, the kitchen looked normal. If dim and dirty.

A hallway to the left led to three more rooms that I could see, and a single door on the other side of the kitchen was open to show a small pantry.

At my signal, the guys headed for the hallway, but Warner stopped on the way to pull a ratty blanket from the back of the couch and drape it over our fallen, gruesomely stuffed brother.

While they searched the back rooms, I kept Abby in the front of the house with me, and I could practically *feel* her revving up for another argument about her own usefulness as an enforcer. But then her focus snagged on a framed photo sitting on an end table next to what at first appeared to be a bronze sculpture of a giant talon, but was, in fact, an *actual* thunderbird talon *dipped* in bronze.

She picked up the frame while I was rifling through kitchen drawers. "Hey, Jace, come look at this."

I joined her in the living room, where she held the photo up for me to see. Two other men were in the picture with Hargrove, and it took all three of them to hold up the body of a well-muscled black cat, at least six feet in length, not including his tail.

I took the picture from her and my hand clenched around the frame. "That's Leo."

Leo had been Mateo's roommate in the east cabin until he'd gone missing several months before. We'd found no sign of him until Abby'd discovered his head hanging on the wall of the hunter's cabin she'd been lured to back in October.

"And that's Steve." She pointed to the hunter on Hargrove's left in the photo, as if I could possibly have forgotten the man who'd tried to kill her. The man whose throat she'd ripped out, putting her on my radar as an adult for the first time. "This other guy has to be Darren, don't you think?" She tapped the third man in the photo.

"I don't want to rule anything out this early, but that's a good possibility."

"Check this out." Abby turned to a set of built-in

shelves to the left of the fireplace, where a dozen more photos had been lined up and pushed to the back of the shelf, not like a woman would display them, with artful angles and pretty frames, but like *I* would. That was a bachelor's work if I'd ever seen it.

"Hargrove's only in a few of these," she pointed out. "But every single one of them shows this guy." She tapped on the face of the unidentified man holding Leo's front half in that first picture. "This has to be his cabin, right?" I nodded, but she was already pulling another frame from the shelf. "Look. In nearly half of these, he's wearing a police jacket."

Sure enough, the picture she shoved at me showed the unidentified man in a navy nylon jacket with the word police written on one side.

"Well, that would explain how he knew to remove those photos of you before the rest of the cops showed up. Especially if he was the one who took them." The implications were startling. A human cop knew about us, but rather than alert the government—or even the internet—he'd decided to hunt us into extinction for his own psychotic pleasure. Which confirmed my longstanding suspicion that most of the world's *true* monsters were human.

"Okay, we're clear." Mateo stepped into the living room. "No one's here, and there's nothing incriminating in either of the bedrooms or in the bathroom. Nothing at all that I can see, except that." He pointed to the blanket-covered taxidermied stray.

"And this." Abby showed him the picture of the hunters posing with his roommate's body.

Teo's hands curled into fists. "I'm going to rip them into *tiny pieces.*"

"The council will want to talk to them first, but I'll

do my best to see that we get to carry out the sentence, when the time comes." But my assurance obviously did little to assuage his rage. "Okay, let's go through everything and see if we can confirm that the cop is Darren and find a last name for him. Or an address, or something."

Abby and I took the first bedroom, while Lucas and Teo tore apart the second. Warner started in the kitchen, then moved into the bathroom.

"This sucks," Abby said hours later, as she sorted the junk in the top nightstand drawer into the "keep" and "trash" piles. So far, "keep" was nearly empty. "What we need is an internet connection. If Darren's a cop, he can't be that hard to track down."

But Darren's email had been right about the spotty connection, and none of us had managed to get a decent signal. Not that that would matter, without Warner's equipment.

"As soon as we're done here, we'll head back to the lodge and let Warner get started." But we had to go through everything first. A single receipt or bill could make all the difference in our hunt for the hunters. Unfortunately, we hadn't found any of those, because their lake cottage obviously wasn't a primary residence.

I was sorting through a closet full of hunting camo when a hinge squealed from the kitchen. I spun around to find Abby frozen, staring at the open bedroom door. I was sniffing the air, tense and on alert, when something crashed.

Abby lunged for the door, but I pulled her back and stepped in front of her. Teo and Lucas were already there when we got to the kitchen, and Warner was on our heels, coming from the bathroom. "What the hell was that?" he demanded.

Teo pointed to the overturned kitchen table, which was propping the busted door open. "Someone just ran out the back door."

"From where?" Abby frowned as she glanced around the kitchen, looking for some nook or alcove we'd missed. But we'd checked everywhere. There'd been no one in the house to run out the back door, and there was no one in the backyard.

"Could a human make it to the tree line that fast?" Lucas asked, staring out the window over the kitchen sink.

"Only one way to find out." I shoved the table aside, clearing a path to the back door. "You and Warner go, but stay within earshot of each other. Teo, you shift, then join them." In cat form, he would be faster, quieter, and have access to much better-developed senses.

The guys left to follow orders, and I righted the table, studying the kitchen for any explanation that made sense.

"There was no one here," Abby mumbled. "We went through the whole house." And that had only taken minutes. "Did anyone look in the pantry?" she asked, and I turned to see what she'd already discovered.

The light was on.

"I did, and Warner rechecked," I assured her. "There's nothing suspicious in there except the thought of an existence sustained by *that* much peanut butter, pork rinds, and domestic beer." One end of the pantry was lined in pine boards stacked on concrete blocks. Shelf after homemade shelf was stacked with canned soup, generic brand sandwich cookies, puffed pork skins, and Miller Genuine Draft.

"Backwoods *haute cuisine*." Abby stepped into the small space and pulled the string to turn off the light bulb hanging from the ceiling. As she was pulling the pantry door closed, she froze, staring at the floor. "Jace," she whispered, backing slowly away from the pantry.

I followed her focus to the thin line of light showing beneath the cheaply paneled wall directly opposite the door.

"That's not a wall." I felt around the edges of the paneled section, then finally pressed in the right place to trigger a crudely fashioned yet well-hidden door. The panel swung backward to reveal a narrow, dimly lit staircase running down and to the left, along what could only be the exterior wall of the house. A wall that had no windows.

"A secret basement?" Abby said, and I nodded. Our backwoods hunters were also amateur craftsmen. "Well, now we know where he was hiding, whoever he is. And it has to be either Hargrove or Darren, right?"

"That's my guess." I inhaled deeply. "Do you smell that?"

"Old blood." Abby sniffed the air. "Strays. And chemicals. Hargrove has another taxidermy studio—or whatever they're called—down there."

I'd drawn the same conclusion. Either he'd been teaching Darren his craft, or Hargrove spent a lot of time at his friend's lake cottage.

"Okay, let's get this over with." She stepped past me toward the stairs, but I grabbed her arm.

"You're not going. Not after what we found in the last basement." And there could still be someone down there. The scent of old blood was strong enough to conceal nearly anything.

"I'm a big girl." Abby tried to push past me again, her jaw set in a stubborn line, as if she *needed* to see whatever was at the bottom of those stairs.

"*Stay here*," I growled. "That's an order."

Her feline eyes narrowed as she glared up at me. "If I stay here, *you* stay with me," she said through clenched teeth, and her irritation caught me off guard. Why would seeing the basement be so important to her? "That's the deal, remember?"

"Abby, your safety trumps our agreement." Protecting her was the whole point of the deal we'd made. "I have to make sure no one's hiding down there."

She wanted to argue—I could see the impulse flashing in the green striations of her feline eyes. "Okay," she said at last, but I recognized anxiety in the frantic cadence of her heartbeat.

Abby wasn't mad; she was *terrified* of letting me go into that basement by myself.

TWELVE

Abby

Jace studied my gaze in the glow from the naked pantry bulb, obviously trying to figure out what was wrong with me. It killed me to let him think I was being pointlessly rebellious and disrespectful.

I felt bad about lying to him, even by omission. *Really* bad. Like, stains-collecting-on-my-soul bad. With every secret I kept and every order I resisted, I was risking our brand-new relationship—the most wonderful thing that had ever happened to me. But no matter how precarious his seat on the council was, with humans being slaughtered in his territory, he wasn't the one with the most to lose on this mission.

Neither was I.

Jace gave me a kiss, then headed downstairs, and each tread creaked beneath his weight. I held my breath, certain that any second, he'd start shouting my name and demand an explanation. I *needed* to be the first person in that basement, even if I couldn't explain that to him.

My pulse whooshed in my ears, counting the seconds as they ticked past. I needed to make a phone call, but he'd hear anything I said, and any conversation I initiated via text message ran the risk of being seen if an alert popped up on my screen at the wrong time.

When Jace's creaky footsteps became solid thumps, I realized he'd stepped off the stairs and onto the basement floor. My heart pounded harder, beyond my control by then. As I reached for the door of the old, yellow refrigerator, hoping for a bottle of water to wet my miserably dry throat, my gaze snagged on the gun rack against the wall.

Hadn't it held three rifles before? Now there were only two.

Shit! The guys needed to know that whoever'd run into the woods was armed.

I pulled my phone from my pocket and opened my mouth to shout for Jace—then froze when something hard poked my back through Robyn's down jacket..

"Set your phone on the counter and shut your mouth, shifter bitch, or I'll blow a hole right through you," a hoarse voice whispered as fear tightened both my chest and my throat. Then I realized he was speaking softly on purpose. If we couldn't hear Jace's footsteps anymore, chances were good that he couldn't hear the whispered threat.

I lifted my left hand into the air slowly, to show him it was empty, then I set my phone on the kitchen counter.

"Push it into the sink." He pressed the rifle harder

into my back.

Damn it. I gave my phone a little shove, and it slid down the grimy Formica countertop into the sink, where it landed with a plop. I groaned. My phone was ruined, and unlike the other enforcers, I hadn't yet been issued a work phone.

"Now turn around. Slowly."

I turned to find Gene Hargrove pointing the missing hunting rifle at my chest.

The broom closet behind him stood open, and with a mental kick to my own backside, I realized he'd opened the back door and knocked over the table to make us think he'd run into the woods, when he'd actually just hidden in the closet, probably expecting all of us to take off after him.

"Your pictures don't do you justice," Hargrove whispered, studying me through grayish blue human eyes. "You would look *stunning* hanging on my wall."

"And you'll be a deconstructed masterpiece once the worms get ahold of you. But only one of those two things is going to happen."

Hargrove actually laughed. "Ambitious for such a tiny little thing. Are you the one who gave Steve and his boys so much trouble?"

"Size means nothing to a shifter." Though that wasn't entirely true. I was nowhere near as strong as my brothers, or even as Faythe, but surely I could give a pudgy, middle-aged human a run for his money. "I could probably throw you across the room with one hand."

"Too bad we'll never find out. You're going to step quietly out the back door and down the steps, then head toward the truck in the driveway. If you even *look* like you're going to run, I'll blow a hole right through you."

"Wouldn't that put a kink in your plan to mount my head on the wall?" If I died in human form, he'd have no cat to stuff.

Hargrove shrugged one shoulder, without compromising his aim. "We've already got an eye on the other little girl cat. What are you called? Tabbies?"

Rage tingled like needles poking me all over, and I silently refused to answer.

"Darren's gonna bring her in tonight. Now march. And keep in mind that if you holler and bring Mr. Hammond or any of his men to your rescue, I have no problem shooting every last one of them."

Chill bumps rose all over my skin, and they had nothing to do with the cold. Hargrove knew who Jace was. Not just his name, but that he was in charge. Before I'd killed Steve, he'd told me that several of the shifters they'd slaughtered and stuffed had given in to interrogation, hoping for a quicker death. Had Leo been one of those?

Hargrove gestured with his gun for me to get moving, and my hands shook. How many bullets did a rifle hold? I knew nothing about guns, except that he wouldn't get a chance to reload.

But that wouldn't help the first couple who got shot.

I backed carefully toward the ruined backdoor, afraid to look away from Hargrove even for a second. "Jace is going to rip your head right off your shoulders."

Hargrove took a soft step forward, forcing me closer to the door. "Those old stairs squeak if you don't know exactly where to step. We'll have plenty of warning if he heads back up. Though it'd be a shame to have to kill an Alpha in human form. No real point in hanging *that* head on the wall, is there?"

A man-shaped shadow fell on the floor behind him, and I had to fight not to look directly at it. Jace stepped silently out of the pantry and deliberately shoved the door open wider. The hinges squealed, and Hargrove turned.

The instant the gun barrel swung away from me, Jace pounced—a denim-clad blur streaking across the kitchen.

He ripped the rifle from the hunter's grasp, then rammed the butt of it into his gut. Hargrove bent over with a breathless grunt. He never even got a chance to shout.

"You okay?" Jace set the rifle on the kitchen counter, and I nodded while he hauled Hargrove up by the back of his thick neck. He wrapped his free hand around the human's throat, digging in lightly, then leaned forward to whisper into his ear. "You're obviously used to dealing with strays. If I didn't want you to see or hear me, you'd already be darkening the devil's doorstep without any clue how you got there."

Jace winked at me, and my heart thudded in my throat. The loss of his rifle didn't make Hargrove any less of a threat to me.

But Jace couldn't know that.

"You so much as twitch before Abby gets back, and I'll rip your throat out," he growled. "Understand?"

Hargrove nodded frantically, his eyes wide. A bead of sweat rolled slowly down the side of his face, in spite of the frigid draft blowing in through the open doorway.

"Where am I going?" I asked, silently scrambling

for a solution to my newest problem—Jace and Hargrove face to face.

"To get a roll of duct tape from the tool bench downstairs. Make it fast, Abby."

I raced into the pantry and down the creaky stairs, thrilled to have caught at least a little bit of a break. Either Jace hadn't found anything he shouldn't have in the basement, or he hadn't had time to look before he heard Hargrove upstairs.

At the bottom of the steps, I glanced around the basement to find a much smaller space than Hargrove had at his own house. The workbench was smaller, the stash of tools and chemicals was meager, and there was no bulletin board at all, though that hadn't stopped the hunters from hanging pictures on the wall with scotch tape.

A quick glance at the photos showed that they were reprints of the ones hung in that other basement—there was nothing I'd need to hide or destroy.

Dried blood caked Hargrove's work surface, but the scents were all unfamiliar and mostly faint from the passage of time and from chemical degradation. A four-drawer metal filing cabinet stood against one wall, but I wouldn't have time to go through that, and an empty three-by-five dog cage took up most of one corner. It smelled like bleach.

"Abby!" Jace shouted, and I jumped.

"Sorry!" I grabbed the duct tape from the workbench and clomped up the creaky stairs again. "I got distracted by all the creepy crap down there."

"Here." Jace took a step back from Hargrove without letting go of his neck. "Tape his hands up. Make it tight."

I tore a long strip of tape from the roll, then knelt and reached between them to wrap the tape around Hargrove's wrists, praying that the next strip would cover his mouth. When I'd stood and backed away, Jace let go of Hargrove and grabbed the rifle from the kitchen counter.

"Abby, call the guys back." He flipped up a lever on the rifle then shoved it back, and the bullet popped out, then rolled around on the floor.

I pushed my sleeve up and reached into a pot full of greasy water to fish my poor phone out. "Can I use yours?"

Jace swore when he saw my cell dripping on the kitchen floor, then handed his to me.

"You move and I start breaking bones," he told Hargrove while I scrolled through his contacts for my brother's number. The hunter looked ready to wet his camouflage pants. "You refuse to answer a single question and I start breaking bones."

Shit. I could *not* let him interrogate Hargrove.

"Jace?" Lucas said into my ear.

"No, it's me. We got Hargrove. Jace wants you all to head back."

"Be there in ten." Lucas hung up, and I tossed Jace's phone back to him.

"Where's Darren?" My Alpha circled Hargrove slowly, sliding his phone into his jacket pocket.

"Hey, aren't you supposed to let the *whole* council question him?" I leaned against the counter, watching them both in profile, trying to project a casual interest.

"I will, once I'm sure no more shifters are in imminent danger."

Damn it.

"Where's Darren?" Jace repeated.

"Is that your girlfriend?" Hargrove was no longer whispering, now that he'd been caught, but his natural voice was still scratchy and distinctive. "She talks back like a girlfriend." He shrugged as his gaze slid down from my neck and kept going. "A little small for my taste, but I bet all those shifter bitches are hellcats in bed."

My fist clenched around the countertop.

"Was Darren here with you?" Jace asked, and I could see from the tension in his arms as he slowly circled his prey that he was itching to punch a hole right through the taxidermist. "Is he a cop?"

"I'd love to get her on my table." Hargrove licked his lips, staring right at me. "Stuffing *that* little showpiece would be a real pleasure."

"She'd rip your balls off and feed them to you." Jace stepped between me and Hargrove, blocking his view. "You take one more look at her, and I'm going to let her do it. Now, is Darren the cop in the photos?"

Hargrove shrugged. "Who's Darren?"

Jace circled him in a blur of movement, and I heard a sudden soft snap. The hunter howled, and I'd never in my life heard such a noise come from a human. When Jace stepped back, Hargrove's left pinkie finger was broken at a ninety-degree angle. Bone showed through a tear in his flesh and a steady dribble of blood dripped into a growing pool on the floor.

"If I have to ask again, I'll break the next one," Jace warned. "Good luck stuffing *anything* with two broken fingers."

Hargrove said nothing, so Jace reached for his

hand again.

"He's a cop!" Hargrove shouted through his sobs. "Ten years on the force in a little town about an hour and a half from here."

"And the other guys in your fucked-up hunting club? I want the names of the ones still breathing."

When Hargrove hesitated, Jace lunged toward him, and I flinched when I heard another soft snap. Hargrove screamed again, and snot dripped from his left nostril.

"Names," Jace demanded, and I tapped the edge of the countertop, growing increasingly desperate for a reasonable excuse to stop the interrogation.

"Carl Wilks and Reggie Lewis are the only others I know by name. But they quit. They got spooked when you guys started picking us off, one by one."

When *we'd*... I exhaled slowly, relieved to realize that the hunters thought they were being killed off by Jace and his enforcers. However, Hargrove still possessed a *fount* of information I couldn't let Jace have.

How the hell was I supposed to stop him from talking, when his silence was rewarded with broken bones?

"Quitting won't keep them safe," Jace said while I clutched the countertop at my back to keep from cutting my palms open with my own nails. "Carl and Reggie are dead men."

Fear tensed every muscle in my body and sharpened my vision. I could see every bead of sweat that formed on Hargrove's forehead and every clogged pore in the crease of his nose. I could smell his terror, but that only made me wonder if Jace could smell mine. If he could, surely he'd think I was still traumatized from behind held at gunpoint.

"Where is Darren now?" Jace demanded, and my chest suddenly felt tight, as if my heart no longer fit. If Hargrove answered many questions along those lines, I was *screwed.*

"Hunting. But he's supposed to be back tonight."

"Where did he go?"

"I don't know, exactly. Hunting is *his* job," the human said. "I mostly just stuff them. And teach the other guys how to do it. Would you believe some of them used to think we could mount a human head with cat eyes? That's what they wanted to do with you, until I told them you can't keep any of the soft tissue. That's why we use glass eyes. But we could keep your *teeth*, if they happened to be feline when you died."

My stomach churned, disgust and fear warring inside me. I needed Hargrove to *shut up*, for multiple reasons.

When my right hand began to twitch, I tucked it behind me. If Jace thought I couldn't handle the interrogation, he'd make me wait outside, and even though *he* shouldn't hear whatever Hargrove had to say, I *had* to hear it in order to plan my next move.

"Who's Darren hunting?" Jace's voice was a snarl so low Hargrove probably hardly heard it.

"He went after the other tabby so we can—" Hargrove's sentence ended so abruptly, I could only imagine how he'd planned to finish it.

My fingers began to itch and burn at my back as the bones moved, rearranging the structure of my hand with no conscious instruction from my brain. I felt threatened on multiple levels, and my body was instinctively preparing me to fight for my life.

"So you can *what?*" Jace demanded, and I shook my head slowly. I didn't want to hear it. I didn't want to think about it. The slaughter. And whatever came before.

Hargrove shrugged, an awkward movement with his hands bound at his back. "We've never had a girl cat. Steve and the others tried with her." He glanced at me, and Jace snarled and stepped between us again. "But she turned out to be much more...spirited than advertised."

A stubborn bolt of pride surged through me in spite of the circumstances. They'd been told by the toms they'd tortured that tabbies were largely overprotected and defenseless, and I'd been thrilled to defy the stereotype.

"So, we thought we'd go after one with less experience," Hargrove finished. "Darren's on his way to get her now."

Jace seemed to swell like a puffer fish, only he was full of pure, homicidal rage. "Darren went after my sister?" he roared, and for a second, I thought he might kill Hargrove and solve my problem for me.

But then he stepped back and took several deep breaths. I could see his internal struggle as he forced his shoulders to relax and his jaw to unclench. He was reining his temper in, as any good Alpha would, and I knew from the movement of his lips that he was counting backward silently. Probably from one thousand.

Yet he'd be ready in an instant if Hargrove moved a single muscle.

For a moment, the only sounds were Jace's steady, controlled inhalations, the pained hitch as Hargrove breathed through a bruised gut and broken fingers, and the steady drip of his blood into a growing puddle on the floor.

Then Hargrove frowned. "She's your sister?"

Jace stiffened, and my fear spiked along with the almost painful jump in my pulse.

Nonononono!

My world was falling apart. Every word Hargrove spoke threatened to split the ground beneath my feet and send me tumbling into an abyss I could never crawl out of. Jace would be furious. My father would be devastated. The council would want my blood, and then everything I'd worked to hide—to *protect*—would be lost.

"Darren will never even get close to her," Jace whispered. "My men will shred him before he even knows they're there."

Hargrove frowned, confusion warring with pain in his features. "But you've left her exposed! Darren probably already has her!"

Jace stepped toward him again, as claws burst from the ends of my fingers. I could see what he was thinking. He'd only brought four enforcers, including me, which left *more* than enough at the lodge to defend Melody. Especially considering that other than defending his Alpha, an enforcer had no greater or more honorable duty than to protect a pregnant tabby.

Hell, Isaac would singlehandedly skin Darren alive to protect his fiancée and unborn child.

But neither the Alpha nor the hunter knew they were taking part in two completely different conversations. And Jace could *not* come to that conclusion.

"We can't figure out why, if girl cats are so rare,

you'd all leave not just one"—Hargrove glanced at me—"but *two* of them totally undefended. We've been watching them, taking pictures, and we never saw a single one of your men. It's almost like you *want* us to—"

Terror squeezed my chest with a brutal pressure. The bones in my hand crackled as they fell into place. The room blurred around me as I lunged at him.

"Abby, no!" Jace shouted, but logic cracked and fell away from me, and the exposed fury burned like fire in every vein in my body. It snapped like static across every synapse.

I have no memory of ripping Hargrove's throat out.

One moment, I was leaning against the grimy kitchen counter, listening to the words that would bring an abrupt halt to life as I knew it, and the next, I was standing in front of Gene Hargrove as his blood arced over my face and my borrowed jacket with each dying beat of his heart. His mouth hung open as he gasped. His eyes were wide but already unfocused, and some primal part of me rejoiced at the thought that I was the last thing that bastard would ever see.

Then he crumpled to the floor in a pool of his own blood.

I stepped back, and the consequence of what I'd just done hit me like a blow to the gut.

That's when the world slid out of focus.

THIRTEEN

Jace

I hardly saw her move, but as soon as I realized her hand had shifted, I knew what she was going to do.

"Abby, no!" I shouted, but I was too late.

One second, she was standing there with her jaw clenched, her heart racing so fast, I was afraid it would explode. The next, she was covered with Hargrove's blood, and he lay dead at her feet, still bleeding all over the linoleum.

She looked down at him for the span of a single heartbeat. Then her eyes lost focus and her hands—one still a claw—fell limp at her sides.

"Abby!" I pulled her away from the body, and my fingers smeared the blood on her sleeve. Only it wasn't even *her* sleeve. She'd ruined her roommate's jacket with arterial spray from the man whose throat she'd just ripped out, and there would be *no way* to explain that to Robyn.

Or to the territorial council.

Fuck. I didn't have clearance to execute any of the human hunters unless they were an imminent threat, and Abby had just killed the only member of the sick shifter taxidermy club we had in custody. The only source who could tell us how many of his fellow humans knew about us and just how big a problem we had. We *needed* that information, and someone would have to pay for the loss of it.

"Abby!" I yelled again, practically in her face, but she only stared at the floor as if she no longer saw the body lying there. As if she no longer saw anything. Footsteps thundered from the back porch, then Lucas pulled her from my grip and wrapped his massive arms around her.

"What the hell happened?" he demanded.

"She *flipped out* and ripped open his throat." Then she'd totally checked out of reality—it probably wasn't true catatonia, but she was definitely in shock. "Abby!" When I reached for her, Luke turned to put her out of my reach, and my temper flared in a white-hot instant. He'd forgotten in his concern and confusion that I was his fucking Alpha and that respect was my fucking *due*.

And, evidently, that I would *never, ever* hurt her. Even if she'd just thrown all of us into a vast world of hurt.

I snarled, and Lucas dropped his gaze but made no move to let go of his sister, who stood motionless in is grip. I took a deep breath and reminded myself that this wasn't about defying his Alpha; it was about being there for his sister. I'd have done the same thing, even back when I was an enforcer. And I didn't even *like* Melody that much. "Okay. See if you can wake her up. Quickly." I grabbed his arm when he started to guide her away. "And don't *ever* let that happen again."

I turned to Mateo while Lucas bent to speak directly into his sister's ear. "Call Isaac and put everyone on alert. Tell him Darren's going after Melody, and we'll be there as soon as we can."

Teo stepped outside to make the call, and as a traumatized feline whine began to leak from Abby, I realized that her throat had shifted along with her right hand. What the *hell* had set her off?

"Why would she do that?" Warner watched Lucas smooth back his sister's curls, still whispering into her ear.

"She must have felt threatened," Luke said.

"Hargrove's hands were bound behind him. He wasn't a threat. She was in no danger." Even when he'd held her at gunpoint, she'd been cool and collected…right up until the moment she ripped his neck open.

"Well, she must have *thought* she was," Lucas insisted, over Abby's head. "She was probably having some kind of flashback."

Warner shrugged. "With everything she's been through, I guess the real surprise is that she hasn't flipped out before."

In theory, that was a rational explanation, but in Abby's case, it didn't make sense. She'd *definitely* been threatened when the hunters had killed her friends in the woods, but she'd held it together in order to track the bad guys, eliminate them, then explain to me exactly what had happened, and how going against my orders was really the right thing to do.

Yet with Hargrove, even though he was restrained

and unarmed, she'd freaked out, lashed out, then checked out. We were missing something.

"Abby," I said as Warner started opening kitchen drawers in search of rags and towels. She still stared at the wall above the gun rack, but now a maelstrom of conflicting emotions flitted over her features. Terror, and desperation, and...caution.

What part of what she'd just done could be considered cautious?

"Abby!" I called again, and finally, she blinked. "Look at me."

She complied, and I saw raw instinct battling shock behind her eyes. She was still mired in the trauma of what she'd done, yet something inside her demanded that she follow her Alpha's orders. Hell, she might actually be easier to deal with as an enforcer without her human stubborn streak getting in the way.

Not that what she'd just done could *possibly* be easy to deal with. Her father and his allies had gone out on a limb to support my leadership of the Appalachian Pride, and so far, all I had to show for it was a serial killer stray and group of human psychos hanging dead shifters on walls. When the council found out I'd let a key informant die—at the hands of an unstable rookie enforcer I never should have hired—they'd have *my* head stuffed and mounted.

It wouldn't matter how much I cared about Abby, or that I'd brought her on the mission in an effort to protect her. An Alpha is responsible for everything that happens in his territory, which meant that if she didn't have a damn good reason for what she'd just done, we were *both* in serious trouble.

"Here." Warner shoved a handful of kitchen

towels at me. "Let's get the blood off her. Maybe that'll help."

Lucas turned her by her shoulders so that she couldn't see the body on the floor, then unzipped her ruined jacket and helped her shrug out of it. She was shaking all over.

"Abby." I used one of the towels to wipe a spray of blood on her cheek, but that only smeared it. "Abby, wake up. I need you to tell me what happened."

She blinked again, struggling to focus on my face. Then she threw her arms around me and I became the third shifter smeared with Hargrove's blood. But I didn't give a damn. I held her as tightly as I could without hurting her.

"I'm so sorry, Jace" she said through chattering teeth, her face buried in the shoulder of my coat.

"It's okay." One way or another, I would *make* it okay, so that I'd never have to let her go. "Just tell me what happened, and we'll deal with it."

Abby stood on her toes and kissed me, and something deep in my chest began to ache. That was a *hungry* kiss. That was the greedy kiss of a woman who knows she'll soon be going without for a very long time. "I am so, so sorry for this," she whispered against my ear, her arms wrapped around my neck to hold me close. "I wish there'd been another way."

"Another way?" I held her at arms length, studying the startling change in her as it happened. Her jaw tightened and an emotional veil dropped over her eyes, shielding her thoughts from me. "Another way for what, Abby?" Had she done it on *purpose*? "Why did you kill him?"

But I already knew that whatever she said wouldn't

be true. Not the whole truth, anyway. She'd locked me out. Hell, she'd practically said good-bye, and that realization sent a terrifying bolt of panic through me.

I couldn't lose her. Not because of this. Not because of *anything.*

"I killed him because he deserved to die." She crossed her arms over her chest, and her gaze narrowed. "He *needed* to die, and *you* obviously weren't going to step up, so I did what had to be done."

A growl rose from deep inside me. Tension filled the room, expanding to occupy the widening gap between us as the guys—even Lucas—stepped back, instinctively distancing themselves from the challenger.

From the five-foot-nothing, one-hundred-pound female challenger, whose strongest muscle by far was that dagger of a tongue.

Abby's words were a deliberate provocation. Her tone, and her stance, and her steady, bold eye contact—they were all intended to provoke me. To elicit a reaction.

They worked.

"That wasn't your call," I growled, struggling to remain calm even knowing she was manipulating my instincts. "Hargrove would have been able to give us names and addresses. He could have told us how far-reaching a problem these hunters are!"

"We can get all that from his records. From his computer," she insisted. "I couldn't recite the phone number of a single person in my contact list, because no one memorizes that stuff anymore. We store the data on devices, which means that Hargrove's cell and laptop are *way* more valuable than he is."

"You better hope you're right," I said. "But that's

not the point. You violated a mandate from the council and disobeyed a direct order from me!"

"It was a *stupid* order." She snatched the towel from me with her bloody left hand and scrubbed at her cheek. "I feel no obligation to follow orders that don't make sense."

Yet I heard a quiver in her voice—more evidence that she didn't believe what she was saying. She was playing a part. Putting on a show.

"Abby!" Lucas whispered fiercely, warning her to shut the hell up. To stop making everything worse, but she knew exactly what she was doing, and so did I.

I just didn't know why.

What I *did* know was that she wouldn't be doing whatever she was doing if she thought she had any other choice. She needed an out.

If she told the right lie, I could give her one.

"You need to think carefully about the next words you say." How she answered my question would dictate what happened to her in the immediate future. Her insistence on being treated like any other enforcer meant she would be punished like any other enforcer. Even if I took the lion's share of the blame, she could lose her claws, her canines, or her freedom.

"Abby did you intentionally disobey my order and kill an unarmed, restrained human?"

Say no. Tell me you had a flashback. A psychological break. Tell me the fucking devil made you do it. Just give me an excuse to make this go away.

"Yes." She met my gaze boldly, and Lucas groaned. "You know damn well I did."

Anger blazed a path up from my gut like heartburn. Every word she said made it harder to help her. Did she have *any concept* of the position she'd put me in?

This is why Alphas shouldn't sleep with their enforcers. Much less fall for them. But it was too late for that, and she'd left me with no choice about what would come next.

"Okay." I took a long, deep breath, and for the first time since taking over the Appalachian Pride, I hated myself for doing my duty. "Abigail Wade, you are hereby permanently relieved of duty as an enforcer." An ache swelled inside me, and I couldn't pinpoint the source because it hurt all over. Why was she making me do this? "I'd tell you to turn in your phone and your credit card, but I haven't issued them to you yet."

I felt like I'd just put a bullet in my best friend, but the lines in Abby's forehead faded and the tension in her jaw relaxed. She'd clearly gotten exactly what she wanted from pushing my buttons, but I had still had no clue what the *hell* was going on in her head. Or how I was going to explain this to the rest of the council.

Why would she manipulate me into hiring her, then provoke me into firing her?

"I understand," she said with a formal nod. "You have no choice."

I wanted to yell and throw things. She could have given me a choice. If there was *ever* a time for her to lie to her Alpha, that was it.

"Don't let them pin this on you," Abby said, as she carefully shifted her right paw back into a human hand, and I saw the first glimpse of regret in her eyes. Of guilt. She turned to glance at the guys, each in turn. "Do *not* let them pin this on Jace. I killed Gene

Hargrove against orders. You all heard that. He told me not to, and I did it anyway. He couldn't have stopped me."

"Abby..." Lucas began, and she cut him off with a fierce look.

"You know what happened here, and if you lie for me, I will *never* forgive you."

No one tried to argue with her that time, so she nodded, as if something had truly been settled. As if emerging from shock had put her back in control not just of herself, but of the rest of us too.

She was wrong on both counts.

Abby swiped at her face one more time, then began scrubbing blood from her left hand with her newly formed right one. We probably weren't supposed to notice that they were both trembling, or that her eyes were standing in tears.

She set the bloody towel on the kitchen counter, then took a backward step toward the door. "Okay, I guess I'll go back to the lodge and let you guys do your job."

"That's no longer an option for you," I said, and every word hurt as if I were carving my own heart from my chest. But again, she'd left me no choice. "Your membership in the Appalachian Pride is hereby revoked. Lucas, take her to the airport and put her on a plane."

I headed straight for the back door, desperate for the shock of cold air. For some distance from the most painful sentence I'd ever uttered.

"No!" Abby grabbed my arm, then planted herself in front of me, pleading with her eyes. "You can fire me. I won't fight that. But don't send me away, Jace. I need to be here. With you."

"Don't you *dare* say that." I ripped my arm from her grip, but the truth was that I was almost relieved to be angry at her. Anger was much easier to deal with than the confusion and betrayal I was starting to associate with her very presence. Abby was hot and cold. Innocent and manipulative. She'd whispered brave truths and shouted bold lies, and I couldn't tell from one moment to the next whether she was going to kiss me or put a knife in my back.

The really scary thing was that she didn't seem to know either.

"Jace, *please...*"

"You broke your vow!" I yelled. "You disobeyed a direct order. You killed someone in *cold blood*! You're finished here. Don't make this worse for yourself." I pushed past her toward the back door, but she shouted after me.

"Do *not* walk away from me!" Desperation echoed in every syllable, but it was her underlying anger that triggered the dangerous rumble rolling up from my throat.

The guys froze, still mired in the tension rising from Abby and me like fog from a lake. I turned slowly, and the room came into crystal focus as my eyes hovered somewhere between human and feline. "If you were anyone else in the *world*, you would lose a tooth for that," I growled. But I couldn't hit her, even if she was the single most insubordinate shifter I'd ever met.

Bar none.

"Everybody out," I snapped.

Logically, I should have left them inside to start cleaning up Abby's mess, but this wasn't a fight I wanted to have outdoors, where it felt like the whole world would be watching. It was bad enough that they'd all seen her push me around like a pawn on a chessboard.

Mateo and Warner headed into the backyard, but Lucas stopped in the doorway. "I'm staying."

He was six inches taller and at least sixty pounds heavier than I was, which made him both stronger and slower. He might only get in one punch before I took him down, but it'd be one hell of a blow, and I couldn't afford to have to fire *another* enforcer. Especially one whose brother had knocked up my sister, and whose sister I was in love with. Even when I wanted to kill her.

No family tie had ever been quite so tangled.

"Get out," I growled, irritated that I had to look up to threaten him. I was losing control of my Pride, my enforcers, and my entire territory, and the only sure way I knew of to get it back would be to unleash more violence. But we'd all seen more than enough spilled blood. "Lucas, I gave you an order. I don't have to explain it. I shouldn't have to repeat it. You should know and trust me well enough to do whatever I tell you, without hesitation."

"Luke—" Abby began.

I snarled at her, and she flinched. He had to go because *I'd told him to go.* Not because she'd given him permission.

"Don't make this worse," I said, turning back to her brother, and finally, Lucas nodded. Then he stepped outside and pulled the busted door shut after him. As shut as he could, anyway.

I turned on Abby the moment the door closed. "What the *hell* is wrong with you?"

"I'm sorry. I haven't done a damn thing right since

we got here." She twisted her fingers together so tightly, I was afraid they'd break, but she didn't seem to notice any pain. "But please don't send me home."

I leaned against the door to keep it closed. "Hell, yes, I'm going to send you home. Even if I had a choice before, I don't now. You're insubordinate and disrespectful, and anyone else would have gotten a fistful for shouting orders at an Alpha." That was standard; for our society to function, an Alpha had to be respected and obeyed without question, and he had to be worthy of both. "But I can't discipline you like I'd discipline one of the guys"—not that that had ever been necessary—"because..."

"Because you love me?" She reached for me, and I pushed her hands away, even though every instinct I had told me to pull her closer.

"Don't muddy the waters," I snapped, fighting to maintain objectivity. "You're half my size. That wouldn't be discipline; that would be assault." Especially considering that she'd only ever been hit by men who followed up their blows by ripping off her clothes and stealing every bit of trust and security she'd ever had. "I would *never* hurt you, even if you broke every rule we have."

What I wanted was to kiss her until she couldn't argue anymore because her mouth was too busy, but that wouldn't exactly make my point.

"And you know that. You're taking advantage of how I feel about you, which means you're getting away with murder. Figuratively speaking." The council would *never* let her get away with what she'd done to Hargrove. "I can't make you obey the rules, but I can't let the guys see you walk all over me. You can't be here anymore, and you know exactly why."

"I'm so sorry, Jace." Her tears spilled over. "I didn't mean for any of this to make you look bad. I would never do that on purpose."

"Any of what?" There it was again—that glimpse of some hidden purpose behind the chaos she'd thrown my entire territory into. "What's going on, Abby?"

"Nothing." She sucked in another shaky breath, then met my gaze again. "I'll go, if that's really what you want. Can you just give me a couple of days to get my stuff packed?"

"No. I'll have it shipped to you." If she stayed one more night, I'd break down and change my mind. Which she clearly knew.

"*Please*, Jace. I won't even go back to the lodge. I'll just go pack up my dorm room, and you'll never even know I'm in the territory."

"No." I crossed my arms so they couldn't reach for her, trying not to be swayed by how upset she was. She'd dug her own grave and had refused to let me pull her out of it. "You need to go home, where you'll be safe. And so your father can start working on your defense."

"I don't care about that. I need to be *here*."

"Why?" I wanted her to say that I was the reason. That she couldn't stand even the *thought* of being away from me, because that was how I felt, after only one night with her. Even after everything she'd done. But I wasn't the reason she wanted to stay.

Not the only reason, anyway.

"What's going on, Abby? If you want to stay, you have to tell me the truth."

"Nothing's going—"

"*Don't lie to me!*" I shouted, and she flinched. "If

you don't tell me what's going on, I will put you on a plane *right now.*"

Her eyes watered, but she held my gaze. And her own tongue, possibly for the first time in her life.

"Abby, don't do this. Tell me what's wrong. I know you wouldn't have killed him unless you had to."

Her tears ran over and her chin began to tremble, and that was all I could take. I wrapped her in my arms, bloody clothes and all, and spoke into her hair. "Let me help you."

"You can't. It's too late," she said into my chest. "I'd only drag you down with me, and I can't let that happen."

"It won't." I held her tighter, breathing in her scent. "Don't make me send you away." I ran my hands down her back, wishing more than anything in the world that we could just rewind the day and wake up in bed together, so I could fix this. So that she would never get blood on her hands and I wouldn't lose her. "Please, Abby. I love you."

Her next breath came with a soft, surprised sound. Then she stiffened and pushed me away. "Don't say that." Her eyes were full of tears again and her voice was strained, as if she was holding back more than she was saying. "Not like this. Please don't tell me you love me, then kick me out of your life."

"Don't *make* me kick you out." A perilous mix of heartache and anger stormed inside me. I wanted to hold her. I wanted to help her. I wanted to *keep* her. But she wouldn't budge. "Tell me what's going on!"

"Stop asking!" she shouted. "*I can't!*"

My temper snapped. I turned and pulled the door open before she could say anything else. "Lucas!" I called, and he jogged up the steps and into the kitchen, obviously having heard every word. "Put her on a plane."

"No!" Abby reached for me, but I stepped back and gave her brother a signal he couldn't possibly misunderstand. He took her by both arms, holding her in physical custody, and glared at me over her head the entire time. He might never forgive me for it, but he would follow my orders, both because I was his Alpha and because I was right.

Any other Alpha would have fired her long before.

"You want me to take her now?" Luke glanced pointedly at the dead body. "What about him?"

"We'll clean this up. Stop somewhere and get her something to change into, then buy her a ticket and give your parents the flight information. I'll tell your dad she's on the way. And that she's all his."

"Jace, please!" Abby tried to reach for me, but she couldn't break her brother's grip. "Please don't do this!"

"Get her out of here." I made myself watch as Lucas hauled his sister out the door and into the woods, even though it felt like he'd just taken my heart with him.

And just like that, Abby was gone.

FOURTEEN

Abby

"Lucas, you have to change his mind," I said, as my brother's truck sped down the highway toward Lexington. "Jace will listen to you."

Lucas snorted. "No he won't. Thanks to you, I'm on his shit-list too." He glanced to the west, where the sun hung low on the horizon, half covered by dark clouds. The forecast called for snow, but I knew he was hoping for rain instead, because we weren't good winter-weather drivers. We hadn't had much practice in South Carolina. "What the hell were you thinking, Abby? You swore an oath! You can't go around disobeying orders and questioning your Alpha's authority just because you're—"

"Don't *do* that!" I snapped, slamming one hand down on his dashboard. "Do *not* assume that everything I do or say is because I'm some fragile kitten suffering from post-traumatic stress. I knew *exactly* what I was doing with Hargrove."

I'd hoped to avoid killing him in front of Jace, to keep him as uninvolved as possible, and I'd kind of lost it for a minute when the whole thing sank in. But other than that, I'd been in control. Doing what had to be done, even if none of the rest of them understood that. And it hadn't escaped my notice that everyone was upset about the fact that I'd killed Hargrove, but not about the fact that he was dead.

Lucas glanced at me with one brow raised. "I was actually going to say, 'You can't go around questioning your Alpha's authority just because *you're sleeping with him.*' Which is really weird for me, by the way. It's my brotherly duty to pound him into the ground, but I swore an oath to respect and obey him."

"Have you ever noticed that the enforcer's oath reads like an archaic marriage vow?" I said. Lucas glared at me and I shrugged. "Okay. Not the point. I'll try to think about *your* comfort level the next time I decide to assert *my* sexual independence."

"That's all I'm asking. Except maybe that you never again use the phrase 'sexual independence' in front of your brother."

The truth was that I didn't want there to *be* a next time. I couldn't imagine wanting anyone other than Jace to touch me. Ever. But things weren't looking good for us, considering he was having me forcibly escorted from the territory the very day after we'd gotten together.

How to lose an Alpha in eighteen hours. My life was a romantic comedy waiting to happen.

Minus the comedy.

"So, wait. What do you mean, you knew what you

were doing with Hargrove?" Lucas gave me a skeptical glance as he mentally replayed my outburst. "You're saying you *intended* to be covered in blood, on your way to the airport to comply with your own exile?"

"Well, no." I sank back against my seat with a frown. "I only meant to get fired. I had no idea Jace would try to get rid of me entirely."

"It's not like you gave him any choice." Lucas glanced at me with his copper-colored brows furrowed. "Please tell me you didn't kill Hargrove just to get out of being an enforcer?"

"No! I killed him because he was a bad guy. He was part of the sick hunting club that mounted Leo's head, slaughtered three of my friends, and would have killed my roommate if I hadn't gotten to her in time. My only regret about Hargrove's death is that it was quicker and easier than he deserved."

"It was also completely unauthorized, but you could have played the PTSD card to keep your job. Or at least keep Jace in your corner. Why did you get yourself fired?"

"Because unlike some of my larger, more brutish coworkers, a girl my size has to be able to think on her feet." To get herself hired, when having a job will get her where she needs to go, then get herself fired, when losing that job will free her up to go where she's truly needed.

Only that last part hadn't worked out so well.

"I don't even know what that means. What's going on, Abby?"

"Nothing."

"You're a terrible liar."

"Then you'll just have to respect my intent." I

twisted on the bench seat to face him, tugging at the shoulder strap of my seatbelt. "Lucas, I need a favor."

"No." His grip on the steering wheel tightened, and the plastic creaked beneath the added stress.

"You don't even know what I—"

"I know you want to stay here, but Jace is right. You need to go home and let Dad work on your defense. They're going to bring you up on charges, Abby. Do you even know how serious that is?"

"Of course I know!" The only thing keeping that understanding from reducing me to a puddle of tears and panic was the more urgent terror Hargrove had driven deep into me right before he'd died.

The charges that would be leveled against me were inevitable, but the Darren problem…that couldn't wait.

"I'll do or say whatever Dad says I should." The scent of Hargrove's drying blood was a constant reminder of how soon I'd have to face the consequences of a crime I'd had no choice but to commit. "I'm not trying to make this worse. I just… I need to be here right now."

"What the *hell* is wrong with you?" Lucas's foot got heavier, and I wondered if accelerator aggression was a trait all toms shared. "I feel like my little sister went to college and a hellcat came back in her place."

He was very nearly right. Only, college hadn't been the trigger.

"I don't expect you to understand." Because I couldn't explain it to him. "But I really am trying to do the right thing."

"Good." Lucas put his right blinker on and swerved onto the off ramp, where a sign advertised food, fuel, and an outlet mall full of discount stores.

I recognized the mall. We were only a few miles from campus and less than half an hour from the airport. My time was running out, and the sun wasn't sinking fast enough.

Lucas pulled into a parking spot near the back of the outlet mall's parking lot. This close to Christmas, most of the lot was full, even with storm clouds rolling in. "Now you're going to stay in the car, and I'm going to get you some clean clothes." Because he could take off his blood-smeared jacket to look presentable, but I was splattered all the way down to my white boots. Which, Lucas had informed me, was why enforcers typically wore all black. "You still wear the same sizes?" he asked, and I nodded. In spite of summers spent training with Faythe, I hadn't put on much muscle, and I hadn't gained even an inch in height since high school. "Any requests?"

"No pink. It clashes with my hair." Which wasn't an issue my redheaded brother had to deal with.

"Got it." Lucas got out of the car, then bent to peer in at me. "I won't be gone long enough for it to get cold in here. Stay put."

I watched him walk toward the entrance to the mall, and where it shone through the clouds, the sinking sun seemed to set his hair on fire. I had *maybe* half an hour of daylight left, but that was half an hour too much.

A glance around the lot showed me more cars than shoppers, and the few people I saw were all headed toward the mall, focused on getting out of the cold before the rain started. They didn't look back once they'd left their cars. No one was watching me.

I wasn't going to get a better shot.

Still watching the parking lot for any unwanted

attention, I stripped out of Robyn's jacket, careful not to get my hands any bloodier than they already were. My green sweater was clean, except for a spot of blood at the hem, which had been exposed when I'd…taken care of the Hargrove problem.

I'd known from the moment Jace started questioning him that I would have to kill Hargrove to keep him from talking, and I would *not* let myself feel too bad about that. Hargrove had tortured and killed many of my fellow shifters, and he'd have done the same—or worse—to me if he'd gotten the chance. And to Jace. And to all of his men, including my brothers. But I'd hoped for a more obviously justified homicide; I'd been prepared to bait him into attacking me.

What I hadn't counted on was Hargrove's cowardly nature. As soon as he'd been disarmed, he'd considered himself helpless. I'd had to act with no obvious provocation, and the only part I regretted was how that would make Jace look. I desperately didn't want my actions to reflect badly upon him, but in that moment, I'd had no other choice.

In this one, you don't either.

I shoved Robyn's jacket onto the floorboard and glanced briefly at my ruined phone, wishing for the millionth time that it hadn't gone for a dive in a pot of greasy water. Or that Lucas had left his accessible. But like Faythe had once told me, wishes are for victims. Survivors make their own luck.

With that in mind, I climbed into the back of the truck cab, where I found several plastic bags wadded up on the floor. Lucas couldn't drive for more than half an hour without a soda and a stick of beef jerky, and he always threw the grocery bags over his shoulder, onto the backseat of the king cab.

I wadded the bag up in my fist, then got out of the truck and closed the door softly, stuffing my hands and the bag into my pockets. The blood splattered across my dark jeans could easily have been water, and no human nose would be able to tell otherwise. There was nothing I could do about the blood on my white boots, although the drier it got, the more it looked like tar and the less it looked like blood.

Shivering from the cold, I walked away from the mall, headed for a gas station across the street. It had recently been upgraded with new credit-card-accepting pumps and a digital sign, but the building itself was old and still had a bathroom built onto the outside, with its own entrance/exit.

The restroom wasn't an ideal place to shed my human disguise, but that was better than stripping down to a blue leotard in a phone booth.

The overgrown field stretching behind the gas station was just a bonus.

I kept my head down as I crossed the street, passing two customers and the large front window, but I already knew that everyone who saw me would remember me. I was the height of a young teenager with enough hair for three girls my size, and I had no coat. They probably all thought I was a runaway.

That wasn't far from the truth.

The restroom had no gender sign, and the door stood open to reveal a small, filthy space. I closed the door from the inside and considered locking it, but I wouldn't be able to unlock it without human hands, so I settled for the desperate hope that no one would try to come in while the door was closed.

A glance at myself in the mirror showed a streak of

blood I'd missed on my left cheek, but the hair hanging in my face would have covered that. My eyes looked glazed with exhaustion—or the remnants of shock?—yet I recognized determination in the set of my jaw. I was out of options and out of time, and the only hope I had for my own future was the possibility that taking out Darren myself, before he could capture or kill his next victim, would be enough to redeem me for killing Hargrove.

Shivering from both the cold and my own nerves, I pulled my sweater over my head and stuffed it into the plastic grocery bag. My boots came off next, followed by my pants, then underwear. Only once I stood naked in a frigid, filthy public restroom did the absurd, dangerous reality of my situation truly sink in.

Would leaving the restroom as a giant cat really be any safer than walking around covered in blood? The police were apt to get involved either way, considering they'd lost three citizens in the past month to a feral wildcat. And that at least one semi-local officer knew about shifters in general, and about me in particular.

Fear and haste fueled my shift, and my bones lengthened and popped, rearranging my skeleton out of some primordial instinct I would never truly understand. My eyes ached with pressure and my jaw crackled as a new structure of bone and teeth was imposed. My limbs popped in and out of joint, burning as if I were made of fuel and flame rather than flesh and bone. An itch washed over my skin in a brutally slow wave as fur grew from my follicles. My nails hardened into claws, lengthening, thickening, and when I tried to grip the floor, they dug into the concrete, chipping away tiny particles of grit.

My tail swished behind me, stirring dirt from the ground. I sniffed, and my nose twitched, my whiskers bobbing on the lower edge of my vision. And as my senses sharpened, the stew of old scents became a foul backdrop for my cruel transformation, but I could only breathe it in, waiting for the pain to fade.

When it finally did, after minutes that felt like hours, I stood tall on four legs, welcoming a configuration of bones and muscle I hadn't taken on in weeks. My ears rotated on top of my head, instinctively listening for danger, but I heard only ordinary sounds. Water running inside the convenience store. Gasoline rushing from thick hoses into rapidly filling tanks. Customers chatting as they pumped gas, lamenting the encroaching clouds and the frigid gusts.

Fighting skittishness—werecats do *not* belong in unlocked public restrooms—I made myself wait until the two cars closest to the restroom drove away. Every moment that passed drew the cloud cover closer and pulled the sun nearer to the horizon, but once I left the restroom, I would be exposed for the entire eighty-foot sprint into the empty field. Anyone who saw me would call the cops, which was why I couldn't leave my blood-covered clothes in the restroom.

Even humans would start to believe in the "impossible" if we kept leaving it around for them to find.

When the convenience store was as quiet as it was going to get during business hours, I took the handles of the plastic bag in my mouth and pressed down on the door lever with one paw. The latch clicked, and the door swung open several inches. I froze, listening again, and when no one started screaming, I dared a peek through the crack.

A woman was getting gas at the pump closest to the road and farthest from the restroom, and I could hear an engine running from a parked car in front of the store. Other than that, the coast was clear.

I burst from the restroom in a flat-out sprint. The white plastic bag swung from my jaw like a pendulum, and the scent of Hargrove's blood was thick in my nostrils as I ran. That scent reminded me of what was at stake. Of why I'd torpedoed my own career—and possibly Jace's—and why this desperate effort *had* to make those sacrifices worth it.

"Holy shit!" A woman cried behind me, as my paws pounded from concrete onto bare earth. My heart pumped blood so quickly, my head began to feel light. "Did you see that? Was that a *dog*?"

I put another burst of energy into my sprint and shot forward into the field. Tall grass slapped my face, snagged in my fur, and caught on the plastic bag, but I kept running until I'd almost forgotten what I was running from.

The overgrown field ended in a steep ditch, then another road, and across that road was a strip mall that had been abandoned, except for a payday loan service. There were two cars in the lot, and not a person in sight.

I looked both ways, then sprinted across the street and through the parking lot into the deep shadows on one side of the building. There I dropped my bag on the ground and rested, shielded from the street by an industrial trash bin speckled with rust and peeling paint. I couldn't stay put for long—when Lucas found me missing, he'd see the same potential escape route I had—but cats aren't long-distance runners, and I needed to think.

Jace is going to kill me. Yet even knowing that, I wished he was right there with me. I could handle the yelling, if that meant I'd get to see him again, and…

But Jace wasn't what I needed to be thinking about.

Which way is north? Thanks to the cloud cover, I couldn't tell by the stars, but there was still a bit more light on one side of the sky than the other. That way must be west.

The first frigid drop of rain fell as I turned to the north, and within four steps, I was drenched and freezing. But minutes later, the sunlight had disappeared and the rain had driven people inside. As long as I stuck to alleyways and deep shadows, I realized, I could move through Lexington like a dark streak in the night. Unseen. Unheard. Unbothered. Which was good, because with a wild cat on the loose, if the police saw me, they'd probably shoot on sight.

I have no idea how long it took me to work my way across town, sticking to shadows and back roads, jumping backyard fences and skirting lighted parking lots. At first, nothing was familiar. I'd never really ventured far from school on my own, and I didn't have a car.

I was starving by the time I got to campus, having shifted and walked several miles without stopping to hunt and eat. In fact, I hadn't eaten since Patricia Malone had put a plate of bacon and biscuits in front of me at seven that morning. Back when I'd been her son's girlfriend, and her daughter's maid of honor, and the aunt of her forthcoming grandson. Back before I'd been a murderer and a dishonored enforcer, on the run from her Alpha and heading *straight* into danger.

You know better, Abby.

I also knew I had no choice.

I entered campus from the south side, avoiding the student center and the apartments, and any other building with lit windows. To my relief, the rest of campus seemed to be deserted, which was no surprise on the first Saturday night of the winter break. Anyone with family had gone home. Anyone who'd stayed at school was either working or partying.

Minutes after I stepped on campus, my dorm came into sight. All the rooms on the front side were dark, but I circled to the back, avoiding flood- and porch lights. From the edge of the parking lot, I counted up three floors and over four windows to find my room. My heart tried to claw its way up through my throat.

My bedside lamp was on, but the form silhouetted in the light did *not* belong to Robyn.

FIFTEEN

Jace

"These are some sick fuckers." Mateo stepped from the bottom tread onto the basement floor, and his gaze immediately found Hargrove's taxidermy table. He shrugged, and I knew what was coming before he even opened his mouth. "Can't really blame Abby for reacting the way she did. Hargrove was part of the group that killed her friends, and she'd just seen her picture all over the second stalker board in two days."

"She took the same oath you did." I stared up at the photo-covered section of wall. We'd packed up everything but the table, the cage, the filing cabinet, and the pictures, but I hadn't thought of a thing since Abby and Lucas left except how empty my bed was going to feel without her next to me. How empty my arms already felt.

Why had she worked so hard to make that happen?

"But the real mistake was mine," I said. "She obviously isn't ready to separate personal grudges from her duty as an enforcer. I should never have hired her."

Not that she'd given me any choice in that, or in firing her either. Abby had an infuriating way of getting exactly what she wanted, consequences be damned, and in retrospect, it was clear that she'd been calling the shots the whole time.

Hell, maybe I should have promoted her. Maybe anyone who could manipulate an Alpha that well shouldn't have been taking orders in the first place.

But that wasn't how our system worked. We didn't just hand out Alpha patches like badges for selling Girl Scout cookies. And we didn't just kill people—even bad guys—against orders.

"Hargrove's group killed one of our men too," I said, thinking aloud. "And lots of Titus's, from the looks of it. What Abby did was about more than those pictures. More than her dead friends." We were missing something.

No, Abby was *hiding* something. She'd practically admitted that much.

Teo frowned. "What else could there be?"

"I don't know. But she was desperate to get into this basement." I ran one gloved hand over the edge of Hargrove's work surface. "In fact, she was hell-bent on coming with us in the first place. I thought that was because she didn't want to be left out, or..." Or because she didn't want to be separated from me. In retrospect, I could see that my ego had gotten in the way of my duty. "...something. But what if it was more than that?"

"It was her idea to stop at Hargrove's house on

the way home from the airport yesterday, right?" Teo said. "Because she knew if you went to the lodge first, you'd leave her there?"

I nodded. He saw it too. Whatever Abby was up to was more important to her than her own career. More important than her own welfare, even. She'd killed Hargrove with full knowledge of the possible consequences. Hell, she'd seen Manx's amputated fingertips up close—Manx had been declawed after the council found her guilty of murder—but Abby hadn't even hesitated.

Teo held up his phone to recapture my attention, reminding me of the call I'd asked him to make.

"Any news?"

"Not yet." He slid his phone into his jacket pocket. "Isaac said the lodge is on lockdown but they've seen nothing suspicious. No intruders. No threats. Not even a prank call. But just to be safe, they've called in backup from the Pride at large."

The most capable non-enforcer members.

"And Titus is coming with three men of his own. They were near the border, hunting the remaining hunters, so they may actually beat us to the lodge."

"Good." That was unprecedented—a group of strays coming to the aid of a US Alpha. Titus knew what was at stake and he knew that his assistance, with adherence to the council's standard rules of engagement, would help his chances in the vote.

Unfortunately, thanks to Abby's crime, my backing would be less help to the cause than I'd hoped.

Mateo shrugged. "Honestly, though, I don't think we're going to need them. It doesn't make any sense for Darren to strike us at the lodge. That's the best-defended spot in the whole territory. It doesn't fit his

MO."

"No, it doesn't." The hunters had only taken stragglers before. Lone strays. Our enforcer Leo on vacation, when he'd had no backup or partner. The most daring thing they'd tried so far was the attempt to catch Abby in the woods. They'd been willing to dispense with her human friends in the process, but they'd brought three armed hunters in order to kill one small tabby.

It made no sense that Darren would be willing to charge into the Appalachian Pride capital—a property crawling with large, angry enforcers—by himself.

"Did Hargrove actually say Darren is going after Melody?" Teo asked, his focus skipping from photo to photo taped up on the wall.

"He said they were going after 'the other tabby.' That has to be Melody. There are no other tabbies in the Appalachian Territory. Or within driving distance in any of the other territories." I frowned, going over what he'd said word by word. "But that doesn't make any sense either, because he said we'd left her undefended. Actually, he said we'd left 'them' undefended, but Abby's the only tabby who hasn't had round-the-clock protection in years." And if I could go back and change that, I'd do it in a heartbeat.

"So, Darren's going after a tabby he thinks is undefended, but we don't know for sure that Melody's the one he's after?"

I nodded, though that made little sense.

"Wait." I spun to face the rest of the underground room. "He said they'd taken pictures of both of the tabbies, and that they'd never seen a single tomcat in all that time."

"But these pictures are all of Abby."

"I know. There must be more somewhere." I crossed the room pulled open the top filing cabinet drawer, then started thumbing through the three hanging folders. They held nothing but receipts for equipment and hunting gear.

"We've been through all of that," Teo said. "There were no pictures."

"I know. But we've missed something." Something Abby *hadn't* missed. Something that had upset her badly enough to make her kill.

I slammed the first drawer and squatted to sort through the middle drawer. "They know that most tabbies would be easy prey, if they can catch one unguarded, and they seemed to think they'd done that. But Melody's never been unguarded, and Hargrove never actually said her name. He just said they were going after the 'other' tabby. Then Abby killed him, and I couldn't ask—"

I dropped onto my knees as the obvious conclusion fell into place. "She killed him to keep him quiet."

"Jace..." Teo sounded doubtful, and I could understand that. It was hard to think of Abby killing anyone out of anything other than self-defense or PTSD, but it was becoming increasingly clear that she'd thought this out, evidently on the fly. "To keep him quiet about what?"

"The other tabby's identity. It has to be." She'd figured out what we hadn't.

"But why would Abby do that? The more of us who know who they're after, the better protected she'll be. Who's the closest of the other tabbies?"

I had to think about that. The East Coast Territory

bordered ours, but Abby was their only tabby. The Southeast Pride—Mateo's home territory—also shared a border, but they'd lost their tabby, his sister Sara, to the same monsters who'd kidnapped Faythe and Abby almost five years ago. That left the New England and Great Lakes Prides, but their capitals were both more than a day's drive away. If he'd headed to either of those territories, Darren would never make it back by nightfall, which had been his plan, according to Hargrove.

"There's no one else close enough." I stood and shoved the middle file drawer closed. "This doesn't make any sense. It's someone Abby knows"—though all the tabbies knew one another—"and someone within a day's drive. And someone the hunters found undefended long enough to camera-stalk." My focus strayed to the stalker wall again, searching for a photo we'd missed. One that wasn't of Abby.

But they were *all* pictures of Abby. The only other girl in any of those photos was her roommate Robyn, and Robyn was…

Human.

"Oh, shit, Mateo, we've messed up." I was across the room in an instant, gloved hands pressed to the grisly surface of the taxidermy table as I stared at the wall above it. "*I've* messed up."

"What? How?"

"It was here the whole time." I pulled a picture down from the wall and held it out to him. The image was taken through the window of Abby's dorm room, and it showed her sitting on the edge of her bed, with one arm around her roommate. Her crying roommate. Her crying roommate who had smudges of dirt on her hands and…was that blood on her mouth?

The focus wasn't sharp enough for me to tell for sure, but suddenly, every move Abby'd made—every lie she'd told—came through in perfect clarity.

"Robyn's a shifter."

Teo shook his head. "She's human. We both saw her in that cabin, after Abby killed those hunters."

"She must have been infected after that, because she's a shifter now, Mateo." I stared at the photo as the ramifications of what we'd just discovered—and the implications of Abby's cover-up—pelted my brain like hail against a window.

Abby knew Robyn had been infected, and she'd hidden that from the council.

She'd hidden that from *me*.

"Wait." Mateo's eyes widened, and he looked like his late sister, the tabby we hadn't been able to save. "You're saying Robyn's a stray? A *female* stray? That's not possible."

"According to Manx, it is." From the beginning, she'd insisted that the warlord shifter bastards who'd used her as a broodmare had also succeeded in creating a female stray, but because we'd never seen one, in the entire history of the US Prides, we'd dismissed her stories as the misrememberings of a tabby traumatized enough to kill multiple men, in the grips of post-traumatic stress disorder.

But Manx had been right all along.

"Okay, but even if that's true—and I'm not going to believe it until I see it," Teo said, "what does that have to do with Abby killing Hargrove? How would she even know he'd known about Robyn, if she didn't know they were being stalked until she saw his board yesterday?"

And I was *sure* that was the case. Abby had been as shocked and horrified to find her pictures on his wall as I was. So, what had she been trying to hide when she'd insisted on going to Hargrove's house—the scene of a murder—if she hadn't known the rogue stray we were after had actually been taking out the hunters? Or that the hunters had been stalking her and Robyn?

What had we gotten from that first crime scene other than the stalker-board?

We'd gotten Darren's name and the names of two other remaining hunters, but she couldn't have anticipated that, because we hadn't known the mauling victims were the hunters. All we'd hoped for, going in, was to identify the scent of whoever'd murdered someone in Hargrove's house, and in the end, we hadn't even been able to isolate that scent. Thanks in no small part to Abby, who'd managed to get her own scent—and Robyn's—all over the place, because of that stupid borrowed…

A groan slid up from my throat.

"What?"

"She did it on purpose. Abby bumped into and rubbed up against everything she could in Hargrove's house so there'd be a legitimate reason for me to smell her there once she let me in. She was planting her own scent to cover up the fact that it was there already."

"Well, you'd think that would have been easier to do if she'd been wearing her own clothes. Thanks to Robyn's jacket, she got her roommate's scent—" Mateo and I came to the same conclusion at virtually the same moment. "She wore that jacket for a reason," he whispered, and I nodded.

"Nothing she's done or said has been an accident. She's not clumsy, or forgetful, or unprofessional. She's been playing us this whole time." I slammed the picture down on the taxidermy table, as the intricacies of Abby's deception finally fell into place. "She wore her roommate's jacket to confuse us with the scent. We smelled Robyn, whom we knew to be human, so we assumed the shifter scent was coming from Abby herself." Which was true, in large part. "And we smelled that scent combination so much, so often, that we mentally began to dismiss it, just like we dismiss our own scents."

Teo whistled. "*Damn*, that girl is smart. Too smart for you."

"Probably," I agreed. "And too smart for her own good."

"But you don't think Abby's the rogue who killed Joe Mathews, in Hargrove's house, do you? Or either of the other hunters? We're thinking that was the roommate?"

I nodded slowly, still puzzling things out, while fear for Abby threatened to overcome all logic. She'd broken nearly every law we had. She was in *much* more trouble than I'd thought. Way more trouble than I could get her out of.

Maybe too much for even her father to get her out of.

"Jace?" Teo cleared his throat to recapture my attention. "You think Robyn's the killer, right?"

"She has to be. Why else would Abby wear that jacket, if not to cover Robyn's scent at the crime scenes? She's protecting her roommate." That was the only conclusion that made sense. Abby would definitely risk her own life to protect those she loved.

Including the roommate who'd helped bring her out of her shell her freshman year, then had seen three of their friends killed for no reason other than their proximity to Abby.

"Why wouldn't she tell us? Why wouldn't she tell *you*? I mean, why hide a new tabby from the people best equipped to protect her?" Teo asked, and my head spun as I tried to pull all the facts, theories, and assumptions into line. I could only think of one reason Abby would keep her secret from me, even after we'd gotten together. After I'd told her I loved her and had threatened to kick her out of the Pride.

"Abby's hiding Robyn because she's the one who infected her." Infection was a capital crime, punishable by execution, if the council convicted her.

My hands clenched into fists at just the *thought* of this new threat. If Abby had infected Robyn, she'd done it by accident, and I could *not* let her pay for that with her life.

Teo's brows rose. "Wait, you think Abby bit her?"

"Abby bit who?" Warner called from the top of the steps, his head hidden by the empty boxes I'd asked him to bring down.

"Robyn," Teo said. "But we don't think that's true, right?" He glanced at me as Warner dropped the empty boxes at his feet. "I mean, that's just a theory."

I shrugged, trying to look less apprehensive about that possibility than I really was. "They are roommates, and Abby's been known to have nightmares. If she partially shifted in her sleep, and Robyn tried to wake her up…who knows? It happened to Faythe."

"Yes, but that was a boyfriend bitten in the height of passion with teeth she didn't realize had shifted.

Total fluke," Teo insisted, as he pulled open the bottom file cabinet drawer. "Although come to think of it, the stray she infected turned out to be a psychotic killer too." He dropped the first file folder into the box. "Maybe it's a good thing most tabbies don't get out much, if they're all gonna infect their friends…"

Warner made an amused noise at the back of his throat. "If it were that easy to infect a woman, Jace would have made enough tabbies by now to keep our numbers well out of the endangered range. Right?"

I answered with a growl.

"Regardless, we're ninety-nine percent sure Robyn's the stray who's been killing the hunters, and that Abby was trying to cover that up," I explained for Warner's benefit. "That's why she signed on as an enforcer and why she just *had* to come to both of the crime scenes." Hargrove's house and Darren's lake cottage.

"So, then, why get herself fired, if being an enforcer helped her keep us in the dark?" Teo asked.

"Well, as an enforcer, she would have had to go back to the lodge with us, when what she probably wanted was to go check on Robyn, to make sure she's not out killing more people," Warner suggested as he began pulling the photos from the wall. He held up a picture of Robyn and Abby walking together on campus, and I took it from him.

"If she thought Robyn was going to kill again, Abby would have fought harder to stay on campus when I came to pick her up." I studied the photo, where Abby had her arm around Robyn's shoulders, even though she was the smaller of the pair. She was clearly comforting her roommate. Guiding her, even.

Robyn didn't look like a cold-blooded killer. She looked like a traumatized, confused young woman who didn't know how to handle what was happening to her. Which was something Abby would understand.

Abby seemed to be acting as the new shifter's mentor or counselor. There was no way she would have participated in Robyn's crimes, even knowing what the hunters had done, but she *would* help cover for Robyn, especially if it was her fault Robyn had become a shifter. And she would try to stop Robyn from killing again.

And she would damn sure try to protect Robyn from the hunter coming after her.

"That's why she got herself fired!" My hand slammed into the taxidermy table hard enough to send a jolt of pain into my shoulder. "Because she knew Darren was going after Robyn, not Melody, but she couldn't tell us that without admitting that Robyn was the rogue stray." That she'd known who the murderer was all along and had been covering for her.

"Oh, shit." Teo froze in the act of pulling another picture from the board. "That's why she didn't want to be sent home. There was nothing she could do for Robyn from South Carolina. Especially since her cell phone is ruined, and she doesn't have any of the stored numbers memorized. She can't even call to warn Robyn."

And neither could we. "Damn it! We sent backup to the wrong tabby." I turned to Teo, already pulling my phone from my pocket. "Call Titus and have him send his men to the Lexington campus instead of the lodge. Abby said Robyn was staying in the dorm over the holiday." Which made sense now. A newly infected stray would have a hard time hiding his—or her—condition from her family in close quarters. "With any luck, the campus will be mostly deserted."

"Should I call Abby's dad?" Warner asked, already holding his own cell, but I shook my head.

"He'll have to tell the rest of the council, and we're not doing that to Abby until we've heard her side of the story."

"But she's probably already on her flight home."

"Then we'll bring her back. Book a return flight as fast as you can, and I'll tell Lucas to stay at the airport and wait for her." I shoved the picture of Abby and Robyn into my pocket on my way up the stairs.

I was halfway across the kitchen, about to call Lucas where the signal was stronger, when my phone rang and his name appeared on the screen. "Luke!" I said into the phone. "I need you to stay at the airport and wait for Abby. Warner's going to—"

"We never made it there," Lucas said, his voice even gruffer than usual with anger and fear.

"Why not?"

"Abby's gone, Jace. I had to leave her in the truck while I bought clean clothes, and when I got back, she was gone. I found her scent in a gas station bathroom across the street and her clothes in a plastic bag behind a Dumpster a quarter mile away. That's where I lost her trail." Because unlike dogs, cats can't track by scent.

"Where are you?" I demanded, my heart hammering against my sternum.

"About half an hour from the airport, west of highway 75."

"So, she's in cat form, in the middle of Lexington?" *Damn it, Abby!* "She's headed for campus. I need you to follow the route she's most likely to take on foot, and see if you can catch up with her. If you haven't found her in an hour, go straight to campus. To her dorm."

"Why would she go there?"

"Because her roommate, Robyn, is the rogue stray."

"Wait, *what*? A female stray?" After a short pause, he exhaled heavily. "Jace, tell me you don't think Abby infected her."

"I don't know." But it worried me that he'd jumped to that same conclusion. "Abby's been covering for her from the beginning, and now she's headed back to campus to protect her from Darren. He wasn't going after Melody; he was going after Robyn, which means the hunters knew she was a shifter before we did. The rest of the council is *not* going to like that."

"That's why she killed Hargrove. To keep him from telling you about Robyn," Lucas said, and from over the line came the sound of flesh hitting flesh as he smacked his own forehead. "She just kept saying she'd had to do it, but that's not like Abby."

"I know. And the only reason I can think of that she'd try to protect Robyn by herself is to hide the fact that she infected her roommate."

Lucas groaned. "What's going to happen to her, Jace?"

"I don't know. I'll do everything I can to protect her from the council, but we have to find her first."

"I'm on it."

"Luke, no one else knows about this. Just you, me, Teo, and Warner. I'd like to keep it that way until we've had a chance to talk to Abby."

"No arguments here. I'll keep you updated."

"Good." I hung up the phone as Teo stomped up the stairs, carrying a manila envelope stuffed with pictures from the basement. "Did you hear that? This is officially a need-to-know situation, and no one but you, me, Warner and Lucas needs to know."

"But Jace—"

"I'd do the same for any of you. We protect our own."

"She's not yours anymore," he pointed out gently as I reached for the backdoor knob. "You kicked her out of the Pride, remember?"

"That does *not* mean she isn't mine."

SIXTEEN

Abby

The only unlit entrance to the dorm had an actual knob rather than a lever or a push bar, and my paws couldn't operate it. Cursing silently, I huddled in the bushes next to the entrance, in the rain, and shifted back into human form. If anyone had been walking by, they would have heard a strange series of gristly pops and animalistic moans as my body rearranged itself, sucking fur back into my pores and spitting red curls out of my scalp. Shortening my feet and retracting my claws.

Though it took more effort than simply letting the process happen, I kept my feline eyes, as well as some small internal bit of cat hearing, because those would give me most of a cat's sensory advantages in my human body. The best of both worlds. And I was going to need every advantage I could get.

Naked, shivering, and instantly soaked again, as

soon as I stepped out of the building's shelter, I jogged up the narrow steps and through the back door into the laundry room, hoping someone my size had left something—anything—in one of the dryers. In what was likely the only stroke of luck I'd ever have again, I found a load of Robyn's workout clothes in the last dryer on the left. Her yoga pants and sports bra were only a size too large.

The minute I spent pulling them over wet skin covered in chill bumps was well worth it.

Barefoot and still shivering, I jogged past the lobby, the main desk, and the administrative office, headed toward the stairs at the end of the hall. My stomach was cramping with hunger and my head swam as I fought disorientation from shifting twice—one hell of a metabolic workout—without eating. And I couldn't make my teeth stop chattering, no matter *how* hard I clenched my jaw.

I flinched when the door to the third floor landing squealed, even though I'd known it would. Darren would probably be able to hear that squeal from inside my dorm room, but he'd have no idea I wasn't just another student staying on campus for the holiday.

I jogged silently down the hall, slowing as I approached my door, and only then realized that if the door was locked, I'd actually have to knock to be let in. I'd left my keys in my bag, back at the lodge.

Holding my breath, I pressed my internally shifted ear to the door and mentally catalogued the sounds from inside. Bedsprings groaned. The bathroom door squealed open, then partially shut, and water ran in the sink.

I closed my eyes and said a silent prayer that I

wasn't too late. That Darren wasn't cleaning himself up after having slaughtered my best friend and roommate. Then I turned the knob and pushed the door open.

Robyn lay on her back on her unmade bed with her arms at her sides. Her eyes were closed. Blood was smeared across her lips and dripping down one cheek toward the pillow. She wasn't moving.

Grief and denial slammed into me like a blow straight to my chest, and I couldn't breathe. I was too late. Darren had killed her, and if I left her body there, he would dismember it and hang her head from…

Wait, why would he kill her in human form? According to Hargrove, unless her teeth had been shifted when she died, her human head would be worthless to mount, and presumably horrifically incriminating, should it ever be seen by the police. But Robyn hadn't yet mastered any form of partial-shift. She'd hardly been able to control the normal full-body shift until recently.

Either way, dead or alive, I couldn't leave her.

A glance at the bathroom showed that the door was only open a crack, and though I could see Darren's shadow moving inside, I couldn't see the psycho himself. Which meant he probably couldn't see me.

Heart pounding, I crept silently across the room, listening for any sign that he might emerge. I was two feet from the bed when I realized Robyn's chest was rising and falling in tiny but steady increments.

She was still alive.

My pulse rushed with sudden hope—and desperate urgency—and my head swam. I glanced at the bathroom door again and saw a sliver of Darren's arm bleeding into the sink as he ran water over an open wound. If he leaned back, he'd see me. But I was out of options and out of time.

I lunged across the last two feet of carpet and almost tripped over a strange black bag near the foot of the bed. It had to belong to Darren, but there was no time to investigate, so I stepped over the bag and slid one arm beneath Robyn's neck and one beneath her knees, praying she wouldn't suddenly wake up and start screaming. But she was out cold.

The room spun around me when I lifted her, and though that should have been an effortless task for a shifter, it nearly cost me my consciousness. I was only operating at about half of my potential strength and speed, thanks to hunger and exhaustion. If I didn't find food soon, Darren would gain a second unconscious shifter through no effort of his own.

Blinking to keep the world in focus, I carried Robyn to the ajar door and pushed it open with my foot. My vision began to darken in the hall, and one knee tried to fold beneath me. Even if I made it to the stairwell, I'd never make it down the steps without passing out, and the subsequent fall could kill us both.

I would have to hide.

Instead of turning right, toward the stairs, I turned left and headed down the empty hall as quickly as I could, counting the doors as I went. When Darren discovered her missing, if he didn't assume we'd gone down the steps, he'd start checking dorm rooms, beginning with the closest. I would walk until I couldn't walk any farther. Or until he came out of the bathroom.

I'd passed seven doors—three on the right, four

on the left—when the bathroom faucet stopped running. *Shit!* I froze, eyes wide, heart slamming against my sternum. Then I set Robyn on the floor next to the nearest room.

Down the hall, the bathroom door squealed open as I grabbed the doorknob in front of me and twisted with both hands. The lock snapped, and the door swung open almost silently. I pulled Robyn inside by both arms, then glanced around. The room Julie Cass had shared with a girl from Montana was empty now, and her closet door stood open. I hauled Robyn inside and propped her against the back wall, then tucked her legs inside, knees bent. As I was backing out of the closet, I noticed something sticking out from under her thigh. Her cell had fallen out of her pocket!

I grabbed her phone and stood, and the room blurred across my vision as I closed the closet door. I leaned with one hand against the wall until my focus steadied, and I knew that hiding Robyn had been the right thing to do. But if I hid with her, Darren would find us, eventually. The only way to stop him from finding and killing Robyn would be to lead him away from her.

And call for backup.

If I called Jace, I'd have to tell him about Robyn. If I didn't, she and I would almost certainly wind up stuffed and mounted wherever Officer Darren kept his grisly keepsakes, now that his lake house had been discovered. But would calling him do me any good?

Lucas had no doubt reported me missing, and Jace was probably already on his way to Lexington. He wouldn't know I was on campus, but he might be close enough to show up soon.

Though maybe only soon enough to stop Darren from carting off our corpses.

From down the hall came the familiar squeal of my bathroom door, followed by sudden silence. "Robyn!" Darren roared, and I cringed. "How the *hell*..."

I sank into a squat behind one of the beds, my arm resting on the bare mattress, and ran one finger over the cell screen to wake it up. Fortunately, the phone wasn't locked. Even more fortunately, Jace's was one of only two numbers I had memorized other than my own, because every Pride member was required to know the Alpha's number.

I dialed, and while the phone rang, I listened to Darren's footsteps as he stomped into the hall. When they got noticeably softer, I realized he'd headed for the stairs. *Please go downstairs... Please go downstairs...*

"Hello?" Jace said into my ear, and I exhaled with relief. "Abby?" He'd recognized me based on nothing more than the sound of my breath.

"I'm sorry. I'm *so* sorry. But I need help," I whispered.

"You're at your dorm?"

"Not in my room, but on the third floor." Had he figured it out, or did he just think I'd come for my stuff? "Darren's here. I can't explain everything now, but Robyn's unconscious. She doesn't have any head wounds, so I think he gave her—"

"Robyn!" Darren roared again, and I squeezed my eyes closed. His voice was louder. He hadn't taken the stairs.

"I'm hiding, but he's getting closer, Jace, and she's helpless. I can't carry her anymore, so I'm going to draw him away from her, but if you could—"

"Don't move. We're already on the way," he said

into the phone, then something scratched against the receiver and his voice was muffled. "Faster, Teo, she's—"

"You don't want to hide from me, pussycat!" Darren shouted. Wood splintered and something thunked against a wall.

"He's kicking in doors. I have to go. But—"

"Abby, do *not* use yourself as bait. Just stay put, and we'll—"

"Jace, I'm so sorry. I know I screwed everything up. In case I never get another chance to say it…I love you too."

"No!" he shouted into the phone, and the first tear ran down my face. "Wait and tell me in person."

"I have to go."

"Abby!" he yelled. "Do not hang up the phone. That's an order!"

"I don't work for you anymore. I love you, Jace."

"Ab—"

I hung up the phone, but I could still hear his voice in my head, until Darren grunted from down the hall and kicked in another door.

Trembling, I stood and shoved Robyn's phone into my back pocket. Darren was a cop. He had a gun and some kind of drug. That's what I'd smelled in my dorm room. That's what was in the black bag. My human corpse would do him no good, so he would probably shoot to wound, until he could try to make me shift.

Shifters are strong and fast, but we can't outrun bullets. Yet I had to try.

I crossed the room and pressed my ear against the door, listening as Darren kicked his way into another room. He was at least three doors down. Five, if he was hitting the rooms across the hall as well. When I heard the soft squeal of another door being opened, I realized he was checking the closets. Which meant he was no longer in the hall.

I quietly opened Julie Cass's door and glanced into the hall. Four rooms were open, and by my best guess, Darren was in the closest of them. I sucked in a deep breath and closed the door softly behind me, then headed toward the stairwell in the opposite direction. I ran as hard as I could, gripping the slick floor with my toes, my legs pushing me faster than any human could have run, my arms pumping at my sides for balance.

The hall swam around me and my vision began to darken, but I kept running, blinking tears from my eyes, wiping sweat from my forehead.

Hinges squealed, and boots clomped into the hall behind me. "Hey!" Darren shouted. "Abby!" His footsteps stopped and that scared me worse than being chased, because that meant he was aiming.

The stairwell was fifteen feet away. Then ten. I heard an odd click, like plastic being broken, then a metallic scraping sound. Five feet from the stairwell, I heard a soft *thwup*, and pain bit into my left thigh. Three steps after that, I grabbed the doorknob and twisted. I pulled the dart from my leg as the stairwell door swung closed behind me, then I was running again, up the steps instead of down, because I was less likely to fall that way.

Heart racing, I gripped the rail. Two steps later, I stumbled and bruised my shin on a metal-edged tread.

"You may as well give up, pussycat!" Darren called through the door as his boots stomped closer. "You've only got minutes at that dosage. Maybe less, since you're a tiny thing."

I ran faster, my pulse racing, my head spinning, and by some miracle I reached the fourth-floor landing before he burst into the stairwell below me. But I couldn't climb any longer without passing out.

"Where'd you stash her?" Darren clomped up the stairs as I threw open the door to the fourth floor. That was as high as I could get, without heading to the roof. "You know I'll find her."

The hallway warped and stretched in front of me, like a carnival mirror maze, and I wasn't sure whether that was from the tranquilizer or exhaustion.

"Not long now!" Darren pushed open the door behind me, but he wasn't running anymore, and he wasn't shooting either. He knew he didn't have to.

When I realized I wasn't going to make it to the stairs at the other end of the long hallway, I stopped and grabbed the nearest doorknob. Twisting it took too much effort, and the click of the broken lock sounded distant, as if I were hearing it through a tunnel. I pushed the door open, listening to the steady rhythm of Darren's footsteps at my back. My legs folded beneath me just inside the room.

Gravity ripped the doorknob from my grip as the floor flew up to meet me, and the side of my skull hit the linoleum with a sickening thud.

A shadowy form appeared over me as I blinked sluggishly, struggling to stay conscious.

"Hello, Abby. I'm officer Darren Park. What do you say we get to know each other?" He lifted me, and as my head fell back against his arm, the world went dark.

***

"Aaaaabby… Wake up, now." The voice was familiar, and just hearing it made my stomach churn, but at first, I couldn't *quite* remember why. "We have a lot to talk about." Something patted my cheek, and my eyes flew open. Darren's face hovered over me, and the memories snapped back into place.

Robyn.

Dart gun.

Hunters.

Nonononono!

I tried to push him away, but my arms wouldn't move. Neither would my legs. I couldn't sit up or roll over. I couldn't move at all except to breathe and to blink. I was frozen. Paralyzed. At the mercy of a psychotic hunter with a badge.

A cold draft stirred my hair from the gap at the bottom of the window. My bare feet were warm from the heating vent over the end of the bed. I couldn't move, yet I could still feel *everything*.

Terror surged through me, and my chest felt too tight. I couldn't breathe. There was nothing covering me but borrowed clothes, yet I felt a brutal pressure crushing me with the weight of my own nightmares. My memories.

I *had* to move.

"Where's Robyn?" Darren sat next to me, and when the mattress sank beneath his weight, panic shot up my spine like a flame fed with fuel. I recognized the creak of the springs. I knew every lump and crack in the plaster overhead. I knew that drafty window. He'd carried me back to my dorm room.

I was going to die in my own bed.

"I've checked every room on this floor," he continued. "If I have to go look for her again, you'll both die slowly and painfully."

Wait, he'd already looked for Robyn but hadn't found her? Where the hell was she? Was this some kind of trick?

My pulse thudded in my ears. How long had I been out?

It would have taken several minutes to check every room on the third floor, and Jace had said he was on the way. Could I stall long enough for help to arrive?

"You may not be able to move yet, but you'll feel every slice." Darren held up a knife, and fresh panic tangled my thoughts.

"Some kind of miracle drug, huh?" he said. "You'd be surprised what can be removed from the evidence room without anyone noticing. After you and Robyn took out Steve and the others, I realized they'd underestimated you. I won't be making the same mistake."

My body was frozen, but my mind raced. Robyn must have crawled out of Julie's closet while Darren was chasing me on the fourth floor. Which meant that her paralytic had at least partially worn off. Which made sense. Darren was a cop, not a doctor, but he'd know that an overdose could kill, and that it'd be safer to err on the side of caution. At least until he had whatever he wanted from his prey.

He'd been washing a fresh bite wound when I'd found him, and if she'd just bitten him, she couldn't have been paralyzed for long. If her paralytic had worn off that quickly, mine probably would too. If I could keep him talking until that happened, I might actually have a chance to escape.

Darren stood and the mattress squealed again, but I breathed easier, thanks to the new distance between us. "Where is she, Abby? What's the matter? Cat got your tongue?"

How was I supposed to—

But when my mouth opened, I understood that my tongue was as functional as my eyes. "Fuck you," I croaked, thanks to my dry throat, and that's when I realized that pissing off the guy with the knife *might* not be the best idea.

Darren bent toward me, holding the knife up, and my heart thumped so hard the whole room seemed to shake with each beat.

"Hargrove's dead."

Darren blinked, and I relished his shock. The only way to ward off his slice-'n'-dice routine would be to keep him off balance.

"I ripped his throat open and watched him bleed out on the floor." I tried to move my right hand, but nothing happened. I'd never felt so helpless in my life. The only weapon available to me was my mouth, and I had no choice but to use it. "I hope you have another sick taxidermy station set up somewhere, because your lake cottage is *crawling* with shifters, and your expert is rotting in a black plastic bag like the human garbage he is."

"You're lying." His grip tightened on the handle of the knife. For a second, I was afraid he'd just stab me and be done with it.

Dial it back, Abby.

"You know I'm not lying. How else would I know about your cottage, with the hidden basement staircase and the stuffed werecat standing guard in your living room? It's over, Darren."

"It won't be over until we've hunted every one of you into extinction."

I didn't bother telling him that really wasn't necessary. With so few tabbies, we were headed in that direction anyway.

"You don't stand a chance." I watched nervously as he started to pace the length of my bed. "There are only a few of you left, and we know all about the last couple of your hunting buddies."

"Couple?" Darren laughed, and chill bumps popped up the length of my arms. "Do you actually think Gene Hargrove and I found out about you and your freak shifter species on our own? I *wish* I could take credit for that, but there are others. All over the world. You guys are a *sport.* Big game hunters pay serious money to learn how and where to hunt shifters, and the only rule is that they gotta die in cat form. Most of those rich bastards will pay *thousands* to have their trophies stuffed and shipped home."

"No." He *had* to be lying. "We would have known."

"You probably *should* have known," he agreed. "But as long as we only picked off the strays, the rest of you seemed to be trying *not* to notice."

Strays. He knew about them, just like he knew about Alphas and tabbies. My blood felt like ice. I tried to move my hand again, but nothing happened.

Damn it!

"You probably never would have noticed if we'd stuck to the free zones. It's like serial killers offing prostitutes—no one really cares. But Steve just *had* to go after a tabby. I told him that was like thumping a hornet's nest, but he wouldn't listen. He thought you'd be an easy kill."

I'd never been happier in my life to prove someone wrong. "If you know better, why are *you* thumping the hornet's nest?"

His grin made me shudder. "I like a challenge."

"The council *will* find you." I tried to move my right foot, and when my big toe twitched, I had to fight to hide my triumph. The paralytic was wearing off!

Darren huffed. "This ain't my first safari, sweetheart. No cat ever born pounces faster than a bullet flies." He patted the pistol strapped to his side for emphasis.

"Maybe not, but we're faster than any human trigger finger. Hargrove had a gun too."

"Hargrove wasn't a hunter. He shot at paper targets and stuffed dead animals."

I swallowed nausea at the thought. "They'll catch you, and you can't *possibly* understand the pain you'll feel before you die." I tried to shrug, but my shoulders wouldn't move. "Maybe they'll skin you and preserve *your* flesh. I bet my dad would love a human skin rug, right in front of his couch, so he can step on you every time he crosses the room."

"Enough." He held the knife up in front of my face. "Where's Robyn?"

"You can't kill me unless I have fur. You told me that yourself."

"A shot of adrenaline will pull the cat right out of you."

Fuck! He knew how to force a shift. The room started to slide out of focus and I fought to slow my respiration. I couldn't afford to hyperventilate.

"Until then, I can hurt you all I like..." The tip of his knife traced the length of my throat and I took a long, slow breath to keep from panicking.

The only thing keeping me alive was the fact that he thought I knew where Robyn was. If I debunked that theory—or refused to talk—he'd be done with me. I'd have to string him along. Keep him talking.

"You'll never find Robyn." My left foot twitched, and when he turned to pace away from me, I tried to curl my right hand into a fist. My fingers jumped a bit on the blanket. That wasn't really triumph, but it was a good start.

"I found her once. I'll find her again." Darren shrugged. "She's a girl and a brand-new cat, right? Not exactly the most dangerous game."

I laughed out loud; he still hadn't figured it out! "There *is* no more dangerous game than a new stray!" Except for an Alpha. "Strays can't control their instincts or their tempers. Robyn killed Joe Mathews and the ones before him. She tracked down Hargrove and went after him in his own home."

"Bullshit." Darren frowned. "That was you and your pack."

"It's a *Pride*, not a pack," I snapped. "And that wasn't us. Our people want Robyn just as badly as you do, because of the attention she's attracted."

Darren didn't seem to believe me. "Tell me where she is, or I'm going to start cutting." He placed the tip of his blade against my left breast. "Five seconds." The metal point bit at my skin through the thin sports bra, and my pulse rushed fast enough to make me dizzy.

"I left her in a closet," I said, trying not to move beneath his knife.

"I checked all the closets." He pressed harder, and I gasped when the blade pierced my skin, just hard enough to draw blood.

"Room 304," I said. I'd actually left her in 312, but all my toes were wiggling behind him by then, and I *needed* him to leave the room. "Maybe she crawled into the bathroom. Or under the bed. Maybe she got out before you checked that room. I swear she's here somewhere."

"I checked everywhere!" Darren shouted, and his blade bit deeper. I whimpered, my heart pounding. If he lost his temper, he might forget about the rules.

He might kill me without a second thought.

Someone hissed, and he stumbled backward, cursing. A form shot out from under my bed and knocked Darren over. I didn't realize I could move my neck until my head turned to follow the hissing blur, and I found my roommate perched on his chest in human form, growling like a cat facing down a large rat.

"Robyn!" She'd been under my bed the whole time. Darren hadn't looked, and I hadn't realized I could smell her, because the entire room already smelled like Robyn.

She turned when I called her name, and Darren's grip on his knife tightened.

"No!" I shouted, and my arm flopped, but I couldn't pick myself up. I couldn't defend her.

Robyn stood as he swung his knife. The blade sank into her thigh instead of her chest, and she hissed. Blood poured from her leg and she collapsed onto one hip. Darren turned back to me, knife high, but already arching toward me.

I screamed as his blade swung, still dripping Robyn's blood.

A dark blur lunged through the open doorway, and

a terrifying snarl filled the room. Jace's front paws hit Darren square in the chest and drove him to the floor. Hard.

Jace's snarl ended in a satisfied note, followed by the gurgle of blood I could smell but couldn't see.

Darren's blood.

I burst into tears of shock and relief as Jace dropped a bloody hunk of flesh onto the floor. I wanted to sit up and hug him, but my arms wouldn't cooperate.

Robyn hissed again and pushed herself into one corner of the room, her hands pressed to the gash in her thigh. Before I could tell her not to worry or tell Jace not to kill her, Lucas and Mateo burst into the room in human form, having followed Jace up both flights of stairs in their inferior bipedal bodies.

They stared at the bloody scene in silence. Then my brother blinked, and his gaze found me. When he saw that I was still breathing and only barely cut, he exhaled and found a grin. Then he turned to offer my roommate a hand. "You must be the new girl. I'm Lucas, Abby's brother." She glanced at me, and when I nodded, she let him pull her up, while Teo pulled the case from the nearest pillow, to use as a tourniquet. "And you..." Lucas turned back to me. "You are *soooo* grounded."

SEVENTEEN

Jace

I knocked on my open bedroom door, and Abby rolled over to face me. Seeing her in my bed—even though I'd hardly touched her all night—triggered a primal satisfaction, like that first deep breath after a long dive. As if having her scent on my sheets meant everything was exactly as it should be, when in reality, everything was falling apart.

She sat up in bed as I crossed the room toward her.

"How'd you sleep?"

Abby shrugged and pushed a mass of red curls back from her face. "You could probably answer that better than I can. How many times did I wake up?"

I sat on the edge of the bed and she scooted closer, dragging the blankets along. "Seven." The nightmares were back, triggered by Darren and his damn paralytic drug. "But I would have had to wake you up once an hour anyway because of the concussion." From the looks of it, she'd hit her head when the drug knocked her out. "Doctor's orders."

As near as I could tell, her dreams were some fucked-up amalgamation of her abduction at age seventeen, the assault on her campsite during fall break, and what went down in her dorm room sixteen hours before. The recurring theme seemed to be helplessness and an inability to protect herself.

I would gladly have killed everyone who'd ever laid a finger on her, if they weren't all already dead, but I couldn't fight her demons. All I could do was rub her back and remind her of where she was when she woke up screaming, and that made *me* feel helpless.

It made me want to rip someone apart, then lick the blood from my claws while the body cooled.

But I'd already done that.

"Did you get any sleep?" Abby straightened her nightshirt, then pulled her hair into a poofy ponytail at the back of her neck, secured with an elastic band she'd left on my bedside table the night before.

"I got enough." Wherein "enough" was defined as almost none. But there'd be time to sleep later, when the chaos had settled. When I was sure she was going to be okay.

My gaze fell to the bedside table again, where her ruined phone lay next to an extra ponytail holder—they were always snapping beneath the pressure of her hair—and a tube of scented lip balm. Strawberry. Seeing her things on my nightstand... That felt right. Normal. Completely at odds with the fact that her parents were on their way from South Carolina, an emergency meeting of the Territorial Council had been called, and two of my men had spent half the night moving the body of a cop whose death would *definitely* be both noticed and investigated.

Mateo and Lucas had left Darren's body in a field behind his home. With any luck, his death would look like exactly what it was—a mauling by a large cat. But even if they'd gone unseen by the only neighbor within viewing distance, the lack of blood at the scene would tell even a bad forensic investigator that Darren had been killed elsewhere, then dumped in the field.

But there was nothing we could do about that.

"Where's Robyn?" Abby glanced at the other side of the bed, where her roommate had slept. Robyn had refused to be separated from Abby, even while her leg was being sewn up, and only hunger had driven her out of bed alone in a house full of strange scents and faces.

"She's having breakfast and probably developing a deep-seated reluctant tolerance for my sister." Melody was *fascinated* by Robyn. Almost as fascinated as she was with herself, which was a miracle all on its own. "Dr. Carver got here early this morning. Melody was going to keep her secret, but when she saw all the attention Robyn was getting, she practically *demanded* a prenatal exam."

Dr. Danny Carver had driven all night to get from Oklahoma to Kentucky. He was actually a medical examiner, but as the only shifter physician in the eastern half of the country, he was constantly on call for injuries beyond the scope of an enforcer's ability to suture.

And for pregnancies.

"So, no problems?" Abby said.

"Well, he didn't come packing stirrups, but he said

that as far as he can tell without doing an ultrasound, all is well."

Since we hadn't previously announced Melody's news and my mother had done a pretty good job on Robyn's leg, I could only assume our new tabby herself was the reason for the doctor's long drive. Carver wanted to examine the first confirmed female stray.

"He took blood samples from Robyn this morning, and he wants to do an exam and a shift observation after lunch."

Abby groaned. "This is *exactly* what I was trying to avoid by keeping her a secret. She's having enough trouble adjusting to the fact that she's not fully human anymore. The last thing she needs is to be poked and prodded."

"*All* strays have trouble with the adjustment. You should have told us—"

"This is different, Jace." Abby pushed back the covers and folded her legs beneath herself. "Other strays don't wake up one day and realize they're responsible for propagating a species they didn't even know existed."

"So, you just decided not to tell her?" Robyn had been hysterical and nearly incoherent in the minutes after we'd met her. Some of that was because she'd just narrowly survived a home invasion by a psychotic shifter-hunting cop. Some of it was probably due to the fact that her first encounter with the local Alpha—yours truly—included seeing him rip that cop's throat out. But it soon became clear that the bulk of her shock and confusion was because *she'd had no idea my men and I existed.*

Robyn knew what she had become and what she

could do, and she knew there were other shifters in the world, somewhere. But she'd had no idea there was any governing body around to hold her responsible for her actions. Or to help her.

"No, I decided to *delay* telling her," Abby insisted. "But I taught her about everything she needed to know immediately—shifting, and instinct, and enhanced senses. About keeping everything a secret. I just left off all the social and political stuff. Alphas, territories, Prides. Procreation. I was trying to give her time to adjust to all the physical stuff first before I threw everything else at her. I was trying to *help* her. She was having a lot of trouble with the transition."

"That's normal, Abby. That's why we monitor strays during their first weeks, whenever possible."

Unfortunately, that was rarely possible. Most strays are infected by other strays, who know little to nothing about their own species, including how transmission works, how to prevent it, and the fact that it's *forbidden* by long-standing council decree. Most of them don't realize that they have a responsibility to help their victims through the transitional period, because *they* weren't helped by the shifters who infected them. It was a vicious, violent cycle, which we had no way to stop unless strays in the free zones were taken into the fold. Given authority, official standing, and organization.

They needed to be counted, educated, and kept in line to protect our secret. Faythe, Marc, Titus, and I were trying to make that happen through our proposed resolution, for the good of our entire species.

But there was resistance from the more conservative members, who believed most adult strays were a lost cause because they lacked the shifter upbringing that would have tempered and informed their feline instincts in the early stages. Certain council members, namely, Blackwell and his supporters, thought the best we could do for strays was to eliminate those who demonstrated uncontrollable violence and leave the rest to their lives. Unaffiliated with ours.

They were wrong, and Robyn was an extreme example of just how badly things could go when strays had a limited—even if well-meaning—support system.

"Abby, you should have told me. I could have helped you." Then we'd only be dealing with the infection issue, instead of insubordination and murder. Not to mention hiding a stray from the council. I couldn't think of an official rule forbidding that, but I was sure they'd be pissed.

"If I'd told you, you would have had to report her to the council, and they would have *taken* her." Abby grabbed my hands. Her eyes were wide, her voice strained. "They would have pulled her out of school and put her through a bunch of tests, and they would have locked her up. I couldn't let them lock her up, Jace. Nobody deserves that."

That's when I understood. Abby'd spent nearly a week in that cage when she was seventeen. She'd been raped and beaten, fed whatever and whenever her captors thought she should eat. She'd had a bucket for a toilet, and she'd lived in utter terror of dying the same way Sara Di Carlo—Vic and Mateo's sister—had. She couldn't willingly put her best friend through that. Even part of it.

But her fear was unfounded. We were talking

about the territorial council, not a band of warlords.

"They wouldn't have had to lock her up if you'd brought her to us immediately, because she wouldn't have killed anyone yet."

"No, they would have locked her up to *stop* her from killing." Abby shrugged, and the gesture carried doubt. "Maybe I should have let them."

"I don't understand."

"She's not well, Jace. In human form, Robyn seems mostly okay, but in cat form, she's practically feral. She's at the mercy of instincts and urges she didn't grow up expecting. She doesn't yet know how to think like a human when her brain is structured like a cat's. It's like there's a disconnect between the two halves of her."

Uh-oh.

Abby studied my grim expression. "What? You know what's wrong with Robyn? What is it?"

I took a deep breath, then squeezed her hand. "It's a dissociative disorder that's specific to the unique psychology of a shifter, and almost exclusively suffered by strays whose introduction to our world was particularly…devastating."

"Dissociative disorder?" Abby's brown eyes widened. "Like…multiple personalities?"

"Not exactly. Shifters *literally* have two forms, and sometimes, the trauma of that initial shift—or of the infection itself—leads a new shifter to disassociate his feline self from his human self. You actually put it pretty well. When Robyn's a cat, she's *completely* a cat. In those moments, she may not even remember or understand that she's also human, which means she doesn't have access to her human conscience and probably lacks the ability to think beyond her immediate needs.

"Kaci had the same problem when puberty brought on a shift she had no way to anticipate. She had *no* understanding of what she'd become and she couldn't think clearly in cat form with feline instincts demanding things she would never have done as a human." Which was how she'd wound up killing her own mother and sister. "But Kaci got better, and so can Robyn."

What I didn't add was that dissociated strays were the ones enforcers were most often required to dispose of. They were the ones we couldn't control. The ones who couldn't control *themselves.*

But things could be different for Robyn. For all strays, if our resolution passed. They'd have the support system they needed to regain control over their bodies and their lives.

"I thought she was getting better. Starting to acclimate." Abby picked at my comforter. "I didn't know she was still killing, at first."

"Wait, *still* killing? You knew about the first one?"

"Yeah, but you guys don't. She's actually killed four hunters, not three, but the first one was in self-defense. He followed us into the woods the first time I took her for a run. He was hunting us, but we didn't know about the large-scale operation at the time. We just knew someone was shooting at us. Robin was in cat form, and she didn't hesitate. She just…took him out." Abby shrugged. "It was a totally justified kill. And I thought that was the end of it."

"But she kept killing?" I prompted.

"I thought she was going for solitary runs, and I thought I should let her, because that looked like progress. Adjustment. I didn't realize she was *killing* until she called me from Hargrove's house last week. She shifted back to human form after she killed Joe Matthews—though I didn't know his name—and she was *totally* freaking out. I went there to bring her home. To calm her down. But I swear that's all I did. I didn't even go into the basement that night. If I'd realized who her victims were, and that they were stalking us, I would have called you, Jace. I swear." She shrugged miserably, and her curls bobbed with the motion. "Then you came to get me and told me about the murders, and I realized she might be the stray you were looking for."

"So, you went along in her jacket to sabotage my investigation."

She nodded. "I'm so sorry. I knew you'd find both her scent and mine at Hargrove's house, and I didn't know what else to do. Then we figured out who Hargrove was, and I realized *why* Robyn's instinct had pointed her at those men in particular. Her human half was scared of them, but didn't know what to do about it. Her cat half knew what to do, but not why she *shouldn't.* I was hoping that since she'd only killed our enemies, everyone would be more concerned with the human hunters than with the stray who was doing our job for us."

"It's not that simple, Abby." Nothing was *ever* that simple.

"So it seems." She exhaled slowly. "How much does Robyn know?"

I shrugged. "We had to tell her *something.*" The previous night clearly hadn't been the time to explain to Robyn that she was now a member of my Pride and thus subject to a long list of rules and responsibilities. But she'd woken up before Abby and had wandered downstairs on her own, where she'd found a kitchen full of shifters—a scent she'd recognized. "She knows this is my house, and that we're all shifters. She knows that the guys work for me, but not in what capacity. We wanted you to be there to explain the bulk of it to her."

"Okay." Abby nodded. "I've been having this discussion with her in my head for weeks." Yet she made no move to get out of bed. "Jace, how much trouble am I in, exactly?"

"Well, the easy answer is 'A lot.' But really, that depends." She'd covered up an infection, disobeyed a direct order, sabotaged an investigation, and murdered a witness in custody—a list of offenses that made her infamously shrewish cousin look meek and agreeable by comparison. But the most serious of all the potential charges was… "Abby, did you infect Robyn?"

Her eyes widened. "No! How could you even…?" She frowned. "Is that what people think?"

"What else are they supposed to think? She's your roommate, and you hid her from us. And you've been living in the same room with her and wearing her clothes for so long that our noses have been trained to associate her scent with yours, since before she was infected. Since before we even met her." Which cast confusion over the scent of her infector, which would forever be woven with Robyn's scent.

"Take an objective scent of her when we haven't been sleeping in the same room or sharing clothes. Her infector's scent is there," Abby insisted. "I can smell it. And I hid Robyn to protect *her*, not to protect myself. She was infected at the hunters' cabin in October. They had a stray in a cage, in the basement. He was dead by the time I got there, but he swiped at her through his cage before he died. It was just a scratch, but by that night, she had a fever." Abby shrugged. "If you'd been there any longer, you'd have known about this all along."

I blinked, stunned. How could I have missed it? Robyn had been bleeding from several minor wounds, but I'd assumed they were all from being dragged through the woods or being roughed up by her abductors.

"Okay." My mind raced, reassembling the puzzle with the new pieces. If I'd paid a *little* more attention, I could have prevented the whole thing. Robyn wouldn't have killed in a maladjusted dissociative state. Abby wouldn't have committed crimes to protect her. "Assuming Robyn will testify to that, that's one charge they'll have to dismiss. And if we can verify her feline dissociative state, they'll probably dismiss *all* the charges against Robyn, in light of her temporary…insanity." And because she was the first verified female stray, and Abby was right; they would want to study her. "Which is why I think you should encourage her to let Dr. Carver do his thing. So he can testify on her behalf, if necessary."

"Okay." Abby nodded. "What about the rest of it?"

"Your hearing will be in two weeks, at the ranch. They've already excluded me from the proceedings."

"Because of *us*?"

I nodded. Ed Taylor had been particularly unhappy to hear about my involvement with his son's ex-fiancée. That—coupled with the fact that on my watch, one tabby been infected, one had gotten pregnant, and two had been kidnapped—had painted my leadership in a less-than-flattering light. "And because I failed to report you missing when you didn't get on your plane. But your dad and Faythe will be there, and they'll do everything they can for you. So, you need to cooperate and make it easy for them."

"Okay."

"Your parents will be here in a couple of hours. You're all three scheduled for a late flight tonight, back to South Carolina, and Robyn can go with you or—"

"No!" Abby stood so fast, I hardly saw her move. "I'm staying here. With you." She pulled her nightshirt off and dropped it on her way to the suitcase lying open in front of my dresser, and suddenly, her parents were the furthest things from my mind.

"They'll just have to cancel my ticket, because I belong here. With you." She bent in front of her suitcase, then stood with a pair of jeans, and I realized I hated her suitcase and the fact that I only ever saw her when she had a reason to use it. I wanted to see her clothes not just on my floor but in my dresser. In my laundry hamper. Hanging from my shower rod. But that had only ever been a remote possibility, and it was even more remote now.

"Abby, you don't work for me anymore. I've already transferred your Pride membership back to your father." I'd done that over the phone the day before, when I'd called to tell him I was sending her back. "He's your Alpha now."

"What?" She dropped the pants, and I realized she was wearing nothing but a pair of purple lace panties. I had to swallow a groan. "No! I never agreed to that."

"You were expelled. That doesn't require your approval."

"So, tell him you changed your mind and you want me back."

Oh, I wanted her, all right. But… "You know he won't give you back to me." Under my leadership and authority, she'd committed at *least* three crimes, any one of which could get her executed if she were a tomcat. The penalty for a tabby wouldn't be so severe—we couldn't afford to lose any women—but it would be permanent and likely painful.

The very thought kindled rage deep in my gut and made claws want to burst from my fingertips.

The Alphas who hadn't wanted Faythe among their ranks—mostly my late stepfather's allies—would want to set an example with Abby to make sure future tabbies didn't think they could just run amok in the new world order. The fact that I couldn't serve on the board that decided her fate *thoroughly* pissed me off.

"So, there's no way out of this?" Her focus volleyed between my eyes, searching for some overlooked possibility. Some miracle that would keep us together.

"No, and there probably shouldn't be. Your dad's in the strongest position to help with your defense, and the best thing I can do for you right now is let him."

"So, then, this is it?" She came closer, and I struggled to maintain eye contact with her so close to naked, and close to my bed, and close to leaving.

"For a while, anyway." I had no idea what would happen after her trial. Whether or not her father would let her leave the territory. Whether he'd let me visit. And frankly, I wouldn't blame him if he refused.

I'd failed her on every level.

"How long until they get here?" Abby closed the distance between us and went up on her toes to kiss me.

"A couple of hours?" I guessed, as her hand slid beneath my shirt and her mouth trailed down my neck, her tongue darting out to taste my skin in hot little increments.

"I know exactly how I want to spend it," she murmured against my skin, and I groaned beneath her touch.

Abby pulled my shirt up, and I lifted my arms to let her remove it. My tee hit the floor near hers. Her kisses continued down my neck while I slid my hands over her shoulders and down her arms. She felt amazing. Warm, and smooth, and soft. She smelled like strawberries and tasted like…Abby.

That was the moment I realized that no matter what her father said, I would *not* be able to let her go.

EIGHTEEN

Abby

Jace tilted my face up, then leaned down to kiss me, and desire exploded deep inside me. My breasts ached in anticipation of his touch. I'd never wanted anyone or anything the way I wanted him, and I couldn't seem to touch enough of him.

And I could see from the bulge straining against his zipper that the feeling was mutual.

"Come here," Jace whispered against my neck. He tugged me toward the armchair in one corner of the room, where he sank onto the edge of the cushion and pulled me close so that I was framed between his thighs. I could feel the heat from his skin through his jeans, but that wasn't enough. My body demanded more.

He reached behind my head to tug the rubber band from my hair, and curls fell across my back and over my shoulders. "You are *so* beautiful."

No, *he* was beautiful. I skimmed his chest lightly with my fingers. I was still getting used to the fact that I could touch him whenever I wanted, and that privilege was about to be ripped away from me.

Surely, separating me from Jace was crueler than any other punishment the council could come up with.

Jace leaned forward and anticipation made my heart race. My eyes closed as he lifted my left breast. He dropped a kiss on my nipple, and when I groaned, his tongue darted out for a taste.

"Mmmm…" I said as his mouth closed over my nipple, sucking gently. I leaned closer, wordlessly asking for more, and he took more into his mouth, teasing the tip with his tongue. The bulge in his pants swelled against my leg, and my body answered with an aching throb of its own, low, hot, and insistent.

Jace's tongue trailed toward my right breast, leaving my left damp and neglected in the cold room. I groaned when he took my right nipple into his mouth, and his hand slid around my waist to my back, then lower, squeezing me through a thin layer of lace.

"Jace." I said, and he sat up to look at me, his pupils dilated from arousal. I held his gaze while I slid my fingers beneath the sides of my panties, intending to step out of them. "I want more."

"Abby, wait." Yet the gruff timbre of his voice said that waiting was the last thing he wanted. "Are you sure? I don't want to rush this just because you think we won't get another chance."

Though I was right about that. I could see the truth in his eyes. If the council locked me up, or if my dad refused my transfer request…

But that wasn't what this was about. "I'm not

rushing it. I *want* you, Jace."

The heat in his eyes burned through me. Touching him was like holding fire in my hand. "Then let me do it."

My heart slammed against my sternum as he slid off the chair to kneel in front of me, angling us so that the wall was at my back. He lifted my hands onto his shoulders and looked up at me, and something about seeing him from that angle—his face inches from my stomach, his hands wrapped around the backs of my thighs—made me ache in sensitive places. His hands slid slowly up my legs, skimming my skin so lightly I wanted to lean into his touch. I let my head fall back against the wall, my eyes closed, content just to feel him.

His fingers hooked the sheer lace stretched across my hips, then tugged it slowly down. So slowly I started to complain—until he kissed the point of my left hip. His mouth was warm, and soft, and...several inches from where I truly wanted it.

A needy sound rose from my throat. Jace bit my hip gently, just the graze of his teeth against flesh, as he slid that scrap of material down my thighs, skimming my overheated skin with his fingers. He let go, and the lace fell, but his hands continued their slow exploration until he lifted first my right foot, then my left, to push the fallen garment away.

His hands crept back up and slid over my backside. Then he lifted my right leg and I caught my breath when he hooked my knee over his shoulder. He forged a trail of kisses up my thigh, and my pulse raced faster with every drop of fire left in the wake of his lips.

Anticipation pooled inside me, hot and aching. At

the first smooth stroke of his tongue where I'd never been tasted before, my eyes fell closed and every muscle in my body tensed beneath the delicious, wet pressure.

Jace groaned, and the sound rumbled through my most sensitive places. His next lick was longer, the next deeper, and by the time his fingers slid inside me, an exquisite spiral of friction and pressure was already building, teasing me toward a peak I'd only ascended once before.

"Oh…" I breathed, and Jace groaned again. His tongue worked faster, his fingers moving gently, applying pressure inside, and my hands slid into his hair. "Oh…" Pleasure erupted in a hot wash of sensation, and I lost all mastery of language. Jace kept moving, stroking, as I clenched around him, until I exhaled and let my head fall back against the wall again.

Then reason returned, and I remembered what I'd *really* wanted. "Oh, no, I wanted to…"

Jace smiled up at me, and new flames kindled where his hand was still nested. "We're not done." His fingers slid out of me slowly, trailing forward and up, and I shuddered as the touch triggered blissful aftershocks. He stood, and I reached for his waistband.

"We should be in my bed," he whispered as I tugged on the denim restraining his button.

"Why? You seem *more* than adept at…upright." I pushed the button through its hole, and his pulse spiked.

Jace groaned as I pushed his jeans down. "I want to do this right, Abby."

"You already are. You're the only thing I need."

"Say that again."

I slid his boxers down to follow the denim, freeing the hard length of him. "I need you, Jace."

He growled and lifted me, his hands digging into my hips. He throbbed against me, hot and ready, and suddenly my eagerness wavered. "Is it… Will it hurt?"

"I don't think so. You're ready, physically," he said, and I could hear how much he wanted me in every word he spoke. "*So* ready." But his self-control was a thing of legend. If I told him to wait, he would wait. "If this is what you want."

I nodded, my pulse racing. "I want you."

Nothing I'd said had ever been truer.

His pupils dilated, and his heart beat harder. "We'll go slow. If you want to stop, just tell me."

I nodded again, and he glanced at the armchair in the corner, just a foot away. "That might be easier, this time." His grip on my hips tightened as he sank into the chair with me on his lap. "You're on top. You're in control."

"But I don't…know what to do."

Jace grinned and pulled me down for a kiss. "We'll figure that out together," he whispered without truly pulling away from my mouth, then he was kissing me again, one hand in my hair, the other on my hip. He arched beneath me, rocking against me, and that simple motion triggered an orgasmic aftershock and pulled a guttural moan from deep in my throat. My body had only ever found pleasure in his touch, and it knew what to expect. What it wanted.

I decided to listen to my body. To forget everything else.

I closed my eyes and rocked against him.

Jace groaned, tense beneath me. Throbbing against

me. "I have never in my life wanted anyone like I want you."

The truth of that echoed deep in his voice. In the cadence of his heartbeat. I could taste it on his skin. I could feel it in my soul. And suddenly, I felt powerful. He wanted something only I could give him. I rocked forward one more time, then leaned down to whisper against his ear. "Show me what to do."

Jace's eyes fluttered closed, and his hand tightened on my hip. "You're already halfway there. Rise up on your knees."

I did, and his fingers slid into me. Testing. Teasing. My body remembered that part, and when I clenched around him, he groaned and removed his hand. "A little higher," he said, and when I complied, he guided himself into position beneath me. Against me. "Do you want to feel?" he asked, and when I nodded, too fascinated by the possibility to articulate, he guided my hand to where our bodies met, and my eyes flew open. My gaze met his, and for once, he wasn't grinning. He was watching me, desire burning behind his eyes. Flushing his skin.

He put both hands on my hips, leaving me to explore the prelude to our union on my own, and I did.

He was hot and hard, yet oddly soft on the surface. I was wet and swollen, and very sensitive. If I lowered myself at all, he would slide inside me. I braced myself against his chest with both hands and held his gaze as I slowly sank…

"Wait!"

I froze, startled, and Jace lifted me by my hips. I groaned when he lowered me onto his thighs instead. *Not* where I wanted to be. He reached for something on the floor, then held up a square packet I hadn't even seen him take from his pocket. I watched while he ripped it open and pulled out a condom. "There are only a couple of rules. This is number one." I watched, fascinated, as he rolled it over his erection. It practically disappeared against his skin except for the ring at the base.

That time, when he lifted me into position, I was ready. He guided and I lowered, and slowly, I slid over him. This felt different than his fingers had. It was blisteringly intimate, in part because I hadn't closed my eyes and he hadn't looked away.

"You don't have to go all the way down," he said, his voice a gruff whisper. "We can work up to that." He guided me with his hands, showing me how to lift myself, then lower myself again, as he rose beneath me, so that we met in the space between. He helped me find the most pleasant angles and the most comfortable depth, and as my confidence grew, I began to relax. To move more freely and discover what I liked. What he liked.

What made his jaw tighten and his eyes flutter closed. What made him sit up beneath me and run his tongue up my neck until he could suck my earlobe into his mouth without ever losing focus.

And then I found my rhythm.

With the right tempo and the right angle came true pleasure, and that intimate pressure began to mount within me again, tightening toward another peak. I moved quickly, almost frantically, desperate to capture that moment again and feel it spill over me with him still inside me.

"Abby…" Jace took my nipple in his mouth, and that pressure built faster. It was like chasing an erotic horizon. I could see it in the distance, stretching from one side of my world to the other. I could *feel* it reaching for me, pulling me…

"Faster," I gasped, and Jace obliged, as a carnal growl rumbled up from deep in his chest. He arched into me, and I rocked against him, and finally, the world exploded all around me. Through me. Jace thrust once, twice more, then groaned as he ground into me, gripping my hips, and each feverish collision of our bodies sent another wave of pleasure through me.

Finally, I collapsed against his damp chest, my head on his shoulder. His arms wound around me. Aftershocks rocked us both, with him still twitching inside me, and I'd never in my entire life felt so comfortable or secure with another living soul.

I could *not* let the council separate us.

"Hey, thanks for letting me stay the night." Robyn tucked a strand of brown hair behind one ear as she set her empty breakfast plate in the sink. "You don't know me, and you guys are already pretty crowded, so that was really awesome of you." She shrugged and smiled at Jace from across the kitchen, but before he could acknowledge her thanks, Melody laughed.

"It's not like he had any choice," my future sister-in-law said, mopping a smear of gravy from her plate with the last of her biscuit. "An Alpha has to provide sanctuary for any Pride member who needs it. But lately, he's been giving Abby a lot more than that, if you know what I mean."

My face flushed and Jace growled.

"Melody!" Patricia scolded. "If you can't be respectful, you can go straight back up to your room."

"But I'm still hungry." She patted her flat stomach. "The baby wants another biscuit."

Jace grabbed a biscuit from the platter and half crushed it as he slammed it down on her plate. "Eat in silence."

"Wait, what?" Robyn frowned, picking at the edge of the thick bandage on her thigh. "I didn't follow much of that." But I could tell which part she *had* understood from the way she looked from me to Jace with a sly grin. "I thought you said he was unattainable."

Jace glanced at me in surprise, and my flush deepened.

"Okay, we can talk about me and Jace later." But we almost certainly would *not*. "Right now, though, we need to have another talk." I sat at the breakfast bar and pushed a stool out for her with my foot. "Come sit down."

"Well, *that* can't be good." Melody dug a glob of grape jelly from an open jar and dropped it onto her biscuit. "The last time someone told me to 'come sit down,' I found out my father was dead." She turned to Robyn with one brow raised. "Has your dad instigated any intra-species civil wars recently?"

"Mel..." Jace growled, and Carver stood from his seat at the table.

"Melody, why don't we go find Isaac so the three of us can talk about what's going to be happening to your body over the next few months." The doctor handed Patricia his gravy-smeared plate. "This is a very important phase in your life, and I'm sure you want to be prepared."

Melody's brown eyes lit up at the thought of a discussion about herself and how important her pregnancy was. "Can I take my biscuit?"

"Of course." Always the gentleman, Dr. Carver picked up her plate. "If you'll excuse us, we have some important things to discuss." He led Melody from the room as if she were precious cargo, and she practically glowed.

"You know, if people keep coddling her, she's never going to grow up," Jace grumbled.

His mother laughed. "Oh, I think childbirth will take care of that."

"So, what's going on?" Robyn limped around the kitchen peninsula and sank onto the barstool, and Patricia turned back to her dishes, giving us the illusion of privacy without sacrificing her ability to eavesdrop. Not that she needed to be in the same room for that.

Jace leaned against the counter on the other side of the breakfast bar, facing us both. "Robyn, I'm assuming you've noticed that our household is larger than most?"

She nodded. "I met your sister and your brothers this morning, and several guys from those cabins out back came in to eat too. They're your employees *and* your tenants?" Her frown said she knew that wasn't quite right but lacked the vocabulary to accurately describe a relationship she didn't understand.

"Not in the typical sense. Room and board are part of their salary, but not because they work construction with me. I don't own the construction company, and they don't all work there. The guys who live in the cabins—all seven of them—are my enforcers."

"Enforcers." Robin swiveled on her stool to face me. "Is this a joke, or are you dating some kind of gangster kingpin?" She was smiling, trying to make light of it, but I could smell the anxiety seeping from her pores. "Is there a shifter mafia?"

"Robyn, I haven't been completely candid with you about my family. Or about shifters in general."

She stood and limped backward, eyes wide, hands out. "Wait, there really *is* a shifter mafia?"

"It's not a mafia," I insisted, but she was already glancing around the room, as if she might escape, if she could only find her purse. "It's a Pride—a group of allied werecats who belong to a specific territory and swear loyalty to the same Alpha. Jace is our Alpha." Though he wasn't mine anymore, technically. "It's his responsibility to protect, defend, and organize the Pride members against outside threats."

"Outside threats?"

I shrugged. "We had a bad patch a few years ago, but lately, there haven't been many outside threats." Well, until the human hunters started targeting Pride cats and Robyn started killing them. "There are ten Alphas in the US—one for each territory—and if you want to visit another territory, for business or vacation, or whatever, you have to get that Alpha's permission first, because trespassing is considered an act of aggression."

Robyn's frown deepened and I could practically see her repeating what I'd just said in her head, trying to understand. "So, how is that *not* a mafia?"

"We're not criminals," I explained. But then I had to backtrack. "Okay, sometimes we have to do things that are *technically* illegal, according to human laws, but we don't profit from crime."

"The laws we have to break include disposing of the man who tried to kill you last night," Jace said, his voice deep but soft. "Protecting you is my job now. I'm your Alpha."

"My Alpha?" Robyn picked at the edge of her bandage again, exposed beneath her borrowed shorts. "As in my…first?"

"As in your dominant," I said, and Robyn's wide-eyed gaze swung back to me. "Jace is the fastest, strongest, and the best equipped to lead, so he's the Alpha of this Pride. The Appalachian Pride. Which you belong to, because this is where you were infected."

Technically, any stray infected in a US territory belonged to that territory, but the *vast* majority of strays were infected in one of the free zones by strays who didn't realize—or care—that they were committing a crime. Those few who *were* infected in one of the recognized territories were almost always rejected by the local Alpha and exiled to the free zone after a brief explanation of the rules.

Marc was a notable exception—he was infected as a young teenager—and Robyn would be too. In fact, the council would probably insist on keeping her, both to protect her and to study the rare infection of a human female.

And in the desperate hope that she would be willing to help propagate the species she now belonged to.

"What if I don't want an Alpha?" Robyn lowered her hands and shifted her weight onto her good leg but looked no closer to reclaiming her seat. The sweat gathering on her upper lip smelled like fear, and I could tell from Jace's forcibly relaxed stance that he could feel her anxiety.

"It doesn't really work like that," he said. "Our laws say that you can't live in my territory unless you belong to my Pride. But beyond that, you *need* an Alpha, maybe more than any other tabby ever has."

Robyn blinked at him for a moment, obviously struggling to make sense of what she was hearing. Then she turned to me, and the fear leaking from her pores developed a sharp tang of panic. "Abby?" She wanted me to tell her that this was all a joke. Or that Jace was wrong and she really did have a choice in the matter. "I didn't sign up for this."

"I know. Me neither. I didn't choose to be born into this any more than you chose to be infected. And for the record, I am *so* sorry. I thought I was protecting you by hiding all this from you, but Jace is right. You need an Alpha. And really, this is sort of a best-case scenario. There are only a few Alphas I'd be happy to see you serve, and Jace is one of them." The others were Faythe, my dad, and Umberto Di Carlo.

"Serve?" Robyn's eyes widened as her panic swelled.

"Well, only in the sense that he's your boss. But that's really more like a supervisory position."

"I'm an adult. I don't need to be supervised," she insisted.

"The string of murders bearing your signature would argue otherwise," Jace said, as gently as I'd ever heard him say anything.

Robyn recoiled, shocked. "You know about that?" If she'd been in a police station, that probably would have been considered an admission of guilt. Obviously, she hadn't realized they knew anything more than that Darren had tried to kill her.

"It's my job to know," Jace said. "You've put our entire species at risk of exposure, and we've been trying to clean up after you. Though Abby was a little less helpful in that regard than she could have been, once she realized you were the stray we were hunting." He shot a censuring glance at me, and I could only bow my head in apology. That was the very least of what I'd get from the other Alphas.

"I didn't mean to." Tears formed in Robyn's eyes. "I can't even remember much of it."

Jace leaned over the counter with both elbows on the tile. "Well, on some level, you *must* have meant to. You found out where they lived and you hunted them like prey."

"That's not how it happened." A tear rolled down her right cheek, and I wanted to hug her, but I was afraid she'd push me away. "I only tracked them down to make sure they hadn't kidnapped someone else. But at every one of their houses, I saw other dead cats, and I smelled blood, and I…lost it. I don't remember shifting. I just woke up naked, covered in blood, every time. But they were monsters!"

She dismissed Jace—something no one born a shifter would ever have done—and implored me with wide blue eyes to understand. "They were just like the men who killed Dani, and Mitch, and Olsen! They're part of some sick club that kidnapped me, and *played* with me, and beat me. They're the reason I turn into this animal I can't control and crave things I never even knew existed. They *deserved* to die! *All* of them!"

"Yes, they did," Jace agreed. "But killing them was my job, not yours."

"I didn't mean to do it," she repeated, and when I gestured to the stool again, she finally limped in my direction. "And I didn't even know the rest of you existed."

"That's my fault." My heart ached, seeing how much I'd put her through by denying her the support of an Alpha and a team of enforcers. "I broke the rules by not telling him about you, and vice versa."

"Why?" Robyn lifted herself gingerly onto the stool, favoring her injured leg. "What were you trying to protect me from? *Him*?" She nodded in Jace's direction, and I shook my head.

"No. He's one of the good guys. Actually, there aren't really any *bad* guys left on the council, but some of them are very old-fashioned, and they care more about the future of our entire species than about any individual member of it."

"I don't understand what that means," Robyn said, as Patricia set a glass of ice water in front of her.

"That means that—" Jace began, but I interrupted, ignoring his irritated growl. The next part would be better coming from a fellow tabby.

"Okay, you met Melody and Patricia this morning, right? And you've known me for years," I said, and Robyn nodded as she lifted her glass. "Well, we're the *only* female shifters in this entire territory. Just the three of us. Only two of us are young enough to...propagate. And Melody's clearly jumped into that role with both feet. But my point is that there are *dozens* of tomcats in the Appalachian territory. Right?" I glanced at Jace for confirmation, and he nodded. "But only a couple of tabbies."

Because Patricia was actually a dam—a mother beyond childbearing years.

"Wait." I frowned and reconsidered. "Technically, I belong to my birth Pride again—my father's territory—which means you and Melody are the only tabbies here, and that's actually a very high ratio of tabbies to toms, compared with the average."

"That's a *high* ratio?" Robyn said, and I could see that she might soon draw for herself the conclusion I was leading up to.

"Yes. Right now in my birth Pride, I'm the only woman of childbearing age, and the Southeast Territory has none, because Sara Di Carlo died almost five years ago." She'd been killed right in front of me, in the cage across from mine.

"So, what, they want you to have a bunch of babies for them?" Robyn forced a laugh, obviously expecting me to say she'd drawn a hilariously inaccurate conclusion. But my silence spoke volumes. "Wait, that can't be what they want from *me*! I'm not having a whole litter of some random tomcat's shifter babies, and they can't make me!"

She stood again, and this time when she backed away from me, the betrayal in her eyes burned all the way to my soul. She thought I'd sold her out.

"No, they can't make you, and they won't even try," Jace assured her.

I sat straighter when I heard the distant rumble of an engine heading toward us. My parents were minutes away, and I wanted Robyn to understand everything before she met my dad, the council chairman.

"But that *is* the expectation for tabbies born into our society," Jace continued. "Which—until you—has been *all* tabbies."

"That's barbaric."

"Actually, it's just very old-fashioned," Patricia insisted, and when she started a fresh pot of coffee, I knew she'd heard the engine too. "It's also somewhat unavoidable, at least until men start growing uteruses. They can't have babies, so we must, or the species will fail. I've had six myself."

"*Six?*" Robyn's voice was practically a squeak.

Patricia nodded. "Five sons before I finally got a girl." She turned to me. "That's about the average, wouldn't you say?"

I nodded. Like Melody, I was the youngest of six. Dams almost *always* stop breeding once they get that precious daughter.

"Okay, but what's with the gender imbalance?" Robyn asked. "Why are girls so rare?"

"Doctors have been trying to figure that out forever," I said, as the car engine rumbled closer. "And you're the very first human woman—at least the first confirmed in the US—to survive being infected. Which means you're our *only* female stray. That makes you very precious, somewhat of a commodity, and a success story to be studied."

Creating strays was forbidden, but understanding why Robyn had survived could only benefit us all. Which I knew. But I also knew that…

"I don't want to be studied." Robyn's pulse was racing. She was terrified, and I wondered if she could hear the car. Her senses were as good as mine, but she'd had much less practice using them. "I don't want to be part of your weird shifter mafia club. I don't need to be protected—"

"You're wrong about that," Jace insisted. "At least for the moment."

"—and I *certainly* don't want to be some kind of anomalous freak baby machine, just so you guys can even out your fucked-up gender ratio."

"I know." I reached for her hand, but she pulled away from me. "That's part of why I hid you from everyone else."

Jace stood as the car pulled to a stop out front. "She broke several very serious rules to protect you, and because of that, Abby is in a lot of trouble."

Robyn turned to me with wide, scared eyes. "What kind of trouble?"

A car door slammed out front, and Jace's brief exhale was his only outward sign of tension. "The kind that might get her executed if she were a tomcat."

"Executed? They would *kill* her if she were a boy?"

"See?" Patricia stirred creamer into a mug of coffee. "The gender imbalance *does* have its advantages."

"Not the point, Mom." Jace listened as one of his brothers let my parents in through the front door, before they could even ring the bell. "The most likely penalties, if she's found guilty, include losing her incisors or her claws, both of which would be permanently disfiguring, not to mention painful. Or incarceration in the capitol of a neutral territory. Which means she'd be locked up in the basement of one of the Alphas who has no blood or personal connection to her."

"Wait, Abby only killed one bad guy." Robyn's heart beat so fast, I was afraid she was about to keel over. "I killed *four* of them. Does that mean I'm in the same trouble?"

"Yes." My father stepped into the kitchen from the hall with my mother on his heels. "But I believe the council will go easy on you, considering the mitigating factors, if you're willing to make a serious concession of your own."

My dad pulled me into a hug, then held one hand out for her to shake, with his left arm still around me. "It's nice to see you again, Robyn, though I am sorry about the circumstances." They'd met a few times before when my parents had come to see me at school.

Robyn took his hand, and for the first time since she'd been infected, she bowed her head, as if the urge felt completely natural. She could *not* have picked a better time to display her new respectful instinct. "Nice to see you," she said. "I think."

"Robyn, this is a man you want to have on your side," Jace said as she took my mother's hand. "Abby's dad is the council chairman, and if he says he can help you, he can. If you cooperate."

"What would I have to do?" Robyn asked as Patricia handed fresh mugs of coffee to each of my parents in greeting.

My father nodded to thank Jace's mom, then turned back to Robyn. "You'd have to agree to remain in one of the US Prides voluntarily and to let our doctor run a few simple tests. And you'd have to undergo training with one of our Alphas until you learn to control your new urges and instincts."

"I don't have to have any babies?" Robyn said, obviously relieved.

My father chuckled. "Of course not. Though no one would object if you were to change your mind. I'm not going to lie—there are council members who see your existence as a precious opportunity for that very reason."

"So, if I agree to belong to one of your Prides, you

won't try to execute me? Or lock me up? Or break off my teeth or anything?"

My father nodded. "That's the gist of my offer, assuming it gets enough support from my fellow Alphas."

Robyn looked to me for an opinion, and I nodded. That was the best offer she was going to get. "Okay, then." She held her hand out for my father to shake again, and that time, *he* looked relieved.

"Now, let's talk about what you can do to help my daughter…"

NINETEEN

Jace

Ed Taylor gripped the arms of his chair and looked at the Alphas seated on either side of him at the Lazy S's formal dining room table. Then he turned back to the woman sitting at the far end, her hands clasped nervously in her lap. "And is it your sworn testimony that Abigail Wade never scratched or bit you, nor injured you in any way that broke the surface of your skin?"

"That's right." Robyn Sheffield took a sip of water from the glass on the table in front of her, then met Taylor's gaze. "Abby would never hurt me."

I exhaled softly from my folding metal chair against the wall. On the surface, the infection charge was Abby's biggest obstacle, but now that the other Alphas had met Robyn, they could tell from her scent that she'd been infected by a stray. Still, formalities had to be observed.

Even though I'd known how Robyn would answer, hearing her official statement was a big relief. She'd been prepped for the hearing, but there was no way to truly prepare someone who'd been born human to sit in a room full of people her brand new-instincts labeled as dangerous, powerful, and commanding.

The Territorial Council was the shifter equivalent of the United Nations—except that *our* leaders could rip each other's throats out with the flick of one wrist.

"Ms. Sheffield, would you please tell the council how and when you were infected?" Rick Wade followed up, from Taylor's right.

Abby's dad had appointed Ed Taylor as the acting council chairman for the duration of his daughter's trial to avoid any appearance of nepotism, so for the first time in more than four years, he was not sitting at the head of the table. The chair to Taylor's left was occupied by Paul Blackwell, who'd made a rare trip to the ranch in spite of his advanced age and failing health.

The entire council had shown up to meet the first female stray ever confirmed to exist in the US. Robyn was a miracle. A violent, largely feral—in feline form, anyway—miracle.

And since I wasn't allowed to participate in the hearing, due to both my involvement with Abby and my responsibility for what had gone down in my territory two weeks before, the council sat at nine members, which meant a tie was impossible. Abby's fate would be decided by the end of the day.

Abby sat several feet from me in another folding chair, but I couldn't see much of her because Michael Sanders—Faythe's oldest brother and an attorney—

sat between us. I hadn't seen or spoken to her since her father had taken her from my house twelve days before, and every hour that had passed without her felt like an hour without oxygen. She'd left a hairband and a tube of lip balm on my nightstand, and I stared at them every night as the minutes ticked past on my alarm clock.

Her father had insisted that the council could view any private contact between me and Abby as an attempt at collusion. As if we were getting our blatantly false stories straight. Even worse—Michael and Rick had decided that I should not testify on her behalf, because the truths I'd be forced to tell would only make things worse for her.

She actually *was* guilty, so their strategy was to elicit sympathy for her and for her motives, rather than falsely claim that she hadn't done anything wrong. Which was where Robyn came in. Our new stray's testimony was supposed to establish the extenuating circumstance that had prompted Abby's actions.

As spectators, Abby and I weren't allowed to speak during the hearing lest we influence the testimony, but Michael, as her advisor, could offer Robyn any help she needed.

"Tell you how I was infected. Sure." Robyn took another sip of her water, and that time, her hand was shaking. Physically, she'd held up well over the past twelve days, though the council had forbidden her to shift except under the supervision of an attending Alpha. But the trial was a source of stress all on its own. "In October, I was abducted from a campsite by three human men who'd come to hunt Abby. Though I didn't know that at the time."

Faythe and Michael had gone over and over

Robyn's testimony with her. Her story hadn't changed, but we'd needed to be sure she could tell it under pressure, without forgetting anything.

"Then what happened, Ms. Sheffield?" Bert Di Carlo asked.

"They took me to a cabin in the woods." Robyn paused for another sip, and again her hand shook. "They kind of *dragged* me there. To this horrible room where there was a big black cat dead on a table, being skinned. I didn't know it was a shifter. I didn't know there *were* shifters. Abby had never told me any of that, because she was following your rules. Even though that meant keeping secrets from her best friend."

Faythe smiled encouragingly from her seat on the left side of the table. As the junior-ranking Alpha—since I'd been excluded—she sat closest to Robyn and farthest from the council chair position. "Please go on."

"There was another cat—a live one—in a cage, and when I got too close to it, he sort of swiped at me with one paw. With his claws out, you know? I think he was scared and just lashing out at anyone who came close. He was already dying from a wound to his stomach. I think he was shot."

Ed Taylor nodded. "And it is your testimony that this scratch from a dying stray is what infected you, triggering your transformation and later your first shift into feline form?"

Robyn shrugged nervously. "I guess. I didn't know any of that at the time, though. I just… Someone knocked me out, and when I woke up, Abby said that the police had come for the men who took me. I was in shock, and I felt sick, so I didn't really question any of it. We stayed in that awful cabin because I didn't feel well enough to travel.

"That night, I got a really high fever and I started hallucinating. Abby took care of me. She explained what was happening, but I wasn't really processing much of anything. Then I started hurting all over, like my body was ripping itself apart. It was excruciating. She stayed with me through that first shift, and she talked me through shifting back into human form."

Paul Blackwell leaned forward with his cane propped on the floor between his knees, both gnarled hands gripping the knob at the top. "And she never told you anything about us? About the council, or her Alpha, or about the rest of our society?"

His skepticism made Robyn bristle. "No. I mean, she told me there were others, but she said I didn't need to meet any of them yet. That I wasn't ready."

"And do you know what she meant by that?"

"Objection!" Michael Sanders stood from his chair against the dining room wall, and I got a peek at Abby behind his back. Her hair was pulled back and she wore a soft green dress, but her hands were clenched so tightly in her lap, she looked like she might snap her own fingers off. "Ms. Sheffield cannot be expected to know what Ms. Wade was thinking," Michael elaborated.

Blackwell scowled. "Mr. Sanders, this isn't a trial."

"But his point is valid," Ed Taylor declared. "We'll ask Ms. Wade about her motivation when *she* sits in that chair." Blackwell frowned again, but remained silent. "Ms. Sheffield," Taylor continued, "why did you kill Joe Mathews and the other human hunters?"

"Objection!" Michael stood again. "Ms. Sheffield has already been pardoned for her crimes, as part of an agreement she made with the council in advance of today's hearing."

"We are *aware*, Mr. Sanders," Taylor said. "I'm trying to establish her frame of mind as it pertains to Ms. Wade's motivation." He tossed a glance at Abby, then his gaze slid my way, and it was less than friendly. Brian's father blamed me for ending his son's engagement. He wasn't the only one.

Michael nodded curtly. "Withdrawn." He sat, gesturing for Robyn to go ahead, now that he was sure the council wasn't going to revoke its promise.

Robyn's leg began to jiggle beneath the table. "I don't know. It wasn't a conscious decision. I never really *decided* to kill anyone." She frowned. "Dr. Carver said my cat half was in charge of my brain when those things happened, which means they weren't my fault. I was dissociated from my conscience and my human decision-making process. Didn't you guys talk to him?"

"We did." Blackwell trained his habitually skeptical focus on her. "Why did you go looking for those men in the first place, Ms. Sheffield? I assume *that* part was done while you had full use of your human faculties?"

Robyn nodded hesitantly. "Well, the first of those men found *me*. Abby had taken me to the woods so we could run in cat form, and I picked up a scent I hadn't even realized I'd smelled at that cabin the day I got scratched. It belonged to a man those hunters worked with who hadn't been there that day. He was following us, and when I smelled him, I just sort of...lost control. My teeth *needed* to break through flesh. I *needed* to taste his blood. I couldn't think about anything else."

She was describing bloodlust; we all knew the

symptoms well.

"When it was over, I shifted back into human form and went through his stuff, trying to figure out who he was. Why I knew his smell. I found a disposable cell phone that only had a few contacts in it. One of the names was Steve's—he's one of the men who took me from the campsite—so I knew the rest of those names were other hunters. Other men out there killing and skinning shifters.

"I texted the addresses to myself, but I didn't tell Abby."

"Why not?" Jerald Pierce asked, from the left side of the table.

"Because she kept telling me how important it was for me to keep the whole thing a secret and to never go anywhere without her. I thought she'd think it was too much of a risk, but I *had* to make sure they weren't doing to someone else what they did to me." Robyn took another sip of her water. "I went to the first address to make sure they weren't holding any more prisoners. I was just gonna wait until the house was empty, then break in and take a look around, but…I don't know what happened. I don't remember shifting, but I must have, because I woke up later, naked and covered in blood."

"You killed those men in a dissociative state, brought on by severe trauma?" Faythe said, reiterating the facts for our fellow Alphas to remind them of Robyn's deal.

"Yeah, I guess. And now I have to have an Alpha, who gets tell me what to do whenever he wants. I have to tell him where I'm going, and I can't leave his territory without getting permission from him and from the Alpha of whatever territory I want to go to.

And if I want to go to one of the free zones, it's this whole big organizational challenge because I can't go by myself, in case I get kidnapped and sold into marriage somewhere in South America. That really wasn't much of a risk for me before I started sprouting fur and claws, you know," Robyn said.

I had to stifle a smile, in spite of the circumstances. In granting her immunity, they'd unmuzzled the new tabby, and several of the older council members were obviously having regrets.

"This system you guys have set up is really anti-American, but it turns out that's not the right opinion for me to have. I'm supposed to be a shifter first, and an American second, but when I do that—when I give in to my cat instincts and urges—you guys threaten to execute me if I don't go along with this bullshit deal you offered me."

Michael stood, unsure what to do, since Robyn had veered off course. "Um, may I have a word with Ms. Sheffield in private, please?" he said, and she turned to glance at him in surprise.

"No," Ed Taylor barked. "Let's let her speak. Ms. Sheffield, what would your reaction have been if Ms. Wade had told you all of this when you were first infected?"

Robyn gave him a bitter huff. "I'd have fucking defected to Canada."

There was a collective gasp from most of the council, who probably hadn't been cursed at by a tabby since Faythe's pre-Alpha days.

"You would have run?" Faythe said, but she already knew the answer. We all knew the answer. She was just trying to drive home the gist of Abby's defense.

Robyn nodded. "You would have had to hunt me down and drag me back by force. You might have had to kill me. I wasn't ready to hear all this then, and if Abby had told me, you guys might be hunting my pale ass all over the great white north right this very minute."

Several of the older Alphas scowled, but Robyn had done her job. As the new stray stood to be dismissed, Faythe caught my gaze, and I knew exactly what had dulled the shine in her eyes and stiffened her posture. The hard part was yet to come.

Abby smiled at me behind Michael's head, and I knew at a glance that she thought we were winning. None of her political science classes had taught her what angry Alphas were like when they felt scared, threatened, and betrayed. She didn't know about behind-the-scenes phone calls or under-the-table deals, or how brutal the survival instinct could be when it applied to an entire species, rather than to an individual.

Abby had no idea what she was walking into, and I'd had no chance to warn her.

All I could do was return her smile and cling to my backup plan. Abby had made herself a target, and I would do whatever it took to draw the council's aim from her.

TWENTY

Abby

Robyn gave me a sympathetic look as she left Faythe's dining room, but I could tell she was relieved. Her part was over. She'd done what she could to help me, swimming upstream in a political current she'd never even known existed until days before, and I was proud of her. Jace was right. She was strong. She'd be fine.

When I stood to take my seat, every gaze in the room followed me. The ambient tension was thick enough to choke me with every breath I took. My father had chosen Ed Taylor to lead the inquisition to show that my broken engagement to Brian had left no rift between the two Alphas, but based on the gruff look Taylor gave me when I sat, he didn't seem to have gotten the memo.

For four years, he'd believed that his son would take over my father's Pride. That I would give him grandchildren. That Brian would follow in his footsteps and maybe ask for fatherly advice. I'd taken all that away from him. I understood his anger. But it had no relevance to my hearing.

"Hi, Abby, and thank you for coming today," Faythe said as I pushed my chair forward. But the encouraging smile she'd had for Robyn was gone. Faythe's obvious anxiety popped my bubble of optimism like a balloon under too much pressure, and all at once my worst-case-scenario fears felt more like an inevitability.

For the past week and a half, I'd lain awake in my childhood bed at night, thinking about Jace. Missing his grin, and his laugh, and that sound he made deep in his throat when he was *really* turned on. Remembering what it felt like to be touched by him and know that the same hands capable of ripping apart every threat he'd ever faced could also bring comfort, and support, and the most blisteringly intimate pleasure I'd ever felt in my life.

My dad had spent those same nights on the phone, having a series of arguments that were evidently well above my need-to-know level. I couldn't identify any of the voices on the other end of the line, and I only caught small bits of what was said, but the gist was clear—everyone was pissed at everyone else.

The thick tension during my hearing supported that conclusion and made me wonder what was going on behind the scenes with the council. Was my trial actually the backdrop for some larger political clash?

If so, was this about the Lion's Den resolution, or about my broken engagement?

Either way, did I really even have a shot?

I twisted in my chair to face Jace, and he gave me a

smile, his blue eyes bright with the spark that blazed between us. But his jaw was tight and his arms were tense. He might not have been on the panel, but he knew what was going on behind all the cordial smiles and formal behavior. And he did *not* look happy.

My father cleared his throat, startling me out of my thoughts. "Abby, why didn't you tell us that your roommate had been infected?"

I took a deep breath, then forged ahead. "Because she got sick really fast, and by the time I realized she had scratch-fever, I thought she was dying." And I was extra glad they'd kicked Robyn out of the room, because she didn't know that part. "I mean, no other woman's ever survived infection that I knew of."

"And after you realized she would live?" Paul Blackwell demanded.

"I didn't tell anyone then because of this." I held both arms out to take in the room full of Alphas—an absolute authority unlike anything that had existed in Robyn's life thus far. "She was scared, and sick, and traumatized. She was having nightmares and flashbacks."

Most of the faces staring back at me seemed completely unmoved.

I exhaled in frustration, then leaned forward with my arms folded on the table. I tried to meet each of their gazes. I wanted them to understand. "Those men killed her friends right in front of her. They hit her and put a knife to her throat. They dragged her away from everything and everyone she'd ever known and locked her in a basement, where her life was *changed forever.*"

Faythe's eyes widened. She knew what that was like. She remembered. But the rest of them...

"You guys have all the power." I glanced at each of the other Alphas in turn. "All the control. You've never been terrified or helpless. You've never sat in a dark room waiting, listening, knowing that the next time the door opens, someone's going to come in and hurt you, and there's *nothing* you can do about it. You don't understand how sometimes, even when it's over, you're still hurt, and scared, and everyone wants you to tell them that you're fine, or that you're not fine, but really you *just want to be left alone.*"

Faythe nodded, and her eyes looked extra shiny. My father's jaw was clenched with the reminder of what I'd been through and why I might over-empathize with Robyn's trauma. Several of the other Alphas looked uncomfortable.

"You wanted my frame of mind? There you go. I knew that Robyn just wanted to be left alone, and that you guys would *never* let that happen. Which was a shame, because Robyn wasn't just healing from a violent crime. She was dealing with bloodlust, and overwhelming new instincts, and radically enhanced senses. Less than a week later, she was back in class, trying to keep up with school on top of everything else.

"Robyn's strong and smart, but she grew up as a twenty-first-century *human* woman with *no concept* of the kind of authority an Alpha wields. Much less an entire council full of them. The last thing she needed was ten strangers telling her she'd have to give up the career she's been working toward since she was sixteen so she can pick a husband and raise a litter of shifter babies. Not to mention the genetic testing and clinical observation. Being kidnapped and infected was unfair enough. I couldn't break the rest of it to her without giving her time to heal. And I wouldn't have had any time to give her, if anyone else knew about her. So I tried to protect her."

Faythe smiled, and for several seconds, no one else seemed to know what to say. I turned to look at Jace, and he gave me the smallest, most Alpha-appropriate nod of approval, but as soon as I turned back to the council, I knew I'd messed up.

Looking at Jace had reminded them of that other thing I'd done wrong. With him.

"And when Robyn started killing people?" Milo Mitchell, Alpha of the Northwest Territory demanded. He'd been one of Jace's stepfather's allies, and our new relationship gave him one more reason to hate Jace. "Why didn't you tell someone about her then?"

"Because I didn't know what she was doing, at first. The guy in the woods was self-defense. I didn't know she'd *kept* killing until she called me from Hargrove's house, but she didn't remember any of what she'd done, and we were in the last week of the semester by then, so I decided to talk my dad into letting me stay on campus during the break. I was going to use that time to tell her everything I hadn't had a chance to tell her before." I shrugged. "But then Jace came to pick me up early, and I realized that Robyn could be the rogue stray he was looking for."

"That's why you forced him to hire you?" Blackwell demanded. "To cover up your roommate's crimes? And your own?"

"Yes, but that was my fault, not his," I insisted.

Ed Taylor glanced over my shoulder at Jace, and my pulse picked up speed. "You would never have been able to manipulate your way onto his staff if he hadn't offered you the job in the first place," Taylor pointed out. "Employment as an enforcer is not candy to be handed out to children in cute costumes."

"I'm not a child!" I snapped, and too late, I realized that was strike number two.

"Many enforcers are hired in their early twenties, or even younger," Faythe pointed out through clenched teeth. "Including both me and Jace."

Milo Mitchell leaned forward, across the table from Faythe. "And there are some who would suggest those weren't the wisest hires either. Age is not just a number, Ms. Sanders."

"A philosophy I'm sure the oldest among us keep close at heart," she snapped with a sharp glance at the elderly Paul Blackwell, and I wanted to cheer.

Instead, I drew everyone's focus back to me, to break the tension. "Jace never really intended for me to accept that job. He thought I'd graduate and go back home, and he had *no* idea what I was up to."

"Well, he *should* have," Mitchell said, and panic swelled inside me when I saw the sentiment echoed on several of the other Alpha's faces. "Tell us about Gene Hargrove. Why did you kill him?"

"Because if he'd kept talking, Jace would have figured out that Robyn was a stray. I was trying to protect her."

"Were you not also trying to protect yourself?" Nick Davidson asked, speaking up for the first time.

"No, I was pretty much already screwed," I said, and when Faythe flinched, I realized they might count "screwed" as profanity. Was that strike three?

"How so?" she asked before anyone could object to my language.

"Well, even if I could have kept everyone from

finding out Robyn was the killer, eventually they'd at least find out she existed, and then everyone would know I'd been hiding her." My open-armed gesture indicated the entire inquisition. "I'd have ended up here anyway, and I knew that from the start."

"I think we've heard enough," Ed Taylor said, and I swear he glanced at my naked ring finger. "Ms. Wade, is there anything else you'd like to say to the council before we dismiss for deliberation?"

"Um..." I began, as my heart tried to launch itself up my throat, and Faythe motioned for me to rise with a subtle openhanded gesture.

I stood, then started over, my hands clutched in front of my skirt to keep them from shaking. "I just want to thank the council for the opportunity to speak in my own defense." My father had made me practice it just like that. "And I want to say that I'm *so* sorry. I was trying to do the best thing for Robyn, and obviously I made the wrong call. But my intent was never to break the council's laws or defy its authority."

"Yet that's exactly what you did," Taylor observed, and my pulse spiked again. "Our rules exist for a reason, Ms. Wade, and your disregard for them led to the slaughter of four humans and a *dangerous* amount of news coverage. Your actions are also responsible for delaying our discovery of the hunting club itself, the consequences of which could be far-reaching." He stood, and my heart dropped into my stomach. "Okay. We're going to take a minute to deliberate, if we could please have the room."

I tried not to assume that he hated me just because I'd dumped his son, but I'd pleaded guilty to several very serious charges, depending on the council's mercy at sentencing, and the temporary chair did *not* seem to be in a generous mood.

"I don't think we'll need very long," Blackwell mumbled as I turned to leave the room. Several of the others nodded in agreement.

My father looked like someone was trying to cut his heart out of his chest, right there in front of everyone.

Faythe looked like she wanted to vomit.

That's when I understood just how badly my inquisition had gone. They weren't just going to cut off the ends of my fingers or take my canines. They were going to lock me up.

In a cage.

The council would see that as a mercy; after all, they were sparing my life. What they didn't understand was that I couldn't survive another cage. I would lose my mind. I would have nothing to do for months—maybe years—on end but remember the last time I'd been locked up.

My chest felt tight and I couldn't draw a breath. My mouth opened, and I sucked at a whole room full of air but couldn't drag any of it in.

Bars. Bruises. Pain.

I bent over with my hands on my knees, fighting the looming panic attack, but the world began to swim around me as I lost the battle.

Locked doors. Blackened windows. Torn clothes.

"You're dismissed, Abigail," Paul Blackwell said, and I tried to stand, but my vision flickered and I stumbled.

My father stepped forward and Faythe reached for me, but then Jace was my side, one arm around my waist. Practically holding me up. "Wait. I'd like to address the council," he said, and the sound of his voice opened my lungs. I sucked in a deep breath, then turned to look up at him, clutching the edge of the table for balance.

The look in his eyes—like a kamikaze in a tailspin—made my heart race in panic.

"No." I let go of the table and blinked to clear my vision. "Jace, whatever you're about to do, don't."

"Sit." He pointed at my chair, and my body obeyed before my mind could think to object.

"Let's hear him," Blackwell said, and I knew from the glee in the old bastard's voice that he knew exactly what was about to happen—and that he'd enjoy every minute of it. He'd never been Jace's biggest fan.

"The council will hear Jace Hammond, Alpha of the Appalachian Pride," Ed Taylor said, sinking back into his seat at the head of Faythe's dining room table.

Jace clasped his hands at his back and looked at each of his fellow council members in turn, ending with Ed Taylor. "As her Alpha during the time in question, I take full responsibility for Abby's actions."

"No!" I stood again, and that time, no one told me to sit.

Jace didn't even look at me. "What happens in my territory is ultimately my responsibility, and I should have seen what was going on. If I'd been more involved, I would have figured it out. So, if you have to punish someone, punish me. But leave her alone."

"Wait a minute!" I turned my back on him to plead with the council. "*I'm* the one who lied. *I* manipulated my way into that job, and *I'm* the one who killed Gene Hargrove. Jace had nothing to do with any of that. He had *no* idea what I was doing."

"But don't you think he should have?" Milo Mitchell leaned back and crossed his hands over his stomach, and anger raced up my spine. He'd *always* hated Jace and had voted against confirming him as Alpha.

Unfortunately, I had no idea how to answer. Claiming that Jace couldn't be held accountable because I'd outsmarted him would *not* help his case. Before I could come up with a suitable response, Jace answered for me.

"Yes. I should have. I move that the council apply the charges brought against Abby Wade against me instead."

"Jace…" I turned to him with tears in my eyes. He was ruining his career for me. He was ruining his *life* for me.

I couldn't let him do it.

"I move to accept the motion," my father said, and I spun on him in shock.

"Dad, no!" But my father looked right into my eyes, and I knew I wouldn't change his mind. He'd found a way to save his only daughter, and he would seize it, no matter who else got hurt.

"I second," Faythe said, one hand on her swollen belly, and the first tears spilled from my eyes to roll down my cheeks. "All in favor?"

A chorus of "Ayes" rang out, and my throat tried to close around a cry of denial. It was unanimous.

Why was the vote never unanimous in favor of any *good* idea?

"No!" But instead of shouting at the council again, I turned on Jace. "What did you *do*?"

"Abby…"

"Take it back!" I shoved him, and he rocked on

his feet, but took the blow without complaint. "Take it *back*!" I pushed him again, and he was against the wall, and everyone was staring. His face blurred beneath my tears, but his blue eyes still burned bright. When I tried to push him again, he pulled me into an embrace, and that's when I totally lost it, sobbing against his shirt.

The severity of the charges against me easily warranted the death penalty, but lockup was the worst they would have thrown at me, because they *needed* me. That was the only true break fate had cut me, to make up for the shitty stick I'd drawn, having been born female in an *overwhelmingly* patriarchal world.

But Jace didn't have gender on his side.

"Get her out of here," Milo Mitchell ordered, and my father growled at him.

One of Mitchell's men grabbed my wrist. Jace snarled, and when the tom didn't let go of me fast enough, Jace seized his arm and gave it a brutal twist. I heard both bones crack.

The tom backed away from us, whimpering and clutching his broken arm. Mitchell cursed softly and waved his injured enforcer out the door for medical care.

No one else tried to touch me. No one yelled at Jace.

You don't cross an Alpha in his prime unless you're looking to get hurt. Or you're stupid.

Jace guided me toward the doorway himself, and I stepped through it because I had no choice.

Faythe followed me into the hall, ostensibly to use the restroom, but as soon as the door closed behind her, she turned to me, an apology written all over her face. "I'm sorry, Abby. I know how hard this must—

"

"Then why would you second the motion?" I demanded, but even with tears in her eyes, she responded calmly.

"There's more at play here than you understand."

"Yeah, I get that. But how could you do that to him? You used to *love* him!"

"And I always will, but not like he loves you." Faythe exhaled slowly, and I got the impression that she was stalling for time. Trying to figure out how much it would be prudent to explain to me. "Jace is determined to protect you, Abby. If we didn't give him this option—the option *he* asked for—he'd find another way, and that would go even worse for him."

There was something in her gaze. Something she wasn't saying...

"You all planned this!" I hissed. Suddenly, the hushed phone calls made sense.

"No. He made us promise to support whatever motion he proposed if your hearing went badly, but your father and I didn't know the details."

"But they're going to execute him!" I whispered, terrified of the words even as I said them.

"No." She wiped tears from my cheeks with her thumbs. "No, Abby, I promise that's not what they want out of this."

The confidence in her steady green-eyed gaze gave me no choice but to believe her, so I sucked in a deep breath, then let it out slowly, counting the beats of my heart as it slowed to a reasonable tempo.

"Jace knows what he's doing," Faythe insisted. "He can handle whatever they throw at him, and if he didn't do everything he could to protect you, he wouldn't be able to live with himself. I know because

I feel the same way. We've failed you enough."

"But I'm grown now—"

"Good." She squared her shoulders, silently demanding I do the same. "Show everyone that by accepting his choice with grace and dignity." I wasn't sure I could do that, but she didn't seem to have any doubt. "Now, if you'll excuse me, I really *do* need the restroom."

A minute later, the dining room door opened again, and Jace was the first one out. His gaze found me immediately, and he led me down the hall, out the back door, and across the backyard to the guesthouse, where'd he'd lived when he was my uncle's enforcer. Mateo sat on the steps, elbows propped on widespread knees, but he stood when his Alpha approached.

"Anyone in there?" Jace nodded at the closed front door of the guesthouse.

Teo shook his head. "They're all in the main house, waiting on the sentence." He obviously didn't know what Jace had just done.

"Good. Make sure we're not disturbed, but knock when the council calls us."

Teo nodded and opened the guesthouse door for us, then closed it as Jace led me inside. I could see Teo through the glass panel in the door, standing with thick arms crossed over his broad chest. No one would get past him without taking a beating. And making one hell of a racket.

Jace gestured toward the stairs, and I turned on him the moment my feet hit the second floor landing.

"Why?" I demanded. He tried to pull me close, but I pushed him away and crossed my arms. I'd had *enough* of Alphas, and politics, and tears. "Why would you *do* that?"

"Because I love you. Because I need to protect you."

Each word was an arrow shot straight through my heart. Love was supposed to make people happy, not tear them apart. "That's not… You can't…" I needed to argue, and he wasn't fighting fair. "That doesn't make any sense."

"No one ever accused love of making sense, Abby. You and Brian made sense, yet that went nowhere because it *meant nothing*. This." He held my arms and looked straight into my eyes. "You and me. No matter how far apart we are or now much time passes, we will never mean nothing." He shrugged, and a hint of a smile tugged at one corner of his mouth. "We may also never make sense, but that just means we'll never be bored."

I leaned against the banister and had to concentrate to think past what he was saying. Past words that triggered every urge I'd ever had to touch him. Words that made me want to crawl into his lap and purr, and write "Back off, bitches!" on his forehead.

It was the words he'd said to the *council* that were a problem. "You're not my Alpha anymore, remember? You kicked me out of your Pride."

"This has nothing to do with the Pride, and you know it." He brushed a tumble of curls off my face, and his hand lingered at the back of my jaw. "I've made mistake after mistake. I missed *so* many things I should have seen, and you stepped up where I failed. You risked everything to protect Robyn when that was my job. She was infected in *my* territory, and I should have been the one helping her through it."

"You would have, if you'd known."

"I would have known if I'd checked on you," he insisted. I tried to argue, but he shook his head. "I stayed away from you because you weren't mine, but I wanted you. I thought I was doing the right thing, but I was just neglecting my duty. I'm not going to mess *this* up, Abby. I'm not going to let them chop off your fingertips to declaw you." He took my right hand and kissed each of my fingers, and my heart suddenly felt too swollen to fit in my body. "Or pull out your teeth." He slid his thumb between my lips and skimmed the tip of my incisor.

I sucked his thumb into my mouth, and Jace's eyes fell closed. I ran my tongue over the pad, my heart slamming against my chest.

"And I sure as hell couldn't let them lock you in a cage." Jace rubbed his thumb across my lower lip, where his gaze seemed stuck. "I can't let that happen to you. Not *ever* again."

I pulled him close and wrapped my arms around his neck, giving in to the sudden urge to touch him. The sudden need to maintain contact with as much of him as possible, because an ominous certainty growing inside me said that I'd soon lose that chance. Even if they weren't going to execute him, they probably wouldn't consider spending more time with his girlfriend an appropriate punishment.

"What do they want from you?"

"Doesn't matter," he whispered as he leaned down to kiss me, but I put one hand on his chest to stop him.

"Yes, it does. What do they want?"

Jace exhaled slowly. "The vocal minority wants me off the council. They're trying to kill our wildcat resolution, and they think Isaac will be easier to manipulate than I am. Especially after they've just spared his only sister and sworn him in as Alpha in record time. Faythe said Mitchell wants to kick me out of the lodge and leave me rank-less in the Appalachian Territory."

"They can't do that." But I knew better even as I said it. Finding him guilty of my crimes would finally give Mitchell and his allies a legitimate excuse to replace Jace as Alpha. Leaving him rank-less would be an extra dose of humiliation.

"I don't want to talk about it." He leaned down for a kiss. "It's done."

"But—"

"No." He shut me up with another kiss. "I don't need to run the Appalachian Pride. I need to be with *you.*" Jace tilted my head for greater access, and his mouth opened against mine. His kiss felt desperate. Urgent.

When we finally came up for air, Jace buried his head in my hair and spoke against my ear, his voice an intimate whisper. "Let's just think about *this.*" He lifted me, and my legs wrapped around his waist. "About *now.*" He carried me three steps forward, and I felt the wall at my back, the cool paint a blissful counterpoint to the heat of his body pressed against me.

"Only now," I whispered, but I would have agreed to anything he'd asked for in that moment, with his arms around me and his mouth on my neck. With our future spread out in tatters before us.

His kisses trailed toward my collarbone and I closed my eyes, concentrating on the heat of his tongue against my skin. The council could take everything away from us any second, but they couldn't take this moment, or the memory of it, once it had passed.

This was mine. *Jace* was mine. And if we were going to make a memory, we were going to make a damn good one.

"Jace." I murmured, tightening my legs around him.

"Mmm…?" he said against the dip at the base of my neck, and his voice sent shivers through me to settle in intimate places.

"Put me down. Just for a second."

Jace growled lightly, but complied, and a second after my feet hit the floor, my dress followed.

"Jace."

He turned to me, buttoning his jeans, and part of me wanted to take them right back off him. "Will you do something for me?"

"Anything." He had his shirt gathered over both arms, but paused before pulling it over his head to kiss me.

"Join the East Coast Pride."

His eyes widened. "What?"

"If you have to be rank-less somewhere, move to South Carolina with me. We could rent a little house and go running on the weekends. I'll transfer and finish school. You can work construction, or do whatever you want. We'll be rank-less together."

"Are you serious? It's only been a couple of weeks, Abby."

I shrugged. "Do you love me?"

"You know I do."

"Any doubts about that?"

His brows rose. "None."

"Any plans to sleep around?"

"Of course not."

"Good, because it may take all five of them, but my brothers *would* kick your ass." I picked up his shirt and handed it to him. "Assuming I leave anything for them to kick."

"I don't want anyone but you." He tugged me closer, but I tripped over my shoe and threw us off balance. Jace righted us with one hand against the wall, then pressed me against it with his whole body. He bent down until his forehead touched mine. "If I come to South Carolina with you, could we do this a lot?"

"Every waking moment. Except those moments when we're doing *other* things."

He gave me a slow, smoldering smile and slid his arms around me. "That sounds amazing."

"Is that a yes?"

"Maybe." He shook his head. "Yes. But Abby, this is crazy."

"So what? I know what I want. And anyway, according to Warner, if it's not crazy—"

"It isn't love. I know." Jace ran one hand through his pale brown waves, and I could practically see the thoughts running through his head. Scrolling past his eyes. "Abby, your dad…"

"He might be pissed at first, but he'll come around. My mom will help. She likes you." I pulled him down for another kiss, then spoke with my lips still brushing his. Then in a couple of years, when my dad's ready to retire..." I let him draw his own conclusion.

"Abby, that's a beautiful idea, but it won't work. They won't let me back on the council after I've been voted off. Even if we get married, eventually, it'll be your Pride. Your council seat. And I think that's the way it should be. I can kick just as much ass behind the scenes, with you wearing the crown. Especially if you promise not to wear anything else…"

The heat in his eyes was stunning. It almost stole my breath.

"But you're an Alpha and that won't change, even if you're not running a Pride." Alphas do *not* take orders. "Do you really think you could go back to being an enforcer? Even my *top* enforcer?"

"Well, our history would suggest I'm no good at being your *boss*." His grin lit me up on the inside. "We both know you were really running the show while you worked for me."

"And you can see how well *that* turned out," I said with a gesture in the general direction of the main house, where his fate was still being decided. "I'm willing to learn, but you belong at the top of the heap with me, Jace. If Marc can co-Alpha, so can you. It's not like the council will have any choice if we're married, right?"

Jace's brows rose. "I don't know. That may be uncharted territory. But if anyone can talk them into it, it's you. You're more than enough to keep a man on his toes."

"I'd rather have you on your back," I said, and Jace growled softly as he kissed his way down my neck. "We can handle whatever they throw at us today, right? We'll make the best of it. Promise me."

"We'll make the best of it. I promise," he

murmured with his lips against my skin. "We'll make history. We'll make love. And if you want, we'll make babies." He stood to look at me, and his blue eyes sparkled. "But only that middle part's set in stone."

"Agreed. Let's tell them we're getting a place together after they read your sentence." Anticipation made me giddy. "I'm *dying* to steal their thunder if they're going to steal your Pride from you."

His brows rose. "Does *nothing* scare you?"

"There's nothing left for me to be scared of."

Jace hesitated for just a second. Then he nodded, and my heart felt like it was going to *explode*. "Let's tell them. They can take my rank, and my home, and my job, but they can't take you away from me." His mouth met mine again, but our kiss was interrupted by a single loud knock on the front door of the guesthouse.

The council was ready to speak Jace's fate.

The Alphas were already waiting for us when we got to the dining room. Jace took his place, standing at the end of the table opposite Ed Taylor, where I'd sat all afternoon. I was relegated to a spot against the wall with Michael.

No one else was allowed in the room except for Victor Di Carlo and Brian Taylor, who closed the door, then stood to either side of it, in a much more formal stance than enforcers typically assumed. That made me nervous, even though they were both Faythe's men.

Why would the council need an obvious display of muscle? Did they think Jace would fight his sentence after voluntarily accepting my charges?

Ed Taylor cleared his throat, and my heart hammered in my chest, even though I already knew what he was going to say. Let them deliver their unjust, politically motivated sentence. Minutes later, I would be driving down the highway with Jace, browsing South Carolina rental listings on my phone.

Screw the council.

"Jace Hammond, the Territorial Council hereby finds you guilty of all the charges leveled against your former Pride member, Abby Wade. Do you have anything to say for yourself before we read the verdict?"

Jace nodded. Then he turned around and held his hand out to me. I glanced nervously at my dad, then took a bold step forward to intertwine my fingers with his. Jace squeezed my hand and looked right at Ed Taylor. "Do what you have to do."

My dad's frown deepened, but I didn't realize something was really wrong until I noticed tears standing in Faythe's eyes. By then, Taylor was already speaking.

"We hereby revoke your status as Alpha of the Appalachian Pride."

But we'd been expecting that. That wasn't bad enough to account for the silent tears trailing down Faythe's cheeks or the strained line of my father's jaw.

"Furthermore," Taylor continued. "In light of the severity of the charges, we sentence you to permanent exile in the Mississippi free zone, effective immediately. If you ever again enter one of the US territories, it will be at the forfeiture of your own life."

Jace's hand tightened around mine, and some inarticulate sound of horror got caught in his throat.

"*What?*" My pulse raced so fast the room had taken on an odd hue. "*Exile?* But that's not even... You can't..."

"There are precedents," Faythe said miserably. "Murder and insubordination have been grounds for exile in the past, even when the offender wasn't an Alpha."

"We *must* hold Alphas to a higher standard," Blackwell added, knowing full well that Jace hadn't committed any of the crimes he'd pled guilty to.

"We were outvoted," Faythe elaborated, with a glance at my father. "There was nothing we could do. I'm *so* sorry."

"Effective immediately?" Jace asked as I clung to his hand, stunned. Devastated.

My father nodded. "I'm sorry, Jace. Faythe will send two of her men to escort you to the border." He waved Vic and Brian forward, and all at once, I understood why they were there.

"No!" I stepped in front of Jace, shielding him with my body as Melody had done for Isaac. "You have to reconsider. *Please!*"

"Young lady, *you* are in no position to make demands," Ed Taylor snapped. "The sentence stands as it was read." He turned to the enforcers by the door. "Vic. Brian. Please take Jace Hammond into custody and escort him straight to the territory border." Taylor turned back to Jace. "If you go peacefully, we'll see that your mother ships your belongings to your forwarding address along with the balance of your personal bank account. If you resist, we'll have no choice but to declare everything you acquired as Alpha of the Appalachian Pride to be fruits of the position and pass them on to your successor."

Unfortunately, there was a precedent for that as well. After the war, one of Jace's brothers had been expelled from his territory without a cent to his name, for crimes committed during the war.

Vic reluctantly came closer, his jaw clenched. Even Brian looked uncomfortable with the order they'd been given. They'd both served as enforcers with Jace, when my uncle was Alpha of the South-Central Territory.

"No." I stepped between Vic and Jace, without turning away from the council, desperate for a way around a sentence we'd had no reason to expect. "I demand a recount of the vote."

"There's no grounds," Taylor said. "Denied."

"Then I refuse to let Jace accept charges originally leveled at me." I turned to Michael, desperate for his legal advice, even though the Territorial Council operated very differently from a human courtroom. "What are my options?"

Michael exhaled deeply and adjusted his glasses on the bridge of his nose. "Unfortunately, you don't have any. That was Jace's decision to make, not yours. Only he can take it back, and it's too late for that, technically."

"Doesn't matter," Jace said, before I could reason with him. "I wouldn't do it even if I could." He reached for me, and I could see resignation in his eyes as he pulled me close.

"You can't give up," I said into his shoulder.

"I'm not," he whispered into my hair. "But our best bet is to accept the sentence for now, then appeal it later, when overheated tempers have cooled."

"No!" I let go of him and turned back to the

council, because I knew his plan wouldn't work. Our appeal would lose. If we accepted the sentence, Jace could *never* come back into any of the US territories. Ever. And my father would never let me spend serious time in the free zone, where I'd be beyond his protection.

Not as long as he had any authority over me, anyway.

I stood straight, fighting to project an outward calm, even as my brain raced and my heart pounded. I only had one option left, and it had never been tried by a tabby. "Fine," I said, relieved when my voice didn't shake. "Kick him out. But I'm going with him."

"Abby, you can't—" my father began, but I spoke over him.

"I renounce my Pride membership and reject the authority of my Alpha and of the council appointed to protect and defend me. I reject all sworn allegiances. I waive all rights to property, resources, lineage, and protection of or by the Pride."

I only knew the right words to say because I'd studied the formalities of our ruling body to contrast it with those of the human world. But I understood the process well enough to know that it was both legal and binding, based on long-standing tradition.

My father stared at me, stunned.

Faythe stood, fresh tears gathering in her eyes. "Abby, please rethink this."

Ed Taylor slammed both hands down on the table and glared at Jace. "Are you going to let her put herself in that kind of danger because of you?"

Jace opened his mouth, already turning to argue with me, but I was faster.

"Jace has no authority over me. He can't stop me.

And the same goes for all of you."

"Abby," my father said, and I could see his heart breaking. I blinked back tears of my own, then rounded the table into the hug he already had open for me.

"I'm sorry," I said as he squeezed me. "They didn't leave me any choice. I have to do this. Tell Mom I love her. You guys are welcome to come visit me. I'll be in Mississippi."

My father's breath hitched—that was as close as I'd ever seen him come to crying. He inhaled deeply, then he slowly, deliberately let me go.

I smiled up at him through my tears, well aware of what that had cost him. Then I turned to Jace as the other Alphas all started arguing at once, most of them demanding that my father try to stop me—one of our few, precious tabbies—from defecting.

"Ready?" I took Jace's hand while he stared at me in shock.

"I can't believe you did that," he whispered as I tugged him from the room, then down the hall, toward the front door. In the chaos, Jace's escort to the border had been forgotten.

Lucas and Teo caught up with us on the front porch. "What the hell happened in there?" Luke demanded. "I've never seen so many Alphas all shouting at the same time.

"They kicked Jace out." I looped my arm through his. "Total exile. Effective immediately."

"Are you serious?" Luke said. "Man, I'm *so* sorry." He frowned, studying us closer. "Why don't you two look more upset?"

I shrugged and gave him a secretive smile. "Part of it's shock."

"The rest is because Abby defected," Jace said, while his former enforcers gaped at us. "By the way, you both now answer to Isaac. Or you will soon, anyway."

"Wait, you're leaving?" My brother looked like he couldn't quite wrap his head around that concept. "I've never heard of a tabby defecting."

"Holy shit!" Teo swore, and I laughed.

Lucas's mouth opened and closed. "I don't know what to say," he finally spat out, after a couple of false starts. "I can't believe you're leaving! Either of you." He scowled with a sudden new realization. "I can't believe I work for my little brother."

"I know. It's crazy, but we have to go." I pulled Lucas down for another hug, anxiously aware that as soon as the Alpha's finished arguing, they'd try to stop me from leaving. We needed to be gone by then. "We'll call you when we know where we're going."

"Take care of her," he warned Jace over my head, while I slowly suffocated against his chest.

"You know I will. You two watch out for Mel and Isaac, okay?" Jace pulled me free from my brother's grip. "They're going to need a lot of help."

"We'll do what we can," Teo promised. He thumped Jace on the back as we clomped down the front steps and onto grass. "We love you guys."

"Love you too. But we gotta go." I gave my brother one more hug, then started pulling Jace toward his rental car.

"The council's not really going to let you go, you know," he whispered, as we waved goodbye to Des and Parker, who were playing in superhero capes on the lawn.

"Then they're going to have to catch me." I dug

the keys to his rental from his pocket on the way toward the car, then slid into the driver's seat, adrenaline buzzing beneath my skin. He got in as I started the engine, and less than a minute later, I pulled out of the long driveway and onto the road. I didn't have so much as a suitcase to my name.

But I'd never felt more in control.

Jace took my hand as I drove, and together, we watched the Lazy S fade into nothing in the rearview mirror.

EPILOGUE

Jace

Abby finally fell asleep about an hour from the border, with her head propped against the window of the locked passenger's side door. Her hair fell over her face, hiding her profile from me, but I could still hear her voice in my head, chattering about all her plans.

Finish college in the free zone.

Get a little house in the free zone.

Make new friends in the free zone.

Do *whatever the hell we want*, in the free zone.

She was high on the possibilities, and I couldn't blame her. But she didn't fully understand the danger. I would fight to the death to protect her, but I was only one man, and the free zone was the equivalent of the Wild West for shifters.

I wanted her to have everything she wanted, and I wanted to share all those things with her—more than

I'd ever thought possible. But she deserved more than an anonymous existence in a lawless place, a constant source of fascination, curiosity, and desire to dozens of strays who'd never seen or smelled a female member of their own species. She deserved the comfort and security she'd grown up with. She deserved a support system and a true community.

And I was damn well going to give it to her.

I dug my phone from my pocket and dialed from the favorites menu.

Titus answered on the third ring. "Today's the big day, right?" he said in lieu of a greeting. "Did it go like you expected?"

"Not even close." I glanced at Abby as she shifted in her bucket seat, but her eyes never opened. "They didn't just take my territory; they kicked me out."

"Ouch. Sorry, man." Something clicked over the line, and a washing machine began to slosh. Titus had been in a fight—he only washed his own clothes when he got blood on them. "But you know my door's always open if you get tired of serving at the pleasure of whoever they gave your spot to."

"Yeah. About that. Exactly how wide open is your door?"

"What does that mean?"

"Abby defected. We're headed your way right now, if you'll have us."

A door closed, and the sloshing got softer. "You're bringing a *tabby* into the free zone? Jace, they'll start a war over this. You have to take her back."

"Not gonna happen, man. I'm ready to put our plan into action with a *drastically* accelerated timeline, but she and I are a package deal. Take it or leave it."

Titus growled, but there was no real anger in the

sound. "You know I can't do this without you."

"That's kind of what I'm counting on," I admitted with another glance at Abby.

Titus took a deep breath, and I recognized both exhilaration and anxiety in the sound. "So, we're really going to do this?"

"Effective immediately."

"Okay. We'll meet you at the border in an hour."

I hung up the phone and couldn't stop smiling.

A couple of minutes from the border, I shook Abby's shoulder. "Ab. We're almost there."

She sat up, wiping a shiny spot from her chin, and her brown eyes brightened instantly as what I'd said sank in. "Mississippi? The free zone?"

I nodded, smiling. "Another word for it might be 'home.'"

Her smile widened and she stared out the windshield, where the Welcome to Mississippi sign had just appeared on the side of the road. Then she held her breath until we'd passed it.

"That's it!" She turned to me, still beaming. "We're home."

"Yup." I put on my right blinker and swerved gently toward the rest stop just past the state line.

"You need a break? I can drive some more." Abby unbuckled her seat belt as I pulled into an empty space near the restroom. Then she froze as five large men stepped out of the shadow of the building, headed straight toward us. "Jace..." She sniffed the air but couldn't have caught much of their scents from inside the car.

"It's okay. They're friendly."

I pulled her jacket from the backseat and set it in her lap, then opened my door and got out. Abby joined me, zipping her coat, and I could hear her heart pound as her hand slid into my grip.

The man at the center of the group stepped forward as I tugged her onto the sidewalk, and her pulse began to race. "Abby, this is Titus Alexander."

Her eyes widened. She recognized the name.

Titus smiled and turned on the charm, but unlike most of the women he met, she only smiled politely and shook his hand. *None* of her clothes fell off at his feet.

"Titus and I are going to turn the free zone into a real territory," I said, and her brown eyes widened. "We're going to make it a home, and you're going to be safe. You're going to have everything you ever wanted. Here. With me."

"And with us." Titus waved his wildcats forward, and they held their hands out for her to shake, each one of them large, and powerful, and polite. "Abby Wade, welcome to the Lion's Den."

Photo credit: Kim Haynes Photography

ABOUT THE AUTHOR

Rachel Vincent is a former English teacher and an eager champion of the Oxford comma. She shares her home in Oklahoma with two cats, two teenagers, and her husband, who's been her # 1 fan from the start. Rachel is older than she looks and younger than she feels, and she remains convinced that writing about the things that scare her is the cheapest form of therapy—but social media is a close second.

Before Wildcats, there were...

SHIFTERS

Rachel Vincent

www.rachelvincent.com